You stay here awhile and be my pillow. And just so you know, if you do anything pervy, I'll make the anomalocaris gnaw at you.

CHIYURI
Haruyuki's childhood friend

"That's game over, Arita—no, *Silver Crow.*"

"Huh...?"

SEIJI NOMI

New student who stands at the top of the school castes

HARUYUKI

Boy in the lowest school caste

"A pleasure. Glad to meet you, too, Corvus."

SKY RAKER
Mysterious female player living as a recluse in Accel World

"It—it has been a while, Master."

"Uh...um...
Ash said
this, but.
He said
you were
the person
in the
accelerated
world who'd
come closest
to the sky..."

ASH ROLLER
A player Silver Crow is stuck with, his first duel opponent

SILVER CROW
Haruyuki's duel avatar

"Ah! Hey!
What are you
doing!"

KUROYUKIHIME

The Black King
Vice president of the Umesato Junior
High School student council,
controlling Black Lotus

HARUYUKI
is the···

"Silver Crow"
in the
Accelerated
World.

"Haruyuki Arita"
in the
Real World.

"Pink Pig"
in the
Umesato Junior
High School's
Local Area
Network.

 ▶▶▶ *ACCEL · WORLD*

THE TWILIGHT MARAUDER

Reki Kawahara
Illustrations: HIMA
Design: bee-pee

YEN ON

NEW YORK

■ Kuroyukihime = Umesato Junior High School student council vice president. Trim and clever girl who has it all. Her background is shrouded in mystery. Her in-school avatar is a spangle butterfly she programmed herself. Her duel avatar is the Black King, "Black Lotus."

■ Haruyuki = Haruyuki Arita. Eighth grader at Umesato Junior High School. Bullied; on the pudgy side. He's good at games but shy. His in-school avatar is a pink pig. His duel avatar is Silver Crow.

■ Chiyuri = Chiyuri Kurashima. Haruyuki's childhood friend. A meddling, energetic girl. Her in-school avatar is a silver cat.

■ Takumu = Takumu Mayuzumi. A boy Haruyuki and Chiyuri have known since childhood. Good at kendo. His duel avatar is Cyan Pile.

■ Seiji Nomi = New seventh grade student at Umesato Junior High. His origins are shrouded in mystery, but he uses Brain Burst in everyday school life and stands at the peak of the student social hierarchy.

■ Neurolinker = A portable terminal that connects with the brain via a wireless quantum connection, and which supports all five senses with enhanced images, sounds, and other stimuli.

■ In-school local net = A local area network established within Umesato Junior High School. Used during classes and to check attendance; Umesato students are required to always be connected to it.

■ Global connection = Connection with the worldwide net. Global connections are forbidden on Umesato Junior High School grounds, where the in-school local net is provided instead.

■ Brain Burst = Neurolinker application sent to Haruyuki by Kuroyukihime.

■ Duel avatar = Player's virtual self, operated when fighting in Brain Burst.

■ Legion = Groups, composed of many duel avatars, with the objective of expanding occupied areas and securing rights. The Seven Kings of Pure Color act as the Legion masters.

■ Territory Battle Time = Time for fighting with special rules, set up for each Saturday evening. Rather than the usual one-on-one fights, groups battle other groups of the same size, regardless of level.

■ Area Control = Privilege given by the system for having an average win ratio above 50 percent during the Territory Battle Time. Within controlled territory, Neurolinkers are given the right to refuse a duel, even if connected globally.

■ Normal Duel Field = The field where normal Brain Burst battles (one-on-one) are carried out. Although the specs do possess elements of reality, the system is essentially on the level of an old-school fighting game.

■ Unlimited Neutral Field = Field for high-level players where only duel avatars at level four and up are allowed. The game system is of a wholly different order than that of the Normal Duel Field, and the level of freedom in this field beats out even the next-generation VRMMO.

■ Enhanced Armament = Items such as weapons or personal armor owned by duel avatars. Can be obtained in ways such as being credited as initial equipment at the start, acquired as a level-up bonus, or purchased at a shop within the Unlimited Neutral Field.

▶▶▶ *ACCEL · WORLD*

It had already been five years since the largest network in the world, known as the Global Net, had transcended the globalness of its name. The Net had been connected to the space elevator station, which was in geostationary orbit above the eastern Pacific Ocean, and also to the international, multipurpose lunar base, such that anyone—if they were so inclined—could dive from their own home into a real-time image of the surface of the moon.

Naturally, countless other nets existed: large-scale closed nets, protected by national and corporate firewalls; local nets in schools and apartment complexes; private nets run by individuals. The assorted systems were multilayered, and if, hypothetically, the signals flying back and forth within them were to be made visible, a dense blanket of intricate stitching, palely glittering, would veil the world.

Although it was quite modest in comparison, the net of most critical significance to Haruyuki Arita was about to appear, at that very moment, in his own bedroom.

"O-okay, I'm connecting, Chiyu," he announced in a slightly shrill voice, and Chiyu—that is to say, Chiyuri Kurashima—replied, without a hint of nervousness crossing her face.

"What're you making such a big deal for? Just do it already."

Howling in his heart that she didn't understand how he felt, Haruyuki took the plug in his left hand and inserted it into the Neurolinker on his neck. Two "wired connection" notices blinked to red life in the center of his vision, then disappeared.

Chiyu, sitting on the bed, had XSB cables stretched out from the two connectors on her violet Neurolinker. One reached out to Haruyuki, who was plopped down on the floor, and the other linked her to Taku's neck—that is to say, Takumu Mayuzumi's—as he sat in a mesh office chair.

Haruyuki shouldn't have been so nervous about making this connection. In fact, the real issue was—

"Y-you don't actually need me to direct link with you guys—" he stammered, and Chiyuri favored him with a long stare from her catlike eyes.

"Noooo way. You promised you'd install it for me if Taku's copy doesn't work. I'm not letting you get away."

"...Fine." He nodded and glanced to his right, where Takumu offered a brief wry smile while pushing up his frameless glasses.

Haruyuki, Chiyuri, and Takumu had been born the same year in a large condo complex in South Koenji and had basically been friends ever since. Going through essentially everything together, they used to hang out every day, occasionally fighting for no reason, then making up for the same. But three years earlier, when they were eleven, Chiyuri and Takumu had started dating, and Haruyuki had pulled back. As a result, the former equilateral triangle of their relationship had stretched into an isosceles, with one corner receding into the distance.

However, with a certain incident the previous year as the catalyst, their relationship had been completely reset, and things had been, in truth, somewhat delicate for the past six months.

Haruyuki simply wanted Chiyuri and Takumu to hurry and make up already. But because Takumu, the cause of the incident, continued to blame himself, he couldn't bring himself to actively reach out to her. Thus the triangle was unstable, stretching and squashing with each new day...exactly like the two cables swinging erratically between the three Neurolinkers at that very moment.

"All right. You ready, Chi?"

Takumu spoke softly, with a tone that gave no hint as to his inner thoughts.

Chiyuri bobbed her head, sending short hair swinging. She clenched both hands on her small knees, which peeked out from under the hem of her skirt.

Takumu returned her nod and flicked a long finger in the air, running it along the virtual desktop only he could see. But once he had grabbed the file, his pale digit lingered in midair, stopped by a slight hesitation.

"Chi. I'm about to send you Brain Burst, but I just want to check one last time. It's a game and it's also not a game. You'll get the most amazing privileges, the total rush of it, and some serious thrills, but it will demand a lot from you in exchange. You...might regret this someday."

Takumu was giving voice to the very misgivings in Haruyuki's own heart.

Once you installed the mysterious game application known as Brain Burst and became a Burst Linker, you gained the ability to "accelerate," and you could never go back. You were caught up in the previously unknown net of the accelerated world, and you had to duel endlessly, for all eternity, to protect the privilege of connecting to that world. The pressure of this could warp personalities; Takumu had set up a backdoor virus in Chiyuri's Neurolinker and temporarily broken off their friendship because he had been backed into a corner by his fear of losing the power of acceleration.

Faced with furrowed foreheads on either side, Chiyuri puffed up her cheeks and sharply announced, "Look! The reason I said I want to be a Burst whatchamacallit isn't because I want this accelerating power thingy. And I *definitely* don't want to be *that girl's* servant! But this whole super-serious thing you two've got going is seriously bugging the hell out of me! Which is why I'm totally going to show you that you need to have more fun with this game!"

Jerking their heads back involuntarily, Haruyuki and Takumu exchanged a look and smiled, strained.

"G-got it, I got it, Chi. Okay. Ready? I'm sending it."

"Go right ahead." Chiyuri jerked her sharp chin upward, urging him on with a wink.

Takumu turned toward her and slid his fingertip through the air and Chiyuri's large eyes became focused on a single point in space. The dialogue to confirm the installation of the application BRAIN BURST 2039 should have opened in front of her. Bringing her right hand up from her lap, she thrust her index finger at the position of the YES button without any sign of hesitation.

"Ah?!" Her small, pink-sweatered body bounced up on the edge of the bed, wide-open eyes rolling from side to side.

Haruyuki recalled the time six months earlier when he himself had received the Brain Burst app. The instant he clicked the YES button, virtual flames had erupted to fill his vision, flames that were displayed to check the acceleration aptitude of the program's installer.

To become a Burst Linker, you needed to clear two bars. The first was having been equipped with a Neurolinker since immediately after birth, and Chiyuri cleared that one with flying colors. The problem, however, was with the second bar: brain reaction speed.

A Neurolinker communicated with the brain of its wearer through wireless quantum signals. But the brain was an organ inside a living body, and its responsiveness differed with the individual. You might have been born with highly reactive nerve circuits or you might be able to improve your reaction speed through long-term training, but either way, if the speed of your brain's responses to your Neurolinker did not exceed a certain threshold, the phantom flames would die out halfway through, and your attempted installation of Brain Burst would fail.

But maybe it would be better if it did fail, Haruyuki thought abruptly, sweaty hands clenched tight. The accelerated world was a swirling morass of the raw emotions of the people who fought there—hatred and resentment, jealousy and desire, and all kinds of other ill will. He definitely did not want to see their cherubically innocent Chiyuri hurt by her exposure to that swamp.

"Haru." Takumu's voice reverberated suddenly inside his head, a voice that only Haruyuki heard. He glanced over and saw his childhood friend on the chair, lightly biting his lip. *"I...I'm scared. Of Chi...changing."*

Haruyuki flicked at his virtual desktop to similarly direct his voice only at Takumu. He replied, *"If we—No, if you protect her, I'm sure she'll be fine, Taku. And it's not for sure that the installation will work. I mean, I feel bad for Chiyu, but it probably won't."*

"R-right. She said she was doing some kind of amazing special training or something, but I can't believe anyone could develop the aptitude in just a couple months—"

At that moment, Chiyuri's eyes abruptly stopped whirling around to take in the various visions, and then came to fix her gaze straight ahead. She pulled her rather thick eyebrows together, and her focus traveled from left to right. Her lips parted slightly, and a real-world murmur slipped out from between them; Haruyuki and Takumu listened with bated breath.

"What is this? W-welcome to the...accelerated world?"

1

The fiercely howling wind beating on the window shattered Haruyuki's thin sleep. In the darkness, his perked ears still covered by his duvet, he listened: the sound of countless water-drops, thrown up by the wind, ringing against the glass. Apparently, it had started to rain at some point.

This overnight storm had almost certainly scattered the blossoms of the sakura trees dotting the grounds of his condo building. However, for reasons having nothing to do with this early destruction of a seasonal symbol, spring was a dismal time for Haruyuki.

Those reasons were twofold. The first was that spring brought with it greater humidity and higher temperatures. With sweat glands twice as active as those of your average person, Haruyuki was already mopping his forehead at 25 degrees Celsius.

The second was that spring was the start of the new school year. He was nothing other than loathe to have the classes shuffled just when the long, seemingly endless days of bullying had finally ended and he may have carved out for himself a harmless and inoffensive niche. He very nearly passed out at the thought of starting all over again, pinging and sounding out his position within a group of students he barely knew. Given this, it wasn't a crime to want to stretch out the last few hours of spring break a bit.

With that thought in mind, Haruyuki fumbled on the shelf above his bed and grabbed his Neurolinker. Once he had attached it to his neck from behind and turned on the power, the lock arm moved to the inside with a faint whir. The startup stage completed the connection check with his senses, and a semitransparent virtual desktop appeared before his eyes.

Glancing at the clock display—2047/04/08 AM 01:22—in the lower right and sighing, Haruyuki took a deep breath and opened his mouth. "Burst—"

Link.

Before he could sing the last note of the magical incantation, the voice call icon blinked palely, and he heard a quiet ringing. He reflexively tapped the icon, only to realize simultaneously that the call was from his childhood friend in the condo two floors below his.

"Haru? You awake?"

He was a little surprised at the voice that sounded in his head. Why on earth was Chiyuri, who always went to bed at ten and slept like the long-dead until seven, calling at this hour? And what could she want?

Pushing his tangled thoughts to one side, Haruyuki mumbled a reply en neuro, *"I woke up a little while ago."*

"The wind's crazy, huh? But that's not the reason I can't sleep."

"You can't sleep?! You?!" he blurted, and in a flash, Chiyuri was shouting.

"Hey! You think I'm a machine or something? And anyway, it's your fault I can't get to sleep!"

"Huh? M-me...?"

"Uh-huh. Today, you—I guess it's already yesterday—when I went to go home last night, you said something weird. You said I might have scary dreams tonight, but that I'm totally not supposed to take off or turn off my Neurolinker. And when someone tells you

something like that, of course you're going to worry about it and not be able to sleep!"

Haruyuki had, in fact, turned to Chiyuri and said that ten or so hours earlier, and for a simple reason. The first night after the installation of Brain Burst, the game searched your memories in the form of a nightmare, to filter through mental scars like past traumas and feelings of inferiority, so it could then create the duel avatar that would be your other self on the battlefield.

Six months earlier, the night after Haruyuki had gotten Brain Burst, he had had the worst nightmare in the history of nightmares. He could only remember the vaguest details, but what the software had created as a result was an extremely lanky body with an enormous helmeted head, the argent avatar Silver Crow. Remembering somewhat fondly his own disappointment at the time, Haruyuki said to Chiyuri, *"Th-there's no way around it. If you don't dream, you can't create your duel avatar, which is essential. Although—I just thought of this, but do you even have any mental scars—"*

"You are so rude! I've been traumatized in my life! Like this one time, a Certain Someone on an elementary school trip was playing this game on the bus and his sense of balance got all messed up and he got super motion sick all over my lap."

"I'm sorry. Really. I'm sorry. Let's just not talk about this anymore," Haruyuki apologized with a groan, his own mental scars threatening to reopen.

But Chiyuri was on a roll, and her complaining tone conjured up her sullen face in Haruyuki's mind. *"And you know, now that I'm thinking about it, you never really apologized for that, did you? Perfect, you can pay me back right now."*

"Wh-what?! That was years ago. The statute of limitations is up!"

"Well, they were saying on the news the other day that 'statute of limitations' is gonna be a dead concept."

The establishment of the social camera net, which recorded video of all public spaces across Japan, had, in fact, several years earlier led to the repeal of the statute of limitations in criminal cases. But if they went by this public standard, Haruyuki probably owed Chiyuri for a lot more than a school trip mishap.

"Well, with the Special Law for Childhood Friends, they decided the statute of limitations is one year, no matter what," Haruyuki muttered in return, before sighing with his real mouth and asking a question in his mind at the same time. *"Well, how am I supposed to pay you back? More jumbo parfaits at Enjiya?"*

"I feel like they're not as good lately. Prob'ly 'cos they switched from milk to that synthetic stuff. So no. Ugh, it's such a hassle to talk like this; come dive into our home net. I'll open a gate for you."

"Huh?"

He blinked rapidly at the unexpected order, and the voice call was disconnected after a cluck of annoyance from Chiyuri's side. Watching the call icon wink into nothingness, Haruyuki cocked his head in puzzlement, wondering what she could possibly be planning at that time of night. But it wasn't as if he had the courage to bail on her now, so, having no other choice, he called out the command in his flesh-and-blood voice as ordered.

"Direct link!"

Instantly, his dim room melted into outward-shooting rays, and then swooshed out of existence altogether. Sensations of body and weight severed, Haruyuki fell gently into the darkness. His consciousness alone was released to the net, through the full-dive function of his Neurolinker.

He felt himself floating briefly as he watched several circular access gates draw near. Each was an entrance to a net he could currently dive into. Among the VR spaces he had bookmarked on the Global Net and his own condo's local net was a gate tagged as the Kurashima home, to which he turned and stretched out an invisible arm.

After a moment, the system generated virtual gravity, and Haruyuki's consciousness was sucked through the small gate. As he flew through with a *pop*, a circle of gentle lemon-yellow light grew before his eyes.

"Wh-whoa!" he cried out at the scene that appeared.

Usually, the VR space of the average household's home net aped the structure of the household: living room, guest room, family bedrooms. Families often had fun customizing this space to create something larger and more inventively embellished than would be possible in the real world. However, below Haruyuki's eyes lay a sea of cushions, an infinite number of them, in various colors and sizes.

There were no walls in any direction. Piles of pastel-colored cushions stretched out to the horizon under a gloriously blue sky. Haruyuki fell smack in the middle of the cushionscape, bounced back up, and hit the ground again on his backside.

"Wh-what is this?" he muttered, eyes stopping on the yellow giraffe-shaped cushion directly in front of him, the elephant cushion next to that, and then the stranger-shaped one beyond that.

"That's an anomalocaris. Creature from the Cambrian period."

Haruyuki whirled around at Chiyuri's voice to where her slender avatar stood behind him, treading on a star-shaped black pillow, likely a crown-of-thorns starfish. The avatar design— body covered in a soft violet fur, clad in a short slip-on dress and looking like what might happen if cats evolved into people— was the one she used on the Umesato Junior High School local net.

Blinking large blue eyes in a face that was 60 percent cat, Chiyuri sniffed haughtily. "You're still using that avatar, huh? Just change it to something else already."

Haruyuki glanced down at his own body and saw the pig-shaped pink body he also used at school. Round limbs on a nearly spherical torso. A flat nose protruded from the center of his face, and although he couldn't see them, he should also have had large ears sprouting from his head. No one was ever going to call this look cool or cute, and the truth was, Haruyuki hadn't even chosen this avatar. But he just sort of kept on using it for some reason.

He twitched his nose defensively and said, "I'm used to how this body feels. It'd just be a hassle to change it after all this time. Anyway, I wasn't asking about this weirdo cushion creature; I meant the VR space itself. Seriously, what is this, this cushion hel—heaven?"

Chiyuri had always liked these stuffed animal cushion things, and he remembered she had a bunch on her bed, but this place was completely over the top. He wondered what the total mass of the objects in the space was as he asked his question, but the cat avatar only laughed proudly, her beribboned tail flicking back and forth.

"Nee-hee-hee! Nice, huh? My parents expanded our home server to make memory just for me, as a present for passing last year. Even at this resolution, it's fifteen kilometers from end to end!"

"S-seriously?!" He recoiled reflexively, sending his round bottom shooting backward and ending up buried between the elephant and the anomalocaris. As he struggled frantically in the pillows, he thought about how, if he had had that much capacity, he could've recreated the battlefield at Kursk in 1943. He could have placed a ton of Tiger and T-34 tanks on the ground and Bf 109 fighter planes in the sky. What a marvelous scene of blood and carnage this could be.

"Hey...Heyyy, Chiyu...If you wanted to share some of that generosi—"

"No!!" Chiyuri snapped, cutting him off. She stuck out her tongue, behind which he spied a mouth full of tiny teeth. "If I let you customize it, you'd totally just fill it full of awful stuff like oil and steel and smoke."

"B-but isn't that a good thing..."

"No! It's! Not! Honestly, I can't even talk to you."

Haruyuki looked up at the cat avatar crossing her thin arms, and he finally remembered the reason he was there in the first place. "Ah…I…I see. So, what would you like me to do?"

"Just sit right there."

"Huh?" Confused, Haruyuki cocked his head to one side, still on the enormous pillow, short legs splayed in front of him. And then—

Pyoing! The cat avatar before him pounced, and with no hesitation whatsoever, laid her slim body across said legs.

"Wh-whoa?!" Haruyuki jumped up to break free, but Chiyuri reached up and caught his nose. Squeezing snugly, she yanked him back down into their original position.

"You stay here awhile and be my pillow. And then I'll forget that time on the school trip. And just so you know, if you do anything pervy, I'll make the anomalocaris gnaw at you."

"I-I won't! But I mean—pillow? What do you…"

Ignoring Haruyuki's now shrill voice, Chiyuri snapped the small claws at the ends of her fingers. Instantly, the calm blue sky above began to rotate, transforming from the horizon into a night sky, complete with an enormous floating moon.

Beneath picture-book stars that twinkled with a faint ringing effect, Chiyuri stretched luxuriously and curled up on Haruyuki's lap. "This isn't serious or anything, you know." The mumbled words tumbled from a mouth Haruyuki couldn't see. "I was just remembering how I used to use you as a pillow and fall asleep right away, back when you came and stayed at our house a lot."

"Wh-when was that?"

"Dunno. A long…long time ago." She yawned widely, and the cat avatar closed her eyes.

Ask Taku to do this kind of stuff, Haruyuki started to say, but then he swallowed the words. He was the only one who had been Chiyuri's substitute pillow when they were kids. Takumu's parents had a strict education policy, and he was almost never allowed to stay over at either of their houses.

But, even so, was this a conditioned reflex left over from so long ago? After all, they were both animal-type avatars in a virtual cushion heaven created by their Neurolinkers. Of course, this sort of behavior absolutely couldn't happen with their real bodies. In fact, he wasn't even sure it was okay in VR, either, if the truth be told.

As his thoughts spun round and round in his brain, to his surprise, he found Chiyuri had dropped into the deep, calm breaths of sleep.

"Come on..." he groaned, and Chiyuri, not quite as asleep as he thought, responded in a muffled, indistinct voice:

"Hey, Haru...I really did try hard..."

"Huh? At what?"

"To become a Burst Linker...I worked so hard...And now, we can go back, right? Like back then...The three of us hanging out every day until it's time for bed...Like...back..."

And now it seemed that Chiyuri had actually fallen into proper sleep. *Suu, suu.* Her avatar made virtual snoozing sounds. Haruyuki ran a gentle hand over the soft fur at the base of her ears and answered her with a sigh in his heart.

There are some things that never change.

But there are some things that do change and never go back to the way they were.

A few minutes later, Chiyuri's Neurolinker detected her deep sleep state and automatically released the full dive. Even after the cat avatar disappeared from his lap with a ringing sound effect, Haruyuki sat quietly for a while among the silent animals.

2

With a mere three classes in each grade, the private Umesato Junior High School in eastern Suginami was in no way large. Even still, the eyes of all three hundred and sixty school students, neatly lined up in the gym, exerted a substantial pressure when focused in one place. If, hypothetically, he himself had been standing at that focal point, Haruyuki was confident the combined force of so many eyeballs would burn an actual hole into him.

However, the person on stage for the welcome ceremony, speaking in a voice so clear it reached even the very back row without the use of a Neurolinker, appeared so cool as to give the impression that the pressure load of those eyes was automatically zero.

"The majority of you are likely feeling anticipation and unease in equal measure. In particular, the new students among you might be deeply perplexed by this unknown school and these unfamiliar schoolmates. However, I want you to consider this: The people behind you right now looking so calm and comfortable were in the exact same uneasy position, sitting in the exact same seats as you, a year ago, two years ago..."

I can't even believe that someone who can say amazing things like this could actually be the destroyer of order in another world, a murderer without mercy, and a demon instructor who'd put even a US Marine to shame.

As he grumbled to himself, Haruyuki turned his gaze to the female student on the stage, with a longing he couldn't entirely suppress—Kuroyukihime, uniform blouse adorned with a deep red ribbon and her long, well-proportioned legs encased in black tights.

With her, he had a special relationship—or so he called it, because, even though it had already been six months since its inception, and it was undeniably special in every way, Haruyuki still couldn't manage to get to a place where he was able to say "girlfriend" and "boyfriend." The general attitude at school seemed to be on that same page, with some even theorizing that Kuroyukihime had rescued the tiny, round, younger student from bullying out of duty or pity and now dragged him around like a beloved pet.

And Haruyuki had no complaints about this theory. He actually even thought it was probably true, although she did hold off on the pet treatment. But he was perfectly satisfied with the idea, serving his princess as a knight—no, a servant—no, no, a page.

"...a year is thirty-one million, five hundred thirty-six thousand seconds, and although this time looms before you now as an eternity, it will pass in a mere instant. Spend it wisely. Thank you."

Bowing her head, long black hair fanning out in front of her before her body bobbed back up along its wave, Kuroyukihime added herself to the line of student council members behind her.

As he clapped earnestly along with the rest of the students, Haruyuki was suddenly struck with the thought, *I'm in eighth grade and she's in ninth. Which means just one more year. And then she'll graduate from Umesato. But, okay, that doesn't mean our relationship has to end. Our bond is much stronger than just students at the same junior high—as Burst Linkers, we're parent and child.*

He squeezed both eyes shut tightly before opening them again to clap his hands even harder when, staring single-mindedly at Kuroyukihime on the distant stage, he got the impression that the detached beauty twitched for a mere instant.

Her narrowed jet-black eyes stopped dead at the very front of where the new seventh graders were lined up, and then quickly faced forward again. Haruyuki furrowed his brow, craned his neck from his seat, and tried to see whom she had pierced with that gaze. But of course, he couldn't make out any one person in the sea of uniforms.

Returning to the school building after the entrance ceremony, Haruyuki almost climbed to the third floor out of habit before hurriedly changing course for his new classroom on the second.

He had been notified of the location of his new homeroom via his Neurolinker, but he wouldn't know the names of his new classmates until he stepped through the door. Fervently praying—*Please don't let there be anyone who'll call me Pig and make me buy him snack bread again!*—Haruyuki slipped through the door of eighth grade class C.

"Haru! Heeey!"

He heard the voice at the same time a pounding came at his back, knocking the breath from him. Haruyuki whirled ninety degrees to his left to see a familiar cat-shaped hairpin holding back familiar front fringe. The face of his childhood friend grinned back at him to reveal fang-like incisors.

"Ch-Chiyu. You're...*here?*"

"What. What is that complicated look for?"

"N-nothing," he replied, cocking his head and wondering if maybe she had had that nightmare last night, given the way she was sniffing and pursing her lips.

Even if he and Chiyuri were in the same class, as long as the bullying didn't start again, he had nothing to be afraid of. But problems were problems, and this was one more. If he and Chiyuri were in the same class, the sides of their triangle could end up—

"Hey, Haru. And Chi, too!"

Pounded on the back once again, Haruyuki spun ninety degrees in the opposite direction to look up and see Takumu's smiling face behind blue glasses.

Apparently all three of them had been put in the same class, which meant their triangle would end up smaller. He remembered Chiyuri talking the night before about how they could go back to the way they were and was aware of a faint fluttering in his heart as he produced a similar smile. "Hey! You're in class C, too, huh, Taku?...Let's see."

He applied a dimly remembered probability formula to the situation and voiced the answer he managed to come up with. "The probability of three students ending up in the same class... is one-third times one-third times one-third, so one-twenty-seventh? Seriously random!"

Takumu shook his head lightly as he walked toward the windows. "No, it's one-ninth."

"Huh? Why?"

"Why?" Chiyuri, having arrived at the same solution as Haruyuki, also raised her voice in surprise.

Entrusting his sharp, tall physique to the window frame, Takumu raised his wireless glasses abruptly and explained, "If it's the probability that all three of us would be in class C, it would be one-twenty-seventh, just like you said, Haru. But in this case, we didn't know which class it would be. So the problem becomes the probability of all three of us ending up in class A or class B or class C, so the number is tripled and you get one-ninth."

"Ah!"

"Right!" Nodding again with Chiyuri, Haruyuki finally laughed and added, "Just like you, Taku. Polishing up your professor character even over spring break—"

"Haru, you seriously need to quit that! If I get stuck with the nickname Professor or Glasses or something in this class, it'll be on your head." Looking honestly put out, Takumu glanced around eighth grade class C, filling up with students, and lowered his voice. "Anyway. There are a lot of coincidences in the world, but if you do the calculation, the probability's unexpectedly greater than your initial impression. So I think we should be ready just in case."

"Huh? For what?"

"The incoming seventh graders," Taku said in an even lower voice, bringing his face closer to the bewildered Haruyuki. "The possibility of an unknown Burst Linker mixed in with those one hundred and twenty people."

Haruyuki took a sharp breath and nodded repeatedly. "Th-that's— I mean, the possibility's not zero, but would anyone go to a different school than their parent? It's one thing to transfer like you did, Taku, but..."

"Yeah, normally, you wouldn't dare make someone your 'child' if they were going to go to a different school from you, right? Because if there were other Burst Linkers at that school, there's a pretty strong possibility your child would end up fighting on their side. I mean, the strongest relationship in the accelerated world is that of parent and child, but school affiliation comes right after."

Just as Takumu noted, Burst Linkers going to the same school would eventually, inevitably find one another "in the real." So if you fought, the battle would have to be to the death, the kind of fight where the rules didn't apply, a fight going beyond the framework of the game itself. In that sort of situation, if both parties wanted to keep Brain Burst, the only thing to be done would be to shake hands and call a truce somewhere, somehow.

Which was why no Burst Linker would choose as their child someone who might go on to a different school. All of which was to say, given that the only Burst Linkers enrolled at Umesato Junior High were Kuroyukihime, Haruyuki, and Takumu—and Chiyuri for the time being—it was basically impossible for an unknown Burst Linker to come to their school as an incoming seventh grader. However, that didn't mean they didn't need to bother checking.

"Um...when exactly do new students first connect to the local net?" Haruyuki asked Takumu, trying to remember what it had been like when he was a new student the previous year.

"Should be right about now. If it's the same here as at my old school, once the entrance ceremony's over and you go back to your classroom, that's when the new accounts are handed out."

Mulling over this answer, Haruyuki finally smiled and said, "Then how about we do this? If we have to spend the Burst Points to see if there are any new Burst Linkers, let's check out Chiyu's duel avatar in the duel field at the same time. After the next homeroom, I'll accelerate and challenge Chiyu. Taku, you join in the Gallery."

Their new homeroom teacher was a young man who taught Japanese History. Sugeno, as this teacher was named, was for his age a surprisingly firm advocate against children needing the net, and, although Haruyuki personally could not get onboard with that idea at all, their new teacher was well received by other students because of his passion.

He ignored Sugeno's policy speech, the general gist of which was, "If you look up everything on the net, you'll all end up adults who can't think for themselves!" and somehow managed to make it through the student self-intro time. As soon as first period was over, he invoked the acceleration command.

"Burst Link!"

Skreeeee!

The dry thunder reverberated loudly in his brain as the scene around him was dyed a single shade of blue. At the same time, Sugeno, on his way down from the podium, and the other students, on their way up from their chairs, froze instantly.

Time hadn't stopped. The Brain Burst program hidden in Haruyuki's Neurolinker had just accelerated his consciousness a thousandfold.

He touched the conspicuously bright, flaming *B* icon on the left side of his virtual desktop and launched the console, then waited for the matching list to refresh with a certain amount of heart pounding.

Silver Crow—the name of Haruyuki's own duel avatar—soon popped up at the very top of the list. The level display to the right read 4. Black Lotus, aka Kuroyukihime, soon followed him. Her level was, obviously, nine. And then Takumu appeared, Cyan Pile, level four like Haruyuki.

After a slight pause, another row of letters sparkled into existence: *Lime Bell. Level one.*

The search list display then disappeared. Which meant that at that moment, there were four Burst Linkers connected to the local Umesato Junior High net. Lime Bell had to be Chiyuri. And since all one hundred and twenty freshmen should have, without exception, finished signing into the local net by now, Haruyuki concluded that there were no new Burst Linkers among the incoming students after all.

However, there was, in fact, just one thing gnawing at him. The way Kuroyukihime had turned momentarily toward the row of new students during the entrance ceremony. What was the meaning of that?

He briefly thought about shooting off a mail to ask, but he thought the better of it. Kuroyukihime, as student council vice president, was probably swamped with a million tasks that had piled up over the break.

As his avatar's finger went to push down on the name of Umesato Junior High's fourth Burst Linker, Haruyuki considered her briefly. Lime, that probably meant a yellow-green. So a little more mid-range than close-range. But he wouldn't know what kind of abilities she actually had until he met her in combat.

The duel avatar is the manifestation of the feelings of inferiority of the person dwelling within it. Kuroyukihime's words from six months earlier came back to life in his ears.

Naturally, it wasn't as if you could immediately intuit a host's mental scars just by looking at his or her avatar. The truth was, even now, Haruyuki couldn't begin to guess at what kind of complexes Takumu and Kuroyukihime had that would produce such powerful avatars. That said, it was true that the avatar was the manifestation of a hidden interior.

In the frozen blue world, Haruyuki glanced over at Chiyuri's back, which was seated in front of him, one row left. Gulping back his slight hesitation, he touched Lime Bell's name and clicked on DUEL in the pop-up menu.

The field that appeared while he changed into the argent Silver Crow was a Factory stage, complete with enormous gears and rumbling conveyor belts. He waited for the flaming FIGHT to explode and scatter, then slowly stood.

His classmates had disappeared, and eighth grade class C was crawling with mysterious machines in their place. Haruyuki looked around and first saw the large, blue Cyan Pile. He nodded slightly in that direction before turning his gaze on the avatar opposite him, small like himself.

Lime Bell was wrapped in a color more verdant than he had expected; it was like the green of fresh leaves. Her body's supple lines were clearly female in nature, with limbs and torso basically as slender as those of Silver Crow, and armor resembling a tree leaf equipped around her waist. On her head was a pointy, wide-brimmed hat rather like a witch's, and below that was a face mask with upturned eyes, reminiscent of a cat's.

What made the greatest impression, however, was the massive hanging bell on her left arm, probably a musical hand bell. Wondering if it was a weapon or just the instrument it appeared to be, Haruyuki took a step toward her.

"This color's kind of...flashy?" Lime Bell—Chiyuri—said, staring fixedly at the bell connected to her hand and cocking her head.

"Don't complain. Basically no one gets a color with that high level of saturation, even if they want it."

"So..." Orange eyes narrowed dubiously beneath the hat. "You're...Haru?"

"I am. And I know what you're going to say, so don't bother!" He added the last bit at tongue-twister speed.

But Chiyuri cried out mercilessly. "So skinny! These game avatars, they're the expression of some trauma? Was that it? Ooh! Wow! I get it!"

"Just drop it." He glanced down at his waist, which was more than half as thin as in real life, and turned away abruptly.

And suddenly, there was Cyan Pile. The blue avatar, pile driver in his right hand, looking down on the yellow-green avatar with eyes somehow full of tension. Eyes Chiyuri met silently.

Before, half a year ago, and unable to bear the fear of losing Cyan Pile, Takumu set up a backdoor program in Chiyuri's Neurolinker. The virus's main purpose was to use Chiyuri's Neurolinker as a stepladder in order to connect to the Umesato Junior High local net from outside. His goal was to hunt Black Lotus, the Black King, the biggest bounty in the accelerated world. However, a secondary effect of the virus allowed Takumu to steal information from Chiyuri's audio and visual feeds, which he used to dig into Chiyuri's true feelings.

When he later confessed his crimes and apologized, Chiyuri was, naturally, furious, and declared that she was breaking up with both Haruyuki and Takumu. It took a full week before she would even talk to them again. The terms of peace she laid out were all the parfaits she could eat at Enjiya, and both of their Neurolinker balances had gotten infinitely lighter meeting these terms, but even so, the relationship among the three of them had been restored and was back to the way it used to be.

Or so Haruyuki had believed, had hoped, anyway. But the fact that the Takumu-Chiyuri line of their triangle still fluctuated unstably could be seen in their eyes as they stared at each other.

"Well, we should get right into the newbie lecture," Haruyuki announced, as if to ease the faint tension, and turned again to the yellow-green avatar. "Chiyu, you already heard the basic rules for Brain Burst from Takumu, right?"

"Yeah. Basically, you win a bunch of fights, get a bunch of points, get to level ten, and you're done. Right?"

"It's not as simple as that. Although I guess it is actually…" Shaking his head at what a certain someone would say if she heard Chiyuri's rather indifferent words, Haruyuki continued. "A-anyway, to win duels, you need to see through to your opponent's weak points and fight in a way that gives you the advantage. And to do that, you have to have a seriously perfect understanding of your own avatar."

I never thought the day would come when I'd be in the position of lecturing someone else. Slightly moved, he continued on, lifting the tip of his right pointer finger.

"In your field of vision right around here, you have your own health gauge, right? Touch that and then open 'Skill List' in the window that pops up." Generally, her parent, Takumu, would be teaching her this, but following the flow of the conversation, Haruyuki took the initiative.

"O-okay." Nodding, Chiyuri stretched out a slightly awkward finger and tapped a point in space. She then flicked around a bit on her virtual desktop. "Umm, it looks like there're three normal attacks, and then one special attack, Citron Call? So, like, this bell in my left hand, it'd be…"

Muttering to herself, Chiyuri aligned her movements with the animated silhouette in the Skill List, whirling her left arm and the enormous bell that began at her elbow until she finally snapped both down from above. But naturally, nothing happened.

"What? It didn't do anything at all."

"Because you have to fill up the blue special-attack gauge below your health gauge to use your special attack."

"So how do I do that?"

"Damage an opponent in a duel or take a blow yourself—" He had gotten that far when Chiyuri slowly brought up the enormous bell and aimed it at Haruyuki's head, so he hurried to add, "A-and you can also fill it by destroying the stage. You can break any of the machines over there!"

"Oh! I can?" Nodding and looking slightly dissatisfied—or maybe that was just his imagination—Chiyuri walked over to a steam engine–like object enshrined in the place where the podium used to be. Without hesitation, she brought her left hand down on the thing as it vigorously puffed out steam. The satisfying sound of an explosion was accompanied by sparks and white smoke.

"Wow! This is fun!"

Haruyuki watched, shivers running up his spine, as the pointy-hatted avatar smashed the gears that made the belt conveyor go round with an innocent cry of delight. She showed not even the slightest appreciation for the reality of the explosions nor the extremely detailed modeling of the stage. This was why girls…

As Haruyuki grumbled on in his head, Takumu, who had been silent up to that point, murmured softly from beside him. "Haru, did you notice? Chi's HP gauge isn't going down at all. I mean, Factory stage mechanical objects are supposed to do some damage when you break them, even if it is just a little."

"Oh! You're right."

"Given her appearance, her relative defensive ability is high. Not a surprise, though. After all, green is the color with the best defense, after the metallics."

At Takumu's cool analysis, Haruyuki suddenly remembered talk he'd heard of the Green King's legendary iron wall.

Lime Bell's armor was clearly harder than Silver Crow's had been at level one. Which probably meant Chiyuri was also a defensive type. He couldn't help feeling, though, that this was the exact opposite of her actual character. As he contemplated Lime Bell, her special-attack gauge grew to nearly half full, shining blue.

"Hey, Chiyu, that's enough," he said, and the avatar turned around and walked briskly back over. Without a moment's hesitation, she brandished the large bell and aimed it straight at him.

"Gah?!" Haruyuki cried out and reflexively brought both hands above his head.

Whirled twice counterclockwise, the bell was suddenly encased in a dazzling yellow-green radiance.

"Citron Call!!" As she uttered the name of the unexpected attack, particles of light began gushing out of the bell. As she lowered her arm to hold steady at a right angle to her torso, the light covered Silver Crow's entire body, accompanied by a magnificent pomp and fanfare sound effect.

"Hng!" Unable to predict what kind of damage it would do, Haruyuki held his breath and pressed his eyes shut. Maybe heat, maybe impact, maybe even an acid melting-attack like the Citron part might—

"Huh?"

"Wha?"

Chiyuri's and Takumu's incredulous voices reached his ears from either side, and Haruyuki carefully opened his eyes a crack.

Looking down at his own body nervously, he still had the same old smooth, silver gleam. He didn't feel any pain or heat at all, and his HP bar hadn't dropped in the slightest.

"What is this?! Nothing happened?!"

"Th-that can't be." Haruyuki reflexively shook his head at Chiyuri's indignant cry. "Your attack definitely hit me. And your special-attack gauge's down, too. It's not anything with continuous damage, either. Maybe it's damage with a timed launch and a delayed effect?" Muttering away, he waited for something to happen, but after several seconds, then several minutes, there was still not the slightest movement in Silver Crow's HP.

"Hmm. Maybe this is, like, a dazzle kind of attack with just the light and sound. I mean, that is a yellow kind of thing."

"That is so boring!" Chiyuri placed her right hand on her hip as if the indignation of it was too much to bear. "Haru, you give me one of your special attacks!!"

"What? That's obviously impossible. And all I have for a special attack is a head butt."

"I can make do with that, if this is what I have."

As their usual song and dance, the same old routine from the real world, unfolded, Takumu abruptly murmured, "No. Your special-attack gauge's gone down too much for it to be just an illusion attack. You had it half full and you used all of it. There should be a more practical effect." Crossing his sturdy arms, Cyan Pile turned a face lined with narrow slits downward. "It's not damage, and it's not weakness. So then…Oh! Hold up! What if—!!"

Haruyuki and Chiyuri simultaneously snapped their heads toward him.

"What, Taku? You think of something?"

"Well, it seems kind of crazy, but…Chi, hit Haru a bit with your bell, just normally."

"Okay, got it."

Kliiing!!

Before Takumu had even really finished speaking, Chiyuri had swung the massive bell without any compunction whatsoever, and Haruyuki, who stood and took the blow to his head, saw countless stars.

"O-ow!" He had barely squeezed out a groan before Takumu's merciless instructions continued.

"You still don't have enough in your gauge. Try maybe three more times."

"Okay, got it."

Klinklinkliiiing!!

Chiyuri's bell is cool. Makes a great sound whenever she hits something. His thoughts swirling deliriously, Haruyuki was soon splayed on the ground like a human X.

In Brain Burst, which was at most a fighting game, your HP, attack power, and defensive power didn't necessarily increase dramatically only when you leveled up. You might get new special attacks or abilities, which would broaden the scope of your battle tactics, but if you were hit without resisting like this, you'd be hit with a suitable amount of damage, regardless of the level of attacker. And Haruyuki's HP gauge went down about 30 percent with the four hits, while in exchange, Chiyuri's

special-attack gauge once again went up to just over half and glittering blue.

Groaning as he stood, Haruyuki saw the bell being swung around once more and the gleaming of a yellow-green light effect.

It's weird. When Kuroyukihime gave me my first lecture, there wasn't anything resembling this "teaching with the master's body" stuff. And why am I the one who's stuck being Chiyu's duel partner here, anyway?

Although it was too late to do anything about it now, these thoughts raced through his mind as Chiyuri gave voice to her attack name for the second time, much more loudly than before.

"Citron Caaaaaall!!"

The crisp ringing of the bell. The ribbons of lime-green light spilling out. And to top it all off, a refreshing citrus scent. All wrapped Silver Crow in several layers.

"Whoa?!" Haruyuki cried out, surprised from the very bottom of his heart. It was the first time in several months he could say that of the accelerated world.

The HP gauge in the top left of his screen, which had been down 30 percent—

It was filling back up before his eyes!

HP recovery.

This was basically an impossible phenomenon in the genre known as fighting games. In fact, up to that point, Haruyuki had never once seen a gauge recover in Brain Burst.

Actually, to be accurate, he had personally seen exactly one example: Chrome Disaster, the cursed Enhanced Armament that they had annihilated and expunged three months earlier in an incredible battle. That avatar had had a power called "Drain," which absorbed the health of cannibalized opponents. However, since the fight with Disaster had been in the Unlimited Neutral Field—where the HP gauges of other avatars could not be seen—he supposed that this was honestly the first time he had witnessed the physical recovery of a gauge.

In a mere ten seconds, his HP had returned to full and the

yellow-green light disappeared. But Haruyuki and Takumu, a little ways off, were both unable to move or produce any sound.

It was Chiyuri's millionth dissatisfied cry that unfroze them. "This sucks! Come on! Your hit points went back to what they were!! No fair, I want a do-over!!"

"I'm not being unfair," he managed to say hoarsely, and then turned his gaze on Takumu, seeking an explanation.

Cyan Pile's blue eyes were wide open beneath the mask's thin slits. "Wh-what *is* this?" he finally moaned in a low voice, shaking his head from side to side. "That was definitely a recovery ability just now. So Chi, your avatar's a healer, then."

"What? So does that mean, like, a monk? Kinda boring." Chiyuri sounded slightly disappointed, and Haruyuki, finally overcoming his shock, simply said the first thing in his head.

"Healer. That's the first I've heard of that. Do they even have healers in Brain Burst?"

In contrast, Takumu lowered his voice even further, as if he were afraid. "It's not boring. It's crazy rare. This is going to blow up when you make your debut in the duels, Chi. Maybe more than when Silver Crow showed up."

3

"What did you say?"

The incredulous utterance and its ensuing silence expressed the enormity of her surprise. Umesato Junior High student council vice president in the real world, leader of the Nega Nebulus Legion in the accelerated world, and Haruyuki's "parent," level nine Burst Linker and Black King, Black Lotus, also known as Kuroyukihime, stared at Haruyuki for at least a full five seconds before finally returning the cup in her right hand to its saucer.

"I had expected that it would be fifty-fifty as to whether Kurashima could even become a Burst Linker. And then she's a Healer, of all things." Brushing back her long black hair, she entrusted her body to the white chair and sighed softly. Her new ribbon was a sleek, deep red shine against her ink-black blouse.

Haruyuki was unintentionally captivated by this beauty, which he felt was only increasing in its incredibleness of late.

April 10, 2047, Wednesday, 3:30 PM.

As usual, there was not another soul in this place, where during lunch break every seat was guaranteed to be filled. The reason was simple: no one was particularly interested in hanging out on campus after school when you couldn't connect to the Global Net.

Two days had already passed since Chiyuri had become a Burst Linker and had stunned Haruyuki and Takumu with the special nature of her avatar, Lime Bell. But Kuroyukihime was insanely busy with student council business, given that it was the start of the school year. She didn't even have time for lunch, so they were only finally able to talk directly today.

Two days earlier, he had reported by mail that Chiyuri had successfully installed the copy from Takumu and what the name of her avatar was. He had actually wanted to mention her avatar's surprising ability at the time, but Takumu had insisted it would be better to tell her in person. So the explanation of that had ended up happening today.

When Haruyuki apologized in a tiny voice for the delayed report, Kuroyukihime finally focused her eyes on him and shook her head. "Takumu's judgment on this was correct. If, by any chance, you had spoken of this matter on the net and another Burst Linker had overheard it, it would be more than a big deal."

"I-it would be that serious?"

"Make no mistake. I have no doubt that Burst Linkers throughout Tokyo would gather in Suginami and try all sorts of tricks to get Kurashima—Lime Bell—on their side before she joined a Legion somewhere," she told him with a faint wry smile, and Haruyuki gazed in wonderment again.

He thought he understood how rare the healing ability was, considering he had never seen or heard of it until that point, even though it had been a full six months since he had set foot in the accelerated world. However, it was unsettling to think it could even cause scouting battles.

When it came to scarce, Haruyuki's flying ability itself was a rarity among rarities. But once he hung out the Nega Nebulus shingle, he had been invited to switch legions maybe two, three times.

"B-but why?" Haruyuki mumbled, feeling greatly surprised. "I mean, she still hasn't made her actual battle debut."

"Mm. True." She seemed to consider her response before popping up a finger. "Perhaps you'll understand if I put it like this. Although seven full years have passed since the birth of the accelerated world, a mere two Burst Linkers with healing ability have appeared. Of these, one managed to dodge the relentless invitations and assassination traps and is still doing quite well, but the other, unable to endure being the center of constant battling, decided to leave the accelerated world."

"Le—"

Left. Which meant he probably deleted his own Brain Burst himself.

Kuroyukihime glanced at the shock-frozen Haruyuki with a cynical expression on her face. "Well, if pressed, I'd say it was more along the lines of a complicated case of princess syndrome, unable to choose one or the other of the two princes petitioning for her hand, and throwing herself from the tower."

"H-harsh…" Haruyuki's cheeks spasmed involuntarily, and Kuroyukihime voiced something even more frightening.

"Fortunately, Kurashima's not that type at all, hmm? Just the opposite, I suppose. Hard to see her as a prize two princes would vie for." She laughed lightly.

"B-but." Haruyuki hurried to return to the topic at hand after glancing reflexively behind her to check that no one was there. "Um, why does everyone lose it just because someone has a healing ability?"

"Use your imagination. Say you work quite hard to reduce the HP of your opponent's advance guard in the public territory team battles. But then he pulls back, returns to the rear, and he's completely recovered. Poof! Put simply—"

"He can't be killed?"

That certainly would be tough. Or rather, awful.

As Haruyuki nodded with a gulp, Kuroyukihime spread out her right hand lightly, adding, "In short, yes. If the enemy team has a healer, you have to subjugate that healer first, above all else. But the other side will clearly anticipate your intentions and have a field day setting up ambushes, pincer attacks, and every other trap imaginable."

"Y-yeah…"

"Frankly, an effective countermeasure has yet to be established for when the enemy side alone has a healer."

"Huh?" Her words were delivered with a catlike smile, and Haruyuki blinked back a daze. "Hold on a minute. You said there was just one active healer right now—I mean, other than Chiyu. That's what you said, right? So then, if the Legion that Burst Linker belongs to wanted to, couldn't they unify the accelerated world?"

"It's possible, yes, certainly. Very much so."

"Why don't they do that, then?"

At Haruyuki's naive question, a wry grin rose briefly to Kuroyukihime's face before quickly melting away. He thought he saw a dangerous glint in her narrowed jet-black eyes. Her voice also contained a cool echo now, different somehow from before.

"A very simple reason. That healer is currently one of the Six Kings of Pure Color. So even if, for instance, the Legion boasts a win ratio of ninety-nine percent in the team battles, if another king hits that king just once, she loses acceleration. Because of this, the healer never appears on the battlefield."

"One of...the kings?!" Haruyuki very nearly dropped the paper cup of oolong tea he had started to bring to his lips, and he hurriedly clutched it with both hands to stop its fall. "What color?!" he asked, coughing violently, but for some reason, her reply was longer in coming.

Eyes lowered, Kuroyukihime seemed to be wrestling with something for quite a while until finally, she shook her head. "I'm sorry. I don't want you to hear her name right now. I don't want you to be even marginally curious about her."

"Huh? Wh-what do you mean?" Haruyuki said dumbly, unable to grasp Kuroyukihime's meaning.

What he got in response to his question was another question. "Now, Haruyuki. Perhaps this is a strange thing to ask, but in these six months, how many times have you been scouted?"

"What?!" His back snapped to attention and his mouth flapped open and closed repeatedly. But he didn't exactly have the option of lying. "Um, twice from the six major legions controlled by the kings, including the thing with Niko three months ago." His voice gradually disappeared as he told her the truth. "And once from a small place outside of that. But I obviously turned them all down, right there right then!!"

He tacked on the last bit rather frantically, but it unfortunately didn't seem to make a deep impression on Kuroyukihime. Or rather, something else seemed to have caught her attention, and she furrowed her eyebrows before questioning him further. "Hmm. The other time from the six major Legions, which color was it exactly?"

"Ummm...I'm pretty sure it was blue?" he replied, and Kuroyukihime exhaled sharply after several seconds.

"Mmm hmm, I see. But blue, well. On top of sending all those assassins every week, they've honestly gone beyond shameless."

"Th-they really have." The beautiful pale face finally cracked a smile, so Haruyuki relaxed his own mouth with relief and cocked his head once again. "But does all that matter?"

"I trust you, of course. I trust that there is honestly no way you would accept an offer from another king. I trust you, but...but I can't help feeling a little uneasy. There is something so absolute about their attraction, to go that far."

Haruyuki didn't know what color king the "their" indicated.

Kuroyukihime abruptly raised her right hand, keeping eyes the color of the night sky on the perplexed Haruyuki. With a supple movement, she caressed the line of his round cheek and murmured in a silken, yet coldly tense voice, "Haruyuki. Listen. You belong to me. Until now and from now. For all eternity. I will not let another have you."

Haruyuki opened his eyes wide and forgot to breathe, turning to stone at this sudden touch and declaration. If it had been just the words, he maybe could've accepted it as a confession of love. But even after she closed her mouth, Haruyuki could still clearly hear a soundless voice in his ears: *Say you're going to another king and I'll cut you down before you get the chance.*

He felt a shiver run down his spine but still managed to reply in his heart: *If that should happen, please have no mercy on me.*

Although what came out of his mouth treated the whole thing like a joke. "Oh, that goes without saying. You can even write your name in permanent marker on my avatar."

"Ha-ha! That's a good idea. And you know, they do exist over there, indelible pens."

"Wh-what?!"

At Haruyuki's surprise, Kuroyukihime finally opened up with her usual smile. She lowered her hand and took another sip of her tea.

"Sorry. I got a little sidetracked there. We were talking about Kurashima, yes? I think you fully understand now just how rare a healer-type avatar is." She nodded briefly, returning her cup to its saucer and letting her gaze drift off a little. "Just as Takumu said, we must therefore handle this all the more discreetly. If the news spreads that a third healer has appeared in the accelerated world, any and all kinds of powers will be maneuvering to scoop up Kurashima."

At that, Haruyuki couldn't help but feel apprehensive. It wasn't that he thought Chiyuri would blithely run out on them at the invitation of another Legion, but when all was said and done, the head of Nega Nebulus was Kuroyukihime, and he couldn't even begin to make the case that the Legion was a good fit for Chiyuri. And if the two of them had a big blowout or something, this was impulsive, straightforward Chiyuri they were talking about. Her quitting the Legion in a fit, getting scooped up by an enemy organization, depending on the circumstances, it was possible that— No, it was fairly likely that...

"...It could happen, yeah," he muttered, a shiver running up his spine. Kuroyukihime let out a long sigh.

"It seems that I'll need to have a real heart-to-heart talk with her about this," she said.

"G-guess so," he assented softly, although he absolutely did not want to be there when it happened. But the thought of not being

there also made his heart beat faster. In any case, all he could do was brainstorm with Takumu in advance to figure out every possible scenario, and then work hard to ensure everything was resolved peacefully.

I can do this. Maximum efforts, he told himself, and the instant he clenched his right fist tightly under the table, Kuroyukihime said something unexpected.

"Well, either way, we've got ten days."

"Huh? Ten days? Why are you going to wait that long?"

"Why?" With a slightly bewildered expression, the black-clad elder student replied smoothly, "*School trip.*"

"Huh?!"

"It was in the annual schedule file handed out in homeroom today. The new ninth graders have a weeklong school trip. We leave in four days, on Sunday. We're going to Okinawa, so think about what you'd like me to bring back for you."

Okinawa?!

In the back of his brain, *rafute*, *mimiga*, *soki soba*, and many other food names scrolled by one after another. *But she prob'ly won't be able to bring those all the way to Tokyo. I guess it'll have to be that, those donut-y things, um*, sata—

"*Andagi*? But those are no good unless you eat them when they're just out of the fryer." Without realizing it, he had apparently started talking out loud. After making this statement to Kuroyukihime, he came back to his senses abruptly and hurriedly shook his head. "W-wait a minute. A whole week?! So you're going to put the Chiyu thing on hold until then? But wait, forget that, what are we supposed to do in the territories at the end of next week?!"

The public Territory Battles, or "Territories" for short, were the team battles held every Saturday evening in which Legions fought for the areas each controlled. The Black Legion, Nega Nebulus, to which Haruyuki belonged, currently controlled the areas Suginami No. 1 through 3—in other words, all of

Suginami City. But to maintain this control, they had to hold onto a 50 percent win ratio against opposing teams who came to challenge them during the Territories.

Victory in team battles was determined by total annihilation of either side, the number of people remaining in the case of timeout or, if this was the same on both sides, by the total amount of HP in all gauges. As of late, even if his opponent was a sniper, Haruyuki was no longer getting unilaterally shot out of the sky like he used to, but it did make him feel secure to have someone like Kuroyukihime, an attacker boasting such overwhelming attack power, as his leader.

But more than that, in the Territories, the system only matched the number of people on both teams when the defending side had three or more people. It was possible for one or two people to come out to defend, but that would be—

"So then Taku and I are going to have to take on three enemies by ourselves?"

"Mmm. Well, I suppose you will," Kuroyukihime agreed crisply, swirling the milk tea in her cup. "The ideal situation would be if Kurashima were able to participate in the Legion by the end of next week. Then you wouldn't have to deal with that. But it seems quite cruel to make her take part in the Territory battles a mere week after becoming a Burst Linker. And you know, with you and Takumu tag-teaming, no three-person team is going to be able to outdo you."

"R-right…" He was definitely not unhappy to hear her say that, and a faint smile rose up onto his face. "We'll do what we can. S-so then I guess we just have to accept that there's nothing we can do about it if we get some kind of wildcard super-team. And we can still get it back the following week, right?"

"No, that won't work." She turned away abruptly. "I couldn't stand it if some other Legion's flag were to be raised in our Suginami. Which is why, Haruyuki, you must defend it to the death."

"To the death?!" Kuroyukihime gave the instantly tearful Haruyuki a fleeting glance, and then smiled in a placating kind of way.

Then, out of the blue, she said, "Mmm, well. Let's do it like this, then. If you succeed in next week's defense, as a reward, I will grant you one wish, anything at all. What do you think?"

"Reward?!"

This word coming from Kuroyukihime's mouth was equipped with a seemingly physical attack force, and it struck him right between the eyebrows, knocking him backward, chair and all. Haruyuki just barely recovered his balance and pulled himself upright again with a clatter, hands trembling visibly.

Anything... What does that mean?! All I can eat from the school cafeteria? Wait, maybe a restaurant even? No, no, this isn't necessarily about eating. Just the two of us going out somewhere... Or maybe she could come to my place... And then she'd let me direct. And the cable could be a meter— No, fifty centimeters— No, thirty centimeters? Could it?!

"Oh, I'll just say this. I can't grant any requests beyond my own abilities. Like eat spaghetti through my nose or something."

"Wh-what would that do for anyone?!" All his rose-colored dreams were instantly wiped from his mind. Haruyuki jerked himself bodily to the side, then shook his head sharply several times to reset his brain. "A-anyway, I'll give it everything I've got. And while you're away, I'll make sure to talk to Chiyu about the basics."

"Mmm. After that, I'll have her apply to the Legion." Here, Kuroyukihime glanced up at the clock display near the edge of her vision. "I should be getting back to the student council office. Which reminds me, didn't you say you had something you wanted to talk about?"

"Oh, right." Nodding, Haruyuki continued rapidly. "No, it was no big deal at all. Just that there are no Burst Linkers in the new seventh graders, that's all."

"You checked as well? I also looked at the matching list a little earlier via the in-school local net, but the only addition there was indeed Kurashima...Lime Bell, was it?"

Even as she confirmed his own finding, Haruyuki sensed a slight evasiveness in her tone. Abruptly, he remembered the entrance ceremony and the glance she shot at the seventh graders when she was onstage.

"Um, just when you were about to finish your speech, did one of the seventh graders catch your attention?" he asked timidly.

Kuroyukihime smiled bitterly and shook her head. "You were watching quite closely, hmm? No, it wasn't so much something caught my attention. If I had to say...I simply *felt* something."

"Felt?"

"You probably know the feeling. Like you're in the sights of a sniper hiding somewhere in the duel field." This was absolutely Haruyuki's most detested sensation in the accelerated world, and he screwed up his face reflexively. Kuroyukihime was quick to wave a dismissive hand. "In the end, though, there were no new Burst Linkers among the freshmen, so it must have been my imagination. And now I will be on my way."

"Oh. I'll head out, too." Haruyuki was now a proper eighth grade student, so he had the right to use the cafeteria's special lounge, but he had absolutely zero courage to stay in this elegant space all by himself. Following Kuroyukihime's lead, he stood, but it was as he tossed his paper cup into the recycling bin that a totally unrelated thought flitted through his brain.

Does that reward of anything apply to Taku, too?

He wanted to reject the idea as impossible, but when it came to Brain Burst, Kuroyukihime treated Haruyuki and Takumu exactly the same. If the reward was for working hard in the Territories, then there'd be nothing strange about it being for both of them.

But I mean, Taku's totally devoted to Chiyu. He wouldn't ask Kuroyukihime for anything weird. His elder reverence is seriously hardcore, though. I mean, he even calls her "Master." Taku's way better in the role of knight than I am. And she probably wouldn't be unhappy if he was...

Puffs of smoke rose up from a heart suddenly overloaded as he trotted along behind Kuroyukihime toward the cafeteria exit, and he blurted, "Um...Uh, Kuroyukihime?"

"Mmm?"

He flapped his mouth, fishlike, at the pale profile peeking through shining black hair, before timidly posing his question. "About that 'two princes for one princess' story you were talking about. If it were you, how would you decide?"

"I wouldn't even have to think about it," Kuroyukihime answered immediately, a daring smile spreading across her lips. "I would fight them and choose the winner."

Then, still walking, she lined up the index and middle fingers of her left hand and aimed straight for Haruyuki's heart.

Eep!

As all the muscles along his spine cramped up and he tripped on the leg of a long cafeteria table, Haruyuki realized all over again:

He would never get to the bottom of her.

4

After school on a bright Thursday, 2:50 PM, Haruyuki was walking briskly toward a section of the school he had essentially no memory of ever having set foot in during the previous full year of his junior high school life.

The fairly dated Umesato Junior High School building was in an *H* shape, with general and classroom wings built in parallel and connected by a sports wing. Haruyuki's destination was in this horizontal part of the *H*—the martial arts area, adjacent to the gymnasium where the entrance ceremony was held. Naturally, however, he wasn't headed there to join the judo team and make use of his bulk. Although, he wouldn't have hesitated to join if there had been something like a "special forces" team that taught marksmanship *and* martial arts, but regrettably, no such thing existed.

Haruyuki, with nothing remotely resembling any interest in participating in any afterschool club or team, ceded the starring role to Takumu today.

Approaching the martial arts area, he could already hear restrained cheers from inside and the dry blows drowning them out. He slipped off his indoor shoes, tucked them into one of the bags provided so he could bring them with him, and stepped up onto the polished wooden floor. In the circle of spectators, of which there were not that many, he found the back of a familiar head with its short-cropped hair, and approached at a trot.

Chiyuri turned and immediately pursed her lips. "Haru. You're late!" she complained in a quiet voice. "They're already doing Taku's match!"

"Sorry. But Taku's gonna kill him. I mean, it's the first round."

"Well, yeah, but still."

He shifted his gaze from Chiyuri's sullen face and, craning his neck for a better look, quickly made out the remarkably calm figure of his childhood friend among the kendo team members. They were lined up on the other side of the tournament area in their defensive gear. Takumu had apparently noticed Haruyuki at the same time, and he signaled with a short wave of his right hand.

Replying with a slight nod, Haruyuki turned his attention back to the tournament area.

"Ehaaah!"

"Sheeeh!"

Two small team members were clashing wooden *shinai* swords together. From their shrill fervor and the green ribbons on their gear, Haruyuki assumed they were both new seventh graders.

Today was the full-participation tournament for the Umesato Junior High School kendo team. The point was to decide who would be on the regular and reserve teams, but it also apparently served the dual purpose of beating the authority of the seniors into the freshmen. Umesato's kendo team was fairly strong, maybe because the school had a specialized dojo, and ten or so new students had joined the team again this year. Of these, the only one in eighth grade was Takumu.

Although Takumu himself had intended to dedicate all his free time to Nega Nebulus after transferring to Umesato at the beginning of the year, Kuroyukihime had strongly urged him not to. When his beloved "master" told him not to make everything in his real life about Brain Burst, Takumu found inside himself the desire to continue the kendo he had been doing for so long, and he was finally able to try out for the team this spring.

Haruyuki interpreted Takumu inviting him and Chiyuri to the tournament as being a sign of his intention not to use acceleration again in kendo, even if it meant he lost. Thus, Haruyuki had brought himself to the domain of the sports teams, which, to be honest, made him nervous.

"*Doh!* Win!" the advising teacher called out, interrupting Haruyuki's thoughts.

One of the seventh graders, back at the start line putting his *shinai* away, returned to the line of team members while stomping with a frustration he couldn't quite fully hide. In contrast, the winning student turned a remarkably small body deftly aside and stepped silently from the tournament area.

Haruyuki narrowed his eyes contemplatively and followed the winner's back, but the teacher's voice yanked him back. "Second match, round one! Red, Takagi. White, Mayuzumi!"

Two students immediately stood up. Takagi was a ninth grader and Mayuzumi—Takumu—was of course a year below. Both were about the same height, with Takagi having the meatier physique. They took three steps from the tournament sign and crouched at the start line. Haruyuki stared at Takumu, who held his *shinai* perfectly steady at mid-level.

Now that he was thinking about it, this was actually the first time he had seen Takumu in his kendo gear in the flesh. Naturally, he had watched tournament videos uploaded to the net before, but obviously, the amount of information you got with the real thing was different. He could practically feel the weight of Takumu's blackly lustrous *shinai* sword, shiny from use, and the stiffness of his kendo uniform. The scent of his protective gear wafted through the air toward him, and he swallowed hard.

Otherwise unchanged for more than a hundred years, the only thing glittering unusually on this kendo practitioner's outfit was the Neurolinker just peeking out from under the mask padding.

It hadn't actually been that long since matches in all kinds of sports had started to be carried out with Neurolinkers equipped. The main purpose was to have a visual overlay display of points earned and match time, but in kendo and fencing in particular, it was also used to judge blows. With the Neurolinker's sensation feedback function, it was easy to judge the beginning and end of a blow, which not uncommonly differed by a few hundredths of a second.

Of course, players were strictly checked for the use of external applications or connections to the Global Net during matches. But there was one super program that could easily make it past this monitoring. It went without saying that this program was Brain Burst.

Takumu had used the acceleration function at the Tokyo Junior High Kendo Tournament the previous summer and won the championship while he was still in seventh grade. But he consumed too many Burst points in doing so, and he was faced with the threat of losing Brain Burst. Driven into that corner, he infected Chiyuri's Neurolinker with a virus and tried to steal all of Kuroyukihime's—Black Lotus's—points.

Takumu still deeply regretted those actions, even now when Chiyuri and Kuroyukihime had both forgiven him. But Haruyuki felt that by coming back to the kendo arena again like this, Takumu was finally trying to make a new start.

"Takuuuu! Take him down!!" Chiyuri let loose next to him with a loud cheer, and even as he hid reflexively, Haruyuki shouted for everything he was worth.

"T-Taku! Go!!"

Against the ninth grade So-and-so Takagi, Takumu won handily, despite missing one blow. And he managed another sweeping victory in the quarterfinals. He secured a win in the semifinals as well, through a verdict, and finally advanced his chess piece to the finals.

However, it wasn't Takumu who was the talk of the tournament, but rather the new seventh grader, who had won all matches with surprising strength, taking each opponent in two blows.

"*K-kote*! Win!!" The slightly high-pitched voice of the teacher/ coach was overpowered by the sudden clamor. The rumor of the "amazing seventh grader" had spread instantly via the local net, and in a mere ten minutes, the area around the tournament space was jammed with students, even with the fact that school was out.

Said seventh grader, smoothly returning to the start line and not appearing to pay any mind at all to the commotion, was the small player from the first match Haruyuki saw. The name embroidered on the number bib read Nomi.

Erring on the side of generosity, Nomi was probably about 155 centimeters tall. His physique was on the slender side and as he faced his older, larger opponent, it seemed like the match would be something more akin to an adult fighting a child and very unlikely to be a proper match.

But he didn't get hit. He lightly dodged blows of his ninth grade opponent—blows so fast Haruyuki had trouble seeing them—as if he had predicted their arrival. Or else he met these blows with his own sword when they were still in their infancy.

According to Haruyuki's fuzzy understanding of the sport, kendo was a contest in which you couldn't really land a point-receiving blow unless you struck when your opponent had yet to begin to strike or had just launched a blow. The former was called *saki no saki*—or first of the first—while the latter was *ato no saki*: first of the last; i.e., the crux of the matter was how fast you could react to your enemy's attack.

On this point, the seventh grader Nomi seemed to have an ability far greater than anyone around him.

Right: *ability*.

"Final match!! Red, Nomi! White, Mayuzumi!"

At the voice of their teacher/coach, Nomi and Takumu stepped into the tournament space. The cheers from the gallery grew even louder.

There was about a twenty-centimeter height difference between Takumu, who was fairly tall for a junior high student, and Nomi, who looked like he was still in elementary school. You didn't have to think too hard to see that Takumu had the advantage. The two had completely different reaches. But Nomi had won all his previous bouts against opponents larger than himself, and without giving up a single point.

Both players bowed their heads and crouched at the start line, *shinai* in position. The large gallery, sensing something perhaps, abruptly fell silent. Haruyuki felt like he could practically see the pale sparks crackling between the swords as the pair faced off.

"*Hajime!!*"

The sharp cry was barely out of the teacher's mouth when the sounds of two shouts and one blow tangled together in the kendo arena.

The first to move was Takumu, or so it looked to Haruyuki. As he stood, he moved forward and struck with the strong *kiai* cry of "*Meeeeen!*" A single, merciless blow aimed straight at his opponent's *men* mask from as far as he could manage. With his short reach, Nomi shouldn't have been able to meet this strike.

However, before Takumu's *shinai* could meet its target, Nomi shouted, "*Teeeh!*" and his *shinai* hit Takumu's left *kote* gauntlet. The slapping sound of the strike shook the air. Takumu started to chase Nomi and lock swords, but Nomi had already created plenty of distance between them and had his *shinai* held high.

"*Kote* hit!"

The raising of a red flag accompanied the shout, and the gallery, together with the more than thirty team members, finally began to chatter noisily.

Standing next to Haruyuki, Chiyuri opened her eyes wide and shouted. "No waaay!"

Haruyuki also felt like that was the only thing anyone could say. Because Takumu had moved first, he was sure of it. And he had aimed for the mask of an opponent who had been just barely within his own reach. How could he have gotten hit on the gauntlet in the middle of that strike?

In other words, Nomi had perfectly grasped the trajectory and timing of Takumu's strike and brought his own *shinai* up first—which made absolutely no sense. It wasn't the first of *saki no saki* or the last of *ato no saki*. If Haruyuki was forced to choose, he would say it was *naka no saki*—the middle of the first.

Forgetting to blink, he momentarily doubted the reality of the world and wondered if he wasn't actually in some virtual one.

If it was a virtual world—if it was an electronic world where everything was decided by the brain's reaction speed—then Nomi's counter might have been possible. But movement in the real world was constrained by several physical laws. Taking into consideration things like the inertia of a heavy body, the transmission speed of nerves, and the contraction speed of muscles, swinging your sword before seeing your opponent's strike was completely and utterly impossible.

Unless you were one of the select few possessing a certain "ability."

Haruyuki felt sweat coating the hands he had clenched tightly into fists as he stared once again at the pair facing off at the starting line.

"Second round!"

This time, the scene developed in the exact opposite way. Takumu maintained his distance, *shinai* held at the ready. His eyes behind the cage of the mask were sharp like a sword, his lips pressed firmly together.

Nomi, on the other hand, didn't seem even vaguely tense as the tip of his sword bobbed lightly up and down. He was backlit, so Haruyuki couldn't see his face, but he could see the faint smile etched out on the lips.

Ten seconds. Twenty seconds.

Time alone passed, neither side reaching out.

Haruyuki opened both eyes wide and focused every nerve in his body on Nomi's face. If his guess—bad feeling—was correct, Nomi would move his mouth ever so slightly at some point. To give a short voice command at a volume no one could hear.

The ticking clock hands were the only things that moved as the teacher/coach finally took a deep breath, on the verge of calling out "stop."

But in that instant, Nomi raised his *shinai* at a speed that could hardly be called fast. And then Haruyuki finally saw it: Nomi's mouth quickly opening and closing in a tight circle.

No mistake. The acceleration command.

This new seventh grader Nomi was a Burst Linker, possessing the mysterious super-app Brain Burst in the Neurolinker around his neck.

"*Dooooh!*" Takumu attacked Nomi's unguarded chest the instant he raised his *shinai*.

Haruyuki also verbally called out, "Burst Link!"

The world froze blue with a screech.

His perception now accelerated a thousand times, Haruyuki watched Takumu's *shinai* inch toward Nomi's torso. Nomi could do whatever he wanted, but he wouldn't be able to evade or defend against this blow now. Even if he were also accelerating at that moment.

Wearing his pink pig avatar, Haruyuki slipped into the tournament space and peeked into the cage of Nomi's mask, semitransparent and blue. Unfortunately, what was beyond the mask was apparently outside the range of the social cameras, and he couldn't see through to Nomi's bare face. Just the mouth cracking a grin was re-created with polygons.

As he stared intently at the shrouded face, Haruyuki launched the Brain Burst console with his left hand. He wasn't clear on how exactly this freshman had managed to slip through the checks he and Kuroyukihime had done immediately after the entrance ceremony. But he had to be connected to the Umesato local net right now, given that he was in the middle of a tournament. And in that case, the full name of this Nomi would have to appear in the matching list.

I'll challenge him to a duel right now, Haruyuki resolved in his heart, and waited for the list to refresh.

Nomi was clearly using the acceleration ability in this kendo team tournament. Which meant he was probably planning to use it in the proficiency tests at the beginning of next week. So Haruyuki would have to teach him—with his virtual fists, if necessary—that Nega Nebulus had an ironclad rule that Burst Linkers at Umesato Junior High were not to use acceleration in tests or tournaments.

The searching display ended, and the names Silver Crow, Black Lotus, Cyan Pile, and Lime Bell were displayed, pop, pop, pop, on the list.

"What...?!" Haruyuki gasped violently, right hand still reaching out to the list.

His name's not here. Just like the other day, there're only the four Burst Linkers we already know about!

"H-how..." he muttered, stunned.

He couldn't believe that it had been his imagination. Takumu had almost certainly launched his first strike without waiting and watching, precisely because he thought this Nomi was a Burst Linker, and he hadn't wanted to give Nomi the chance to call out the acceleration command.

After toying with the thought that maybe, impossibly, the backdoor program Takumu had used six months earlier was going around again, he quickly tossed the idea aside. That program was to connect from outside a closed network, using someone as a stepladder. However, at that moment, Nomi was clearly in the Umesato Junior High kendo area. And that meant that he had to be connected to the in-school local net. So he had to be registered on the matching list, he absolutely had to.

Haruyuki crossed his short pig avatar arms, dropped his head, and seriously racked his brain. He needed a full minute to organize the up-to-three possibilities that could explain this situation.

One: Nomi was not a Burst Linker, but instead, a kendo genius.

Two: Nomi was a Burst Linker, but he was not connected to the in-school local net.

Three: Nomi was a Burst Linker and he was connected to the local net, but he could refuse to be registered on the matching list.

One of these had to be the truth. But whichever one it ended up being, there was still something that couldn't be explained.

Haruyuki exhaled at length, with frustration and a foreboding he couldn't quite pinpoint. But it was useless to keep thinking about it now. All he could do was talk with Takumu and the others about it later.

He returned to his own frozen blue body and stared once more at Nomi.

Perhaps recklessly aiming for Takumu's *men* mask, he was leaping forward, his *shinai* sword raised high. Takumu's timing in going for the blow on the exposed *doh* stomach was perfect to Haruyuki's layperson eyes.

If, hypothetically, Nomi happened to be a Burst Linker or a kendo genius or even both, there was nothing he could do about it at that moment. Deciding to at least properly witness with his own eyeballs Takumu taking a point, Haruyuki shouted the acceleration stop command, eyes wide open.

"Burst out!"

From off in the distance, the sound of the real world approached, while the blue world gradually regained its color. Takumu's and Nomi's movements steadily, bit by bit, returned to their original speed—

"......?!" Haruyuki was slapped in the face with a new shock for the nth time in these last few minutes.

Nomi's body had slid to the right.

It wasn't anything approaching footwork. Only the tiptoes of his left foot were in contact with the tournament floor. And yet, with this single point as an axis, the little body rotated left, like a figure skater, and slid to the right. Takumu's *shinai* gave chase, but the torso fled, escaped...

Which is where the acceleration of Haruyuki's senses was completely released.

The *saki-gawa* tip of Takumu's *shinai* bounced off Nomi's torso. But lightly.

Then Nomi's casually deployed *shinai* caught Takumu's mask cage spectacularly. As he followed through, he stomped the floor hard with his right foot.

"*Meeeen*!!" A faultless counterstroke accompanied the *kiai* cry.

The kendo area fell back into silence until there finally came the cry of, "*Men*! Hit! We have a winner!!"

Fwump. The bag containing Haruyuki's jacket fell from his hand.

5

Unable to rank the priority of the things he needed to be investigating, Haruyuki stared for a while at the small shrimp. It sat on top of the pizza slice he held in his hand.

Making up his mind, he took a big bite, raised his head, and asked, "Taku. He...Is Nomi a Burst Linker?"

"Wow, you cut straight to the chase, huh?" Takumu raised the right side of his mouth in a wry smile and bit into his own slice.

Eight thirty at night, Haruyuki's bedroom. Takumu had finished his team practice and taken a shower at his own place before coming over, so it had gotten a bit late.

As a rule, Haruyuki's mother didn't come home before midnight, and in his elementary school days, Takumu knew his parents would never have allowed him to eat supper at a friend's house like this. Takumu had also fought battle after war with his parents about the transfer to Umesato at the beginning of the year, although he had stubbornly refused to tell them why he wanted the transfer.

In the end, he had finally managed to get them to allow it by voluntarily offering several conditions, but naturally, Haruyuki didn't know all the details of that deal. And although he bowed his head to all the struggle Takumu had gone through, he also selfishly wondered which way worked out better for a kid:

Takumu's life or his own, with parents who paid him absolutely no attention.

"Oh! You're eating stuff like that again?!" Haruyuki had just taken his second bite when a voice suddenly shattered his thoughts.

"Honestly!" Sidling in through the open door, Chiyuri placed her right hand on her hip and continued on her tirade. "I've been telling you forever that you have to learn how to cook for yourself!"

"I-I do."

"You mean you take stuff out of a box or the freezer!"

"I-I serve it on a plate."

"That is not a meal!" She got Haruyuki's nose in her sights with a snap of her index finger, and then held high the paper bag in her left hand. "I figured this is what would happen, so I had Mom make some lasagna. See? Smart!"

It's not like you made it yourself! he grumbled internally, but when the fragrance of baked cheese came wafting from the bag, Haruyuki was compelled to throw himself down before her.

The lasagna, tightly packed in the heat-resistant square container, was a rare treat jam-packed with Chiyuri's mother's special Bolognese sauce, and it had a flavor with which—although it was also Italian food—the frozen pizza could not compare. They moved to the living room, where it took a mere fifteen minutes for Haruyuki to polish off a fourth of the whole thing and Takumu and Chiyuri to finish a third each.

"That was delicious. Your mom should open a restaurant, Chi," Takumu said with a satisfied expression, and Haruyuki seconded his words immediately.

"For real. She can make anything: Japanese, Western, Chinese, whatever."

"Oh, no, no way. Mom's cooking output's at fifty percent when she's not making food for Dad," Chiyuri said, looking very serious, and Haruyuki unconsciously looked down at the now empty lasagna dish.

"S-seriously? This deliciousness is only half her real power?"

"Oh, this is about ninety-five percent here. If Mom's cooking for a candidate for my future husband— Aah what are you making me say? I'll kill you!!" she shouted suddenly, and actually launched a kick under the table at the shins of Haruyuki before carrying a clattering pile of plates and forks into the kitchen.

After exchanging a slightly bitter smile with Takumu, who was nearly fainting in agony, Haruyuki cleared his throat and forced them back on topic. "So, about Nomi. Right. So what's this guy's first name?"

"Seiji? He spells it like this." Takumu generated holo-paper on the table and moved his fingertip briskly. The characters he wrote on the virtual paper with his virtual pen read SEIJI.

"Hmm. I wonder if he's got any older brothers or sisters," Haruyuki muttered, and Takumu made the paper disappear, nodding.

"Yeah. I checked the graduation yearbook, and there was a student three years ahead of us called 'Yuichi Nomi.' But the address's encrypted, and only graduates from the same year can read it, so I'm not sure if that's our Nomi's older brother or not."

"Three grades ahead? Age-wise, he'd just barely meet the first condition..."

Because the ones able to fulfill the first condition of Burst Linker compatibility—being equipped with a Neurolinker from immediately after birth—would inevitably be the children born in the year the first Neurolinkers went on sale. This so-called "first generation" would be in grade eleven that year—that is to say, three years older than Haruyuki and his friends.

"If this Yuichi is a Burst Linker, Master would've gone to school with him for a year. But I've never heard her say anything about there being any older Burst Linkers at Umesato."

"Right. That's true." Humming thoughtfully, Haruyuki switched tracks and said, "Well, let's leave Yuichi for now. Either way, the problem is the seventh grader Nomi. Taku, he...He accelerated during the match with you, right? Otherwise, there's no way you could lose like that."

"It wasn't that big of a deal for me, you know." Takumu smiled like the ends of his large mouth were twisting. "I mean, it's not weird at all to lose after the first two bouts. Even without acceleration, that's just how it is."

"That's not how it is. You were definitely stronger than that team captain you got in the semis!" Haruyuki was suddenly serious, protesting Takumu's self-deprecating comments, and then lowered his voice. "Anyway, what do you think? I'm sure I saw Nomi calling out the acceleration command or something."

After a long silence, Takumu nodded slightly. "Yeah. I saw it, too."

"What?!"

It was Chiyuri who cried out in a high-pitched voice, back in the living room having finished washing up. Slamming a plastic bottle of green tea and three glasses down on the table, she squawked, "No way! He's a Burst Linker?! But I mean, you guys both said there weren't any in the newbies!"

"There aren't. That's the problem," Haruyuki returned, pouting his lips and ransacking his brain. "The instant I thought he had accelerated, I accelerated, too, and checked the matching list. But Nomi wasn't there. Taku, he was connected to the local net, right?"

"Yeah. You can't even compete if you're not."

"Right. But that kind of reaction without acceleration...Taku, he dodged the first blow to the mask and the second to the side of his stomach, almost like he knew in advance you were gonna do that. Especially the second time, I dunno, it was almost as if he moved his real body while accelerated...Although I guess you can't actually do that."

"Uh!" Takumu cried in a strange voice, so Haruyuki responded, "Huh? Wh-what is it?"

"It's just...Haru, you don't know?"

"Wait a second." Those words and that look sent a wave of déjà vu crashing over him. "Quit it. This sounds like another bit of accelerated world common sense that I don't know. Like the Unlimited Neutral Field or the Judgment Blow, any time either of those comes up, it's totally embarrassing."

"Yeah, well this is the third time." Whatever he was thinking, Takumu grinned as he grabbed a glass and filled it halfway with green tea from the plastic bottle.

He held the tea-bearing glass in his right hand, and his gaze firmly focused on the yellow-green liquid—

"Physical Burst!!"

Takumu shouted the naggingly familiar command before hurling the tea in the glass straight up with a splash.

"Wha—"

"Aah!"

Haruyuki and Chiyuri yelped in tandem, and then were, immediately, doubly shocked, eyes and mouths gaping at what they saw.

High in the air, the green tea drew long and thin arcs, and Takumu, glass in hand, caught the entire quantity while maintaining that structure!

Moving his right hand in tiny increments in line with the amorphous fluid, at the end he kept splash back to a minimum by lowering the glass in a swoosh as he caught the liquid. A second later, when its bottom hit the table with a *konk*, the glass contained the exact same amount of tea as when he poured it, rocking gently. A mere four drops had fallen onto the table.

"No way…" Chiyuri murmured, and Haruyuki finally remembered where he had heard a command like this one.

He was surprised he had forgotten, however briefly. It was the forbidden Physical Full Burst command, which Kuroyukihime had used to save Haruyuki from an out-of-control car plunging toward them six months earlier. Only level-nine Burst Linkers could use this function, which accelerated the movements of your physical body a hundredfold and used 99 percent of your total points to do so.

The command Takumu had just used was no doubt the low-level version. Not a "Full" Physical Burst. It was like the same command, but in an earlier stage of development.

"So then...that's the command to accelerate your consciousness in your physical body?" Haruyuki asked in a low voice.

"Right." Takumu nodded slowly, looking serious. "Tenfold for three seconds, uses five points. The movements of your physical body themselves aren't accelerated, but it's pretty easy to avoid an opponent's attack in hand-to-hand combat or meet it with a counterattack."

"So if you turn it on in baseball, you hit a home run. Huh... Nomi for sure used it to avoid your stomach attack, Taku," Haruyuki added with a sigh. He understood now why Kuroyukihime hadn't taught him the command. Unlike the basic command required to fight—Burst Link—Physical Burst was only required by people using their acceleration abilities for fame or the limelight. And there was probably no end to it once you started using it. Simply imagining the ridiculous number of points you would end up using if you relied on Physical Burst for even just a few things sent a chill up his spine.

"Seiji Nomi is just like how I was until last year," Takumu said, the edges of his mouth bleeding into the self-deprecating smile that had stained his lips lately. "Everything about him. He's winning at tournaments with the power of acceleration and avoiding at all costs the risks of the fight, risks that are supposed to be the price you pay for the wins you get. So even if I did lose to him, I'm in no place to say—"

Chiyuri, up and standing behind Takumu in the blink of an eye, rapped him on the head with a small fist, cutting him off. "You're wrong." She sniffed contemptuously at Takumu, who was dumbfounded, blue glasses sliding down his nose. "You're not the same. You were trying to win those tournaments for me,

Taku. I mean, right after you won, the first thing you'd do was wave a hand at me, right?"

"Y-yeah."

"But he's different. This Nomi kid, he didn't look at anyone after the tournament. He just looked at himself and smiled. He's totally different from you, Taku!"

Haruyuki's eyes moved from Chiyuri and her resolute declaration back to Takumu, and he nodded fiercely. "She's right, Taku. You're not the you from back then anymore. And more importantly, if he's a Burst Linker, he must already know our real identities. We can't just let him do whatever he wants and break our law against abusing the acceleration ability in our home base like this. No matter what it takes, we need to figure out how he keeps from showing up on the matching list and then beat him black and blue in a duel."

"Exactly! And don't worry! He can attack you guys all he wants, but I'll just heal you right up again!"

"......" Digging a deep ravine in the space between his eyebrows, Takumu continued to stare at the floor for a while. But finally, he moved his lips stiffly and a quiet "Thanks" slipped out.

When he brought his face back up, it was wearing his usual unfettered expression. "Got it," he said in a low, strained voice, after nodding once. "I'll look into it somehow during practice. Leave him to me for a while, Haru."

6

However, two days quickly passed with no change at all in the situation.

Haruyuki was desperately focused on trying to learn the faces, names, and personalities of all the students in his homeroom, and honestly he had no extra time for thinking about the matter with Seiji Nomi.

Having for a long time been very bad at hanging out with anyone, to the point that the only people even talking to him were groups of bullies, Haruyuki could not believe how quickly Chiyuri became friendly with several girls. She was already sitting with them at lunch and things. And even Takumu, a transfer student, had melted into the brainy group, chatting with them over lunch, surrounded by torturous equations displayed in 3-D standing models.

Of course, if Haruyuki had asked them to, they would have declined to join their new friends and eaten with him. But the last thing he wanted was for Chiyuri and Takumu to treat him with kid gloves.

So just like in the accelerated world, he had to break free of his shell and get to the point where he could make new friends. Intent on this purpose, he kept his ears open while aimlessly wandering within the local net, attempting to find other guys he might have something in common with. But any and everyone were talking about sports or music or fashion, with not even a mere micro-second of talk about games or anime.

Well, I just have to take my time and keep trying. I mean, technically, I have someone I can eat lunch with. And she's the most popular person in school.

He really and truly wanted to be as strong as this thought, but this popular person he could technically have lunch with was the vice president of the student council, and she was currently caught up in a whirlwind of busyness dealing with everything that needed to be dealt with before the school trip in a few days. So he didn't even see her on the net, much less during lunch.

The situation being what it was, the next time Haruyuki got the chance to talk with her was on the Territories' duel field at the end of the week.

"Eeeyaaah!"

Haruyuki watched Black Lotus's jet-black right leg kick out at right angles, drawing a beam of blue-purple light as it did.

Cut abruptly in a straight line from waist to shoulder, the enemy close-range attacker shot up into the air, spinning round and round, before it crashed into a building in the distance and stopped moving.

Haruyuki gazed at the team victory display that popped up in front of him and ran over to his Legion Master, relieved that their total win rate for the battles that day was 80 percent.

"Hey, nice work, Silver Crow, Cyan Pile."

"You, too!"

"Excellent work." Cyan Pile's large bulk materialized from the entrance of a collapsed building nearby, only to follow Haruyuki. As he bowed, his voice was quiet. "Please excuse me. I'm right in the middle of my team practice break, so I have to go. Master, do please have fun on your trip to Okinawa tomorrow. Take care."

They watched Takumu as he said his hurried good-byes and burst out, and then Kuroyukihime laughed quietly.

"He's so thoroughly a kendo guy. They started him on the regular team right away, didn't they?"

"Yeah. Well. Anyway, um, about the kendo team." Haruyuki glanced around to check that the three members of the enemy team and every one of the ten or so people in the Gallery had all disconnected, and then continued in a whisper. "We don't have any proof yet, but that new seventh grader who joined the regular team with Taku might be a Burst Linker."

"...What?"

Black Lotus's violet eyes narrowed, and she brought her swords up to intersect, as if crossing her arms. Haruyuki turned toward her and explained what had happened at the tournament two days earlier.

Kuroyukihime remained silent for several seconds, even after he was finished. Finally, she glanced up and muttered, "Still plenty close," before seating herself elegantly on some nearby rubble. Haruyuki sat down timidly across from her.

"Nomi...Seiji, hmm? I don't have any recollection of the older brother, Yuichi. There were no Burst Linkers ahead of me last year or the year before. So even if this Yuichi were Seiji's 'parent,' he must have lost Brain Burst by the time I started at Umesato."

"In that case"—Haruyuki shook his head, digesting Kuroyukihime's smooth statement—"if Nomi Seiji's a Burst Linker, maybe he went to a different school than his parent?"

"It's rare, but it does happen on occasion. I did it myself, in fact. But before we get to that...Are you certain? That this freshman Nomi accelerated during the tournament?"

"We don't have any proof. Just— I mean, it'd happen in kendo if it was going to happen in any sport, right? Taku used the Physical Burst command in kendo, too, so I think he totally knew what he was seeing."

"Hmm." Black Lotus nodded slightly and let slip a sigh somehow like a wry smile. "But all of this does mean you've finally learned of the existence of the physical acceleration command. I won't tell you not to use it, but you do know that using the command to become a baseball hero or anything of that nature is banned in Nega Nebulus."

"I-I won't use it! If I'm going to pay five points for just three seconds, I'd be way better off using ten points to dive into the Unlimited Neutral Field. Anyway, the real problem here is the reason why Nomi doesn't show up on the matching list."

"It is quite hard to believe, to be honest," Kuroyukihime murmured, further narrowing both eyes. "A patch was applied after the backdoor program incident six months ago, so it should be impossible now to use the same kind of underhanded trick. If Nomi is a Burst Linker and he's connected to the Umesato local net, he has to be registered on the matching list. If he's not on the list, then that means he's not connected to the local net."

"B-but for a student not to be connected to the in-school net while on school grounds... is that even possible? Especially during lessons and kendo tournaments, good Lord!"

"It's certainly unlikely." Mirrored black goggles shook gently from side to side at Haruyuki's rebuttal. "If you infiltrated the local in-school net main server or— No, it's simply too risky. This might be junior high, but if you were discovered, you'd be expelled. Perhaps... He might be masking himself from other Burst Linkers with some kind of illegal program."

"It has happened once before," Haruyuki responded in a low voice, turning his silver helmet to face the ground. "I feel like... that's the most likely thing."

"But even if that were it, what's Nomi's objective? If he wanted to hide the fact that he's a Burst Linker, using the Physical Burst command basically does the opposite. This is, indeed, the reason we're largely suspicious of him. And despite the fact that he's no doubt got information on our real identities, he doesn't use it to challenge us to duels. What exactly does he want?"

Haruyuki, of course, had no answer to Kuroyukihime's question. "I think the only thing we can do is figure out how he's not appearing on the list, challenge him to a duel, and ask him," he said, after thinking about it for a while. His tone was uncertain.

"Well…Hmm. For Burst Linkers, everything starts with the duel. I'd like to fight him straightaway, but unfortunately, I'll be away from Tokyo for a week, starting tomorrow. Perhaps I can fake an illness and stay behind—"

"Y-you can't do that!!" Haruyuki cried out, waving both arms frantically to stop her from finishing the unthinkable sentence. "Your junior high school trip only happens once in your whole life! Go. The rest of us will work something out with this Nomi thing!!"

"Mmm. You will? But don't be reckless. Oh right, have you decided what you'd like me to bring you?"

"Oh, that. I'd feel bad asking for something too bulky. If you just showed me some videos you took or something…"

Or to be more accurate, video taken of you or something.

To go into further detail, high-resolution video taken of you in a bathing suit or something.

And throwing in that reward for defending our territory without our master, all this via a thirty-centimeter direct cable.

While listening to the request to which he added these mental notes, Kuroyukihime cocked her head and said, "What, that's all you want? Okay, then. I'll take plenty of video and mail it to you. I'll record all the Okinawan food I eat during the trip."

And then the morning of the next day, a Sunday, Kuroyukihime got on a flight departing Haneda Airport with 120 other Umesato Junior High School ninth graders and flew off toward the distant southern country.

Haruyuki could, of course, still contact her with a voice call or during a full dive. But when he thought about her physical coordinates being several thousand kilometers away, it in fact made him a bit anxious, and even after waking up and going back to bed, he continued to toss and turn.

Why can't I be in the same grade as her?

If they were in the same grade, he might have been able to do things like see her in her bathing suit with his own eyes, graduate with her, and go to high school together…Although it was pretty doubtful they'd be able to go to the same high school…

These thoughts spinning freely around his brain were interrupted by the voice-mail icon flashing in the center of his field of view. As soon as he realized it was from Taku, Haruyuki sprang up and hit the icon with his fingertip.

"Morning, Haru. About Nomi, sorry to be reporting in so late. I thought I'd try and connect to his Neurolinker somehow and see whether or not he had the Brain Burst program, but I didn't manage to find an opening. I finally got ahold of a photo at least, so I'm sending you that. I'll be practicing with the team again this morning, so if I find out anything else, I'll let you know. Okay, 'bye."

The icon for the attached file started flashing as soon as the message playback finished. He furrowed his brow when he noticed that the data file was excessively large, but he soon understood why when he opened the file. Displayed was a group photo of all the new seventh graders on the kendo team.

Since Neurolinkers were equipped with built-in cameras, it was technologically possible to take a static image or video of your field of view at any time. But this also meant that peep shots could be taken with an ease that was unimaginable with the old generation's camera-equipped cell phones.

Thus, the function was currently limited so that people within range of the photo would not appear in any screenshots unless they gave permission via the net. It was a different story, of course, if you happened to be using some doubtful means to avoid this regulation, like Kuroyukihime.

Haruyuki, and Takumu like him, was not that knowledgeable or handy with Neurolinkers, so to get a photo of Nomi's face, their only real chance was a commemorative photo like this. Haruyuki ran his eyes over the photo filling his field of view and found the name SEIJI NOMI, GRADE SEVEN, CLASS A among the attached tags popping up and disappearing in succession.

Nomi's visible face—he was simply a boy with no special

features, features still plenty childish. Slightly brownish hair in a bowl cut hung long over his forehead. His eyes and nose were cute like a girl's, but the mouth, with a slight smile playing on it, had the roughness you'd expect from a member of the kendo team.

"You're...a Burst Linker...?" he murmured, but of course, the Nomi in the still image did not reply.

Haruyuki carved the face of the mysterious seventh grade student into the back of his brain, closed the photo, and got out of bed. He had been thinking about going to Shinjuku or Shibuya that afternoon to have a duel but, deciding to exchange those plans for a trip to the school, he got dressed in his uniform. If Takumu and Nomi were at kendo practice, there might be some change in the situation.

After hitting up the kitchen and there restlessly eating a couple slices of bread with some ham and cheese wedged in between them, Haruyuki left a short message for his mother, who was apparently still asleep, opened the door quietly, and went outside. As soon as he saw the ridiculously blue sky above another wing of the skyscraper condo, his vision blinked and flickered. Now that he thought about it, this was probably the first time since he had started junior high that he was going to school on a day off.

He changed his shoes at the school entrance and glanced at the clock. Getting ready and actually moving had eaten up an unexpected amount of time, and the clock was already rolling around to 12:15 PM. He thought about shooting off a mail to check if Takumu was still there but changed his mind, figuring it would be faster just to go and check himself.

The school on a Sunday afternoon was surprisingly deserted. It wasn't as if there wasn't anyone around. From the sports grounds, he could hear the shouts of the softball and the track and field teams, and if he had gone to the cafeteria, he would have found students from the culture club hanging around.

But the inside of the school building was dim, with the lights shut off and hallways shrouded in silence, making Haruyuki feel confused, like he had wandered into the wrong place somehow.

Quieting his breathing for no reason, he walked down the first-floor hallway and passed through to the sports wing. Slipping around the corner of the gym, which echoed with the squeak of basketball shoes, and heading toward the martial arts area—

"Sheaaah!" The sharp cry of a martial artist stopped him in his tracks.

Several other voices joined to form a chorus, but even among those harsh cries, repeated as a rhythmic chant, Haruyuki could definitely tell that this one was the high, piercing voice he had heard the other day—the voice of Nomi.

Making himself even more invisible, he descended into the graveled courtyard, advanced several meters while hugging the wall of the martial arts area, and peered in through a window.

Apparently, the full-team kendo practice was already over; only a few team members remained in the large, wooden-floored practice space. All of them seemed to be seventh graders, and they were all lined up and waving their *shinai* swords. Maybe an older student had ordered them to stay and practice or something. From where he was, Haruyuki could only see their backs, but given the small stature and the brownish, subdued hairstyle, the one on the right-hand end had to be Seiji Nomi.

Even through Haruyuki's amateur eyes, Nomi's bearing was infinitely more assured than that of his fellows, leaving no doubt about the strength of his actual abilities.

So if he has this kind of skill, why's he going to all the trouble of accelerating during tournaments? Haruyuki bit his lip. *Maybe he's stuck in some situation where he's totally screwed if he loses? Like the way Taku tormented himself?*

Haruyuki let out a small breath and Nomi alone halted abruptly. Haruyuki shrunk into himself, worried his spying had been discovered, but that apparently was not the issue. Back still turned to him, Nomi walked briskly to the wall and put away his *shinai*.

"Hey! Nomi! You didn't finish your reps yet!" one of the other seventh graders said, still brandishing his own *shinai*.

Nomi said nothing in response, lifted his sports bag, and started walking toward the entrance of the dojo, as if practice for him, at least, was finished. The team member who had called out clucked his tongue showily, and the student next to him raised his own voice. "Mr. Regular Team's not like us, huh?"

Even at this flagrant barb, Nomi did not break stride. Still in his kendo uniform, he left the dojo and turned toward the gym where Haruyuki was hiding, so Haruyuki hurriedly moved away from the window and crammed his body into the shadow of some nearby shrubbery. Nomi seemed not to notice him and proceeded straight through the passage, disappearing down the stairs toward the gym basement. There was housed the facility Haruyuki had the least to do with in the entire school: the heated swimming pool.

The idea that Nomi might actually be going for a swim baffled him, and he quickly put that guess out to pasture; the pool probably also had a shower room. Maybe he was going to get out of his kendo uniform and rinse off all the sweat he had worked up during practice.

The shower room.

"......!" Haruyuki inhaled sharply.

Given the situation, the remaining seventh grade kendo members would likely be continuing their fundamentals for the time being. And he couldn't see any students from any other sports teams anywhere. In other words, Seiji Nomi would, for a few minutes, be completely alone.

Maybe this was his chance? His once-in-a-lifetime perfect opportunity to question Nomi about why he refused to be registered on the matching list and why he was ignoring the other Burst Linkers who went to the same school as him?

Of course, if he feigned ignorance, that'd be the end of that. But Nomi had dared to use the Physical Burst command in front of Haruyuki and Takumu, who he had to know were also Burst

Linkers...Almost like he was showing himself to Takumu during the tournament. When he thought about it like that, it almost seemed like Nomi might be encouraging contact.

Still wrestling with conflicting desires, Haruyuki followed Nomi, paying attention to his surroundings. He tiptoed down the stairs, along the wall right by the gym entrance. At Umesato, swimming was an elective, and Haruyuki had never had any reason to select such a thing, so it was no exaggeration to say that this was the first time he had ever been down these stairs.

When he peered carefully around the corner to his left, Nomi was already nowhere to be seen in the short hallway. On the left-hand wall, he could see the entrance to the split shower/changing rooms. He glanced up at the ceiling, but there was no familiar black social camera dome. This passage up to the shower room interior was out of the cameras' range.

After hesitating another ten seconds or so in the shadow of the janitorial cart around the corner, Haruyuki steadied himself and approached the locker room.

On the wall at the main entrance, the directional display signs were excessively vivid: to the left, girls, in pink; boys, to the right, in blue. He looked back at the stairs before making the expected right-hand turn, took a few steps forward, and cleared his ears. If there were any students in there besides Nomi, he would, of course, have no choice but to sadly retreat. However, there were no voices to be heard. At some point, the palms of his hands had become drenched with sweat, and he wiped them briskly on his pants.

There's no reason to freak out here. I mean, I'm a boy who goes to this school. So if I keep going, no one can get mad at me or say anything about it. I'm just trying to spend a moment alone with Nomi here and ask him some questions about what he's really up to. Haruyuki reprimanded himself once again and took a few clumsy steps to finally slip into the shower room.

The space was much larger than he had expected, with lockers lined up against the wall on his right. In the center was a long table, and on this was a single, school-mandated sports bag. Several shower stalls were set up along the wall to his left, hidden behind a smoke-colored plastic panel, and along with the sound of water, he could see steam rising from one stall. Otherwise, the room was completely deserted.

I'm too late? Haruyuki sighed softly. Nomi had apparently gotten into the shower while he was fretting and being indecisive. And he naturally didn't have the guts to spring himself on someone taking a shower. He figured he would just go and come back later, and he started to quietly withdraw, but at that moment something glittered in the half-open sports bag on the long table, reflecting the light. He could only see a fraction of the object, but there was no doubt that this thing, with its smooth curve, was a Neurolinker.

Normally, if you were a security-conscious person, you would never leave this device, which was basically your second brain, anywhere out of sight. Even if you were taking a shower, you would keep it on or at least put it in a secure locker. But at school, when there's no one but you around, you might let your guard down, not wanting the tiny hassle of turning the mechanical key on a locker.

In that case, maybe you would also not bother turning off your Neurolinker? As long as the power was off, no one would be able to touch it, since a brain-wave authentication was needed to power it back on. But if it was left in standby mode, anybody could direct with it and search the memory areas. This was exactly the same trick the Red King Scarlet Rain had used in January when she had gotten ahold of Haruyuki's mother's Neurolinker and set up a fake mail address in it.

Of course, this was strictly forbidden, in terms of both morals and school regulations. If a teacher found out he had secretly directed with another student's Neurolinker without permission, he wouldn't get off with just a reprimand.

But however pervasive the social camera net was, constantly monitoring the nation's citizens, it didn't cover school wash- and shower rooms. And the educational authorities did not deign to concern themselves with violations of regulations for which there was no video evidence. Like how they had so magnificently let things slide when other students had beaten and blackmailed Haruyuki outside the view of the cameras. Furthermore, if Haruyuki directed and took a peek at Nomi's physical memory, there was a strong possibility that he would not only find out whether Nomi was a Burst Linker, but also that he would resolve the mystery of the mechanism that kept Nomi from appearing on the matching list.

After getting this far with a couple seconds' thought, Haruyuki made his decision.

He held his breath, listening to the sound of water echoing from the shower stall, and approached the bag to pull it up slightly. Inside was a neatly folded jersey and on top of that, a pale purple Neurolinker, indicator flashing a pale blue. It was in standby.

He yanked a cable out of his pocket and promptly inserted one end into his own Neurolinker before grabbing the other end dangling in the air. Then the Neurolinker inside the bag—

No, wait.

This color. Purple-tinged satin silver. He knew this Neurolinker almost as well as he knew his own, and it wasn't Seiji Nomi's.

As he stood there, frozen, gripping the plug, thoughts at a standstill, he heard the sound of the shower taps being twisted shut. The sound of water was cut off. He raised a dumbfounded face as the swinging panel creaked open, and his gaze crashed into Chiyuri Kurashima stepping out, wrapping a large towel around shoulder-length hair. Two sets of eyes popped open wide.

The gears of his deactivated brain exploded with a bang, and Haruyuki simply continued to stare at Chiyuri's face, not having the mental leeway to shift the focal points of his eyes downward— a slight saving grace in this situation. Likewise, she froze as well, still in her hair-drying pose.

"Chiyu," Haruyuki whispered almost soundlessly, finally regaining control over his mouth somehow. "Why're you in the boys'—"

"Haru," Chiyuri said at the same time, after blinking hard once. "What're you doing in the girls' shower?"

What?

Which was when Haruyuki at last noticed that the keynote color of the space around him was not blue, but pink. The floor treated with an anti-slip finish, the smooth walls and ceiling, the table before his eyes, all of it was tied together by a light grayish-pink.

But— I mean— So stupid!! Haruyuki shouted inside, peeling back his eyelids as far as they would go. *I'm sure I went down the side with the boys' sign. And it was painted right on the wall, so there's no way someone could have switched it as a prank. Or maybe someone just painted over it with something? No, no one would have had the time to do something as big as that.*

While Haruyuki was putting his brain through furious paces, Chiyuri seemed to finally remember her current state. She glanced down at her body, and her eyes immediately turned into perfect circles, ears blooming blood red. She yanked both arms down to cover as much surface area as possible; lifted her face again; drew in a deep breath; and, right before she began shrieking and freaking out at maximum volume—

He heard the voices of several female students coming closer in the passage outside. Instantly, although quite belatedly, Haruyuki understood that this situation would not be dismissed as a joke or a simple misunderstanding. This was a genuine crisis. If the school authorities found out, he could be suspended or expelled— No, he could even be reported to the police.

As Chiyuri seemed to come to the same conclusion at the same time, the color drained abruptly from cheeks flushed bright red. While they stared at each other's frozen faces, the girls' voices grew steadily louder.

Chiyuri thrust out her right hand, grabbed Haruyuki's tie and his collar along with it, yanked him forward with such force he was unable to speak, and shoved him into the shower stall she had been using until a moment ago. She got in after him, pressing Haruyuki up against the wall, and hung her towel over the top of the smoke-colored door. Grabbing the showerhead, she cranked the temperature to the maximum of sixty degrees Celsius, and then turned the tap all the way on. A stream of water gushed out against the wall to his right, and scaldingly hot water bounced back, immediately obscuring the stall in white steam.

"Don't say anything! Don't even move!" Chiyuri hissed, and he felt a minimum of three girls coming into the shower room, separated from them by a single panel.

"Ah, ugh! I'm covered in sweat!"

"Right? I want to pull out our summer gear already."

"Maybe we should just change to mesh for our Linker pads?"

They were probably on the track team with Chiyuri.

The sound of zippers being pulled down followed the voices. But Haruyuki obviously did not have the luxury of imagining the scene outside as he pressed his face to the wall, closed his eyes tightly, and desperately muffled his breathing.

Panic ruled approximately 90 percent of his brain, but the remaining 10 percent continuing to consider exactly how he had ended up in this situation. He simply could not believe he had misread the signs for the boys' and girls' shower rooms. And physically switching the signs was impossible. In which case, there was only one trick that would explain it.

Quantum masking of his visual field. Overwriting the visual signal from his Neurolinker. Someone had used a program to paint over the shower room signs with a fake image, making the boys' into the girls' and the girls' into the boys'. As soon as he reached this conclusion, he belatedly realized that the signs he had seen a few minutes earlier had been excessively vivid in the dim hallway. Almost as if they had been emitting light themselves.

How a program like this had gotten into his system was still a mystery, but he was pretty sure he knew who had gotten it in there.

Seiji Nomi.

It was all a trap set by Nomi. He knew that Haruyuki was spying on the kendo team. And so he led him to the showers, made him get the signs wrong, and sent him to the girls' side, thereby ensnaring him in this precarious situation. To get him expelled, and thereby wipe every trace of Haruyuki, the Burst Linker Silver Crow, from Umesato Junior High School.

A strategy so brilliant, cold, and merciless, it was terrifying. On the same level as the time Kuroyukihime had a student by the name of Araya removed—maybe even more so.

"Huh? Chi? You're still in there?" The voice of one of the girls came abruptly from the other side of the swing door.

Cringing with fear, Haruyuki heard Chiyuri reply right next to his ear. "Yeah. I managed to sweat a ton!"

"You must have. I know it's right before the regional prelims, but, man, you were pushing too hard."

Haruyuki was drenched in sweat. Steamed as he was in the extremely hot water vapor—wearing a jacket over a blazer over a button-up shirt over a T-shirt—he didn't feel the heat at all. Quite the opposite; his skin was so chilled his teeth were almost chattering.

If that girl outside decided right now to play a joke on Chiyuri and open the partition, Haruyuki wouldn't be the only one with his neck on the chopping block; Chiyuri would also be in serious trouble. She wouldn't be able to play the victim of his peeping; she'd probably be punished just as harshly as he.

"But Chi? Isn't the water too hot? It's crazy steamy."

"Huh? It feels better hot. Gets the blood moving, too."

"Ugh, you sound like my grandma!"

The other students laughed loudly. Chiyuri laughed along with them, and Haruyuki could feel her muscles shaking lightly through his back glued to her body.

Sorry. I'm sorry. Forgive me. I was an idiot. If I hadn't been looking for the Neurolinker in that bag, none of this would be happening! he cried out in his heart, clenching his teeth so hard they threatened to break.

Then he heard the creak of a door swinging open, and his feet left the ground.

But it was the sound of a girl going into the neighboring stall. He heard two more doors opening and closing, and then the sound of showers all starting at nearly the same time. Several seconds later, he felt Chiyuri peel away from him and step outside.

When she came back after a moment, Haruyuki looked over his shoulder at her, and she said, only her lips moving, *Now! Get out!*

Unable to voice his gratitude at Chiyuri's quick thinking because he was still holding his breath, Haruyuki simply nodded and staggered out of the stall. He forced himself to focus on nothing but the exit and worked hard to make his stiff body move: one, then two steps in a half-crouched posture. If he fell or something now— Or if another girl were to come in …

Just thinking about it was enough to make him pass out, but, somehow, he miraculously succeeded in escaping from the shower room without tripping on his own feet. He half jogged along the curved C-shape of the passage, reached his starting point of the boy/girl bifurcation, and leaned back against the wall, rubbery with exhaustion. The last of his strength drained from his legs, and he nearly slumped to the ground. But it was indignation, abruptly erupting within him, that kept him on his feet.

"Bastard!" he shouted in his mouth and raised his head abruptly, before charging into the real boys' shower room on the opposite end of the hallway.

But the pale blue-gray-painted space was absolutely deserted. There wasn't even any trace of the shower stalls having been used. Most likely, while Haruyuki was busting into the girls' side, Nomi had gotten pretty far pretty quickly.

"Dammit!" Haruyuki shouted and slammed his fist into the wall behind him.

Two hours later, at his own condo building's twenty-first floor. The Kurashimas, Chiyuri's bedroom.

"Excuse me, sorry, my bad, I really am sorry!!" Haruyuki repeated his apology chant again for the millionth time and pressed his forehead against the laminate floor with each word.

The owner of the room sat on the edge of the bed, still in her school uniform, arms crossed, emitting a fiercely murderous aura. The fact that she had said almost nothing since she invited the contrite Haruyuki in made her even more frightening.

He understood only too well that the mess he had made was essentially an act of barbarism of such magnitude that it would be stricken from the realm of possibly funny things for the rest of time—or he thought he understood that. But Haruyuki, being a boy, wasn't equipped to truly relate to the enormity of the shock Chiyuri had suffered.

He had witnessed her naked as the day she was born from extremely close up: a mere one meter away. It went without saying that this was a greater crime than Takumu infecting Chiyuri's Neurolinker with that virus last year. It was different from when they were kids and got in the bath together. Everything about it was different. Her collarbone clearly defined now, pectoral muscles connecting shoulders to chest, and the unexpectedly voluminous, very real, white—

"You're remembering it, aren't you?" she said abruptly in a low voice, and Haruyuki jumped at least a centimeter, still prostrate before her.

"I-I'm not! I wasn't!"

"Liar. Your ears are bright red. Let me tell you one thing right now. If you use that for anything weird, I will make you dive into that—what's it called, that U-Unlimited Neutral Field until you lose your memory. For like a hundred years."

He jumped up again with a small squeal. "I-I won't! I won't use it!"

It was true that he would end up spending more than forty days inside if she did make him use the Unlimited Burst command right then and there and keep watch over him for an hour. There was no doubt that the images stored in his brain would degrade in line with that lived time. But if another Burst Linker or an Enemy were to pursue him during that time, forget about his memory, he would end up dying of overwork instead.

"I-I'll forget it! I'll totally forget it!" Haruyuki shook his head and his extra chins desperately.

"Well, for real, I'm still going to think about what kind of penance you need to do for me, Haru. I'll hold off on it for now, though."

Something thumped into Haruyuki's head with an indignant sniff. Glancing up, he saw that it was a large stuffed animal cushion.

"So you can quit with the bowing and scraping. Sit up already."

"O-okay." Nodding, he picked up the cushion. He had thought it was an elephant, but the nose was too short, and it had six legs, three on each side. "Wh-what is this?"

"Water bear. Strongest creature on earth...Anyway! You said the reason you snuck into the girls' shower room was because of this virus, and the one who infected you with the virus was this Nomi kid. Really?"

"I'm totally positive." Haruyuki hurried to sit in a proper kneeling position on the strange creature and jerked his head up and down. "I know I went in the side with the boys' shower sign. I might be a total scatterbrained alien, but I'm not going to get pink and blue signs mixed up."

"But when would he have done that? I mean, you haven't even talked to Nomi, right?"

"Y-yeah." He nodded sharply.

The truth was, how he had been infected with the virus was a total mystery. At some time during the week between the entrance ceremony and that day, someone else had apparently handled his Neurolinker, but Haruyuki couldn't believe he had left an opening like that.

If he could isolate the virus, he would be able to determine the date and time it had been uploaded, but no matter how many times he poked around in his physical memory, he couldn't find anything that looked suspicious. When he checked his Neurolinker's operation log, he found traces of a single unknown file being automatically deleted immediately after he went into the girls' shower room. Since he had no recollection of performing this operation, the virus had most likely been set to launch and then self-destruct immediately after fulfilling its objective—i.e., applying a mask to Haruyuki's vision.

"But..." Chiyuri brought her thick eyebrows together tightly and cocked her head. "If he can do something like that, why didn't he just mess up the OS on your Neurolinker or delete the Brain Burst program or something? If he wanted to make it so you can't duel, wouldn't that work better?"

"No matter what kind of crazy virus you use, you won't be able to destroy system files with it. The best you can do is use its functionality to play tricks. And if you're already a Burst Linker, you can redownload the Brain Burst program itself anytime. Otherwise, you wouldn't be able to change Linkers or anything, would you? Of course, you have to put your core card in the new Linker, but..."

Having made these rebuttals, Haruyuki scowled suddenly. "But wait...if he's doing such serious and seriously hard stuff like overriding my vision, that's not at the prank level anymore. He's crossed over into really rough territory. I mean, taken to the extreme, he could basically kill me, couldn't he? If he made me mistake a red light for a green one or if he completely masked a moving car from all my senses?"

"K-kill—" Chiyuri cried out unconsciously, before remembering that her mother was probably in the living room and clapping a hand over her mouth before speaking once more. "Kill you? What are you even saying?! W-we're talking about a game here!"

All Haruyuki could do was smile weakly and shake his head from side to side. "Brain Burst both is and isn't a game. A guy like Nomi, who's using acceleration for status in the real world, will do anything to protect that power. Think about it. If it hadn't been you who'd come out of that shower stall then, but some other girl, right about now I'd be—"

"At the police," Chiyuri murmured, and a belated tremor ran up his back. "But...So then, does this mean that that Nomi kid is going to set up traps like this from now on? Not just targeting you, Haru, but...Taku, Kuroyukihime, me...?"

"No. I won't let him," Haruyuki declared, uncharacteristically firm, trying to reassure Chiyuri. "Now that we know how he works, we just have to wait and watch. Maybe Taku and I will take him on tomorrow. I don't want to, but...if we have to, we'll force him to direct, and we'll get to the bottom of why he doesn't show up on the matching list."

"Haru." Chiyuri looked even more anxious, biting her lip and turning her face downward. "I...I dunno, I don't like it. I feel like there's a mistake somewhere. I mean, it's a game...But you, and Taku, and Nomi, you don't seem to be having any fun at all."

He quickly shook his head, but at the same time, he wasn't surprised in the least that she would feel that way. Because Chiyuri was in possession of a rare healer avatar, she still had not experienced a normal duel even once. Right away, he wanted more than anything to show her the size and details of the field, the excitement of battle, and the exhilaration of victory, but for that, he would have to wait a week for Kuroyukihime's return to Tokyo.

"I-I've changed since I came across Brain Burst, at the very least. I went up against Taku for real, and I feel like my groveling parameters have gone down a little...p-probably," he stammered.

Chiyuri blinked hard, and a meaningful smile rose up on her face. "Well, I guess that's true. If the old Haru had seen me naked, he would've spent a whole month running away from me without even trying to apologize."

Gulp.

His throat closed up, and the screen in his mind generated a problematic image once again. "Excuse me, sorry, my bad, I really am sorry!!" Haruyuki prostrated himself once more, this time to hide the band of heat coloring his face.

"Enough already!" Another cushion came flying at him, hitting him squarely in the head.

"And one more thing," Chiyuri proclaimed quietly, her voice taking on that dangerous edge again. "If you tell Taku about the shower room thing, I really will kill you. And I'll tell Kuroyuki, too."

"What?" Haruyuki froze like a block of ice.

Although it was true that he had not the slightest intention of telling Kuroyukihime, he had thought to report to Takumu once his apology was finished. "N-not even Taku?"

"Obviously not! What are you even thinking?!"

Taking a third cushion to the crown of his head, Haruyuki wondered how it was so obvious. But if he couldn't tell Taku, then how was he supposed to explain Nomi's attack? Maybe he could just say that he was mistakenly led into the girls' shower room and not say anything about bumping into Chiyuri there. He was slightly ashamed at the idea of creating secrets to keep from his good friend and partner, but he took a deep breath and shook it off.

This wasn't the time to be dragging out a shower room incident.

This had been Nomi's declaration of war. For the battle about to begin, Haruyuki needed to muster every bit of willpower he had in him. And then, if possible, take care of the problem before Kuroyukihime came back from Okinawa. He couldn't be exposing that level-nine fighter to danger.

Haruyuki chanted this to himself as he left the Kurashimas' and returned to his own condo, two floors up.

He was wrong, however. He had misread the situation so badly that there would be no coming back from it.

The battle had already started and ended before he even realized it.

7

"That's game over, Arita—no, *Silver Crow*."

These were the first words spoken by Seiji Nomi at their initial meeting.

If you set north as up, Umesato Junior High School was shaped like an *H* on its side, with the main gate to the east. Of the two vacant spaces wedged in between the crossbar Sports Wing—which connected the northern Special Classroom and the southern General Classroom wings—the eastern section was called the "front garden" while the western section was the "courtyard."

In this courtyard, rows of incredibly ancient camphor and oak trees stretched along all sides, making the garden dim even during the day. It had no benches or lawns, so the majority of students never went near it, and there were no social cameras.

Immediately after first period on Monday, Haruyuki received a text mail from Nomi, inviting him to meet in this courtyard. At the end of the short text, in a tiny font, he saw the word *alone*, and he immediately glanced over Takumu's back, seated ahead of him in a row to the right.

Haruyuki hadn't, in the end, been able to tell Takumu about the shower room incident the previous day. He was good up to the part about being infected with the virus and charging into the girls' side, but he would have to touch on the fact that he had run into Chiyuri if he was to explain how he managed to make it out alive. However, Chiyuri herself had forbidden him to speak of it, so to keep that bit secret, he would have to lie, no matter how he told the story.

He absolutely did not want to lie to Takumu. But he could also easily understand that Chiyuri didn't want to be embarrassed by it any more than she already was. And now, as he moaned and groaned, torn between his loyalties to both of his friends, he was called out by the instigator of the whole situation himself. Bowing to the inevitable, Haruyuki decided he would report to Takumu after the face-to-face. And the mail insisted he come alone....If he went with Taku, Nomi wouldn't show.

When the designated time arrived—the twenty-minute break between second and third periods—Haruyuki got up from his seat and flew out into the hallway. He ran down the stairs, grabbed his sneakers from the shoe lockers, headed down the gravel path alongside the gym, and stepped into the courtyard.

It wasn't a particularly happy place for him. It was outside the range of the social cameras, and those bullies had made him come here far too many times. His memories of this place were all miserable—being shoved around, falling on his ass on top of wet, fallen leaves.

But that's all in the past. The me now is different from the me then, he murmured to himself as he walked over to the remarkably thick Mongolian oak in the middle of the gloomy copse. He heard the crunch of footfalls, and a person appeared from the other side of the oak, facing him.

Convinced as he was that he would be the first to arrive, Haruyuki was momentarily taken aback at this, and he took a half step in retreat. Now that they were face-to-face, he could see that Seiji Nomi was indeed fairly small in stature. Even compared with Haruyuki, who was slightly below average in his class, Nomi was yet another ten centimeters shorter. His limbs, his torso, and his neck—equipped with a dark gray Neurolinker—were all slim like those of a child. He probably weighed half of what Haruyuki did; his face, too, was cherubic enough to be mistaken for that of a girl. So much so that, despite having memorized the face from the photo Takumu sent, Haruyuki wondered for a moment if this could really be the person who had set such a ruthless trap for him.

Nomi bowed lightly, soft, bowl-cut hair swinging. The smile that started on his small, neatly shaped lips spread to big, beautiful eyes fringed with long eyelashes.

"That's game over, Arita—no, *Silver Crow*."

So said Seiji Nomi.

"Huh? Wh-what is?" Attacked and caught off guard, Haruyuki could only stammer a question in response.

"The match. My victory," Nomi said, smile still dancing across his face, and he shrugged his slender shoulders.

"What are you— Victory..." Haruyuki took a deep breath, got his thoughts in order, and scowled at his opponent. "We haven't had a duel yet. Because you've got something set up so you don't show up on the matching list."

"There's no need for duels and the like anymore. As long as I have this." Nomi pulled his right hand out of his pocket and made a show of fiddling with his virtual desktop. A holo-dialogue confirming the receipt of a file blinked in Haruyuki's vision.

"Please be reassured. It doesn't contain any viruses."

"......" Unable to readily trust that, Haruyuki glared at Nomi with suspicious eyes. In a whisper, he asked, "How did you apply a visual mask to my Neurolinker?"

"Goodness! You even managed to figure that out? Then as your reward, I shall reveal the secret. It was the photo! The photo! Takumu Mayuzumi forwarded one to you, didn't he?"

"Th-the photo?" As soon as he heard the word, Haruyuki belatedly understood. The group photo he had gotten from Takumu, of the new seventh grade students on the kendo team. Right before he opened it, he had definitely had the thought that it was a ridiculously huge file.

"I was the one who embedded the name tags. And it's a simple matter to embed a program to tamper with vision along with tags, because the Neurolinker image viewer and the augmented reality information display use the same engine," Nomi explained with a smile, but Haruyuki, given what he knew from his own recent low-level forays into the programming aspects of a Neurolinker, was pretty sure that this "simple matter" required some high-level skill.

Most likely, Nomi here was, like Kuroyukihime and the Red King Niko, an expert Burst Linker whose appearance and mental age no longer matched up. It would be a mistake to underestimate him just because he was younger.

As he made this mental note, he timidly accepted the file Nomi had sent—after also launching more than just the default virus checker on it this time. Nomi had forwarded what appeared to be a short video. He checked before playing it, but there was nothing unnatural about the file size given the resolution and length. Pinching his lips together tightly, he hit the icon with a fingertip.

A square play window opened, filling his vision. The image projected was clear, although there was a little noise. It appeared to be a school hallway recorded from a high vantage point.

It seemed to be in the basement, as there were no windows on the walls to either side. The hall didn't go very far; indeed, not too far ahead, at the end of the leftmost wall, there stood an entrance with no door. This quickly split to the left and the right, with two signs lined up on the wall at the bifurcation point: boys in light blue and girls in pink. This was—

The entrance to the shower rooms in the gym basement.

The instant he realized this, Haruyuki felt fairly certain he knew what he would be seeing next in the video. All the same, goose bumps broke out on his arms and up his back.

A second later, from the lower right, a round male student

inched into the frame. Hair an unkempt mess. Aluminum silver Neurolinker. Arriving at the shower room entrance in the center of the screen, the boy glanced back at the camera. The face captured from head-on belonged to none other than Haruyuki.

After hesitating briefly, the Haruyuki in the video proceeded at a trot down the right-hand passage, following the girls' sign.

"Goodness! I was quite surprised!" Nomi's cheerful voice reached Haruyuki, who simply stood vacantly once the video ended, face drained of color. "Normally, you'd realize the mistake when you saw that everything inside was pink and come running out! And yet you just did not come out. I really wondered what I should do."

What Nomi meant by this was a mystery, but Haruyuki first had to deal with the unbelievable fact that the video itself existed. "Y-you…" Haruyuki squeezed out hoarsely. "How did you… There was nowhere to hide in that hallway…"

Nomi chuckled as if this were actually very funny, and then shook his head. "Kids these days…At least, that's the sort of thing I'd like to say right now. You don't think that the only portable devices in this world are Neurolinkers, do you? They've been selling things like this for at least ten years now." He plucked from his pocket a streamlined device, lens inlaid on the front surface and small enough to fit in the palm of his hand. "Well, I guess when you say digital camera these days, it's all about those large-diameter SLRs. But this little thing has more than enough resolution. After all, anyone can tell that it's you in the video. I set it up on top of the tool shelf in the hall."

"You…You did all this to get me out of this school…?" Haruyuki asked, half automatically, staring dumbfounded at the toylike machine. "Are you trying to force me to drop out?"

"No, no, of course not! Not at all!" The cute, round eyes grew even rounder, and he shook his head, almost as if to say, *Don't be ridiculous!* "How would it profit me to have you drop out? No, all this effort would be wasted if you, pushed to such despairing lengths, were to attack me in the real. I was just thinking that from now on, at school"—Nomi Seiji paused for a beat, and a cherubic, and yet excessively cunning and controlled, smile filled his face—"you, Arita, could be my faithful and diligent dog. My obedient pet, bringing me the Burst points I use each day."

"I won't let you do that."

The voice shook the heavy air of the courtyard.

Haruyuki shrank back with a start, and Nomi, smile still strong, turned to face the direction from whence the words had come.

Appearing from the depths of the stand of trees was Chiyuri, catlike eyes blazing. There was no Takumu next to her. Somehow, she must have followed Haruyuki and overheard the entire conversation.

Chiyuri approached them, crunching along the underbrush, until she confronted Nomi at an extremely close range.

"I called Haru from inside the girls' shower room," Chiyuri snapped with a sharp tongue. "I'll testify to that if you make that video public. Maybe I did it because I happened to fall and twist my ankle so I couldn't stand up? Then Haru would have had a perfectly valid reason for going into the girls' side. Which means, of course, he wouldn't be suspended or expelled."

Haruyuki forgot his predicament and opened his eyes wide in mute amazement. Her explanation certainly was persuasive. Moreover, if he had been there for peeping purposes, it would be ridiculous to slip in through the front so obviously.

However.

Even after Chiyuri closed her mouth, Nomi's thin smile did not disappear.

He smoothly tucked away the small video camera before bringing his hands together in a slow, insincere applause. "That's good, that's quite good, Kurashima," he said. "That is, for a brand-new acceleration user still wet behind the ears."

"Quit with the bluffing. That video you took is completely useless now."

"Hmm, I wonder about that. For instance..." Nomi popped a single finger up in a theatrical gesture. "What if right about now, a hidden camera were to be discovered in a locker in the girls' shower room? The whole school would certainly be in an uproar. And if this video were to be uploaded to the local net after they started looking for the perpetrator...I wonder if you would be able to really cover for Arita, Kurashima?"

"......!" Haruyuki took a sharp breath together with Chiyuri. "You wouldn't...To go that far," he gasped, mouth dry, and suddenly, a red light began flashing before his eyes.

The words *emergency report* began scrolling across the top of his vision in a pompous, excessively bolded Mincho font, and the ringing of bells filled his ears, without leaving him even the time to be surprised. Unlike the bell for the start of class, the tone of this ringing was tinged with a sense of urgency. It was followed by an announcement in a synthetic female voice.

"This emergency announcement is from the Umesato Junior High School administrative division. As of the present moment, all student access to the following areas will be limited. Students in these areas are requested to leave promptly. To repeat..."

A transparent, 3-D map of Umesato then filled his view. An area in the center was colored bright red. The gym basement and hallway area. Naturally, the girls' shower room was also included.

Even after the image shrank to a small icon and he could see the world around him again, Haruyuki continued to stare in astonishment at his nemesis's face.

"It seems that the camera was finally found," the brand-new seventh grader said brightly, smile unchanged. "But I suppose that's only natural; I did set it to start making a shutter sound right about now."

His voice was half drowned out by the commotion erupting throughout the school building to the south.

"You…" Chiyuri murmured, almost inaudibly, staggering back a step. "Are you insane? Doing…Doing something so huge…All for the sake of just a game…"

"I'd like to ask you something myself, Kurashima. Do you really think that Brain Burst is 'just a game'?"

Haruyuki watched as, in an instant, Nomi's smiling face, so cheerful to that point, changed completely. The corners of his mouth were yanked up sharply, and a cold light spilled out from his narrowed eyes. His tongue flicked out to lick his lower lip, as if he were throwing it out to make fun of them.

Chiyuri's entire body shook, and Nomi's right hand shot out like a snake to grab the blue ribbon at her chest. Ribbon casually in hand, he yanked her over roughly.

"Aaah?!" Chiyuri released a thin cry, pulled so close to Nomi that their noses were almost touching.

"Please don't ever speak so rudely to me again." His cool voice housed both a childish quality and resolute determination. "You have no choice but to obey me. If you want to help Arita, that is… That said, being at level one, you won't be able to earn me many points, Kurashima."

Slipping suddenly and smoothly behind Chiyuri, Nomi wrapped his left arm tightly below her chest. He rested his chin on her shoulder and murmured directly into her ear. "Rather than a hunting dog, I'll make you a beloved lap dog. When I fight duels, you will ensure you are in the Gallery to wait upon me. Heh-heh-heh… my own pet, not even the six kings have that. Oh, don't worry. I'm not intending to make you do anything in the real world. For now, at least."

With each word from Nomi's mouth, Haruyuki's temple throbbed powerfully. He didn't realize right away that the strange creaking sound was the squealing of his own teeth grinding.

"You…bastard," Haruyuki growled, and went to take a step forward.

"Who said you could move, dog—I mean, Arita." He let the contemptuous words fly with a cold laugh. "I told you at the start, this is game over. You don't have any options left. Please be a good boy and sit there quietly for a moment." As he spoke, Nomi took something long and thin out of his blazer pocket. Haruyuki didn't have to look closely to quickly see that it was an XSB cable. And what its target was.

Readjusting his hold on Chiyuri's body from behind with his left arm, Nomi brought the small plug toward her neck. A thin layer of tears started to build up in Chiyuri's wide eyes.

And then when he saw the incremental chattering of her perfectly white teeth, Haruyuki heard a noise go off inside of him and he burst forth with it.

"Bastaaaaard!!"

Before he was even aware that he was the one yelling, Haruyuki kicked off against the damp ground. He pulled his hand into an unfamiliar fist and lunged at Nomi. In the moment, he was not aware of just what he was actually doing.

He was making a real opponent yield with a real fist—with violence in the real world, in other words—to destroy his pride and make him submit to Haruyuki's will. This was exactly the kind of lowest of low behavior that had made Haruyuki's own life a living hell in the past, but any sense of reason or irony had flown from his head. All that existed was the impulse to pound on this boy named Nomi, who was much smaller than he was.

Nomi's thin smile still did not disappear, even as he watched Haruyuki's enormous bulk charging toward him. He shoved Chiyuri away, sending her crashing to the ground; crouched low; and opened his mouth slightly.

Instantly, Haruyuki grasped what his opponent was trying to do.

Accelerate. And not the usual way. Physical acceleration, dropping his consciousness into his flesh body and making it ten times faster.

The moment he realized it, Haruyuki instinctively shouted the command he had never once used before—and he did it at the same time as Nomi.

*   *   *

"Physical Burst!!"

Whrrrrrr. The pitch of all the sounds around him dropped. The color of the sunlight grew duller, and the density of the air increased. It was almost like being inside a colorless, transparent, but viscous fluid. A single step forward took an extremely long time.

This isn't acceleration, it's deceleration, he thought before quickly rejecting the idea. The command accelerated his perception by a factor of ten while his consciousness stayed in the real world. Which meant, in other words, that the speed of his own body and everything else dropped by a tenth.

Nomi, a mere meter in front of him, was also moving at a dully sluggish pace. Cold smile still pasted on his lips, he brandished his right fist. Having brought the fist up to shoulder height, he slowly pushed it forward. The trajectory of this punch, which would normally not be visible at all, could be clearly predicted now.

Haruyuki went to throw his body to the right in the gluey, heavy air. At the same time, he started to thrust his left fist up from below. His aim was to counterattack: to ram his fist into Nomi's stomach at the same time as he dodged the boy's attack.

Is this really a good idea? The thought popped up quietly from the froth of his thoughts, to the water's surface of his heart. *I can't allow this; I can't let Nomi get away with this. I mean, it's not just me. Him going so far as to threaten and scare Chiyuri, and on top of that—what did he say? She'd be his lap dog?*

I can't let that happen. I won't.

Haruyuki took his time in determining his target, the place where his fist should strike: Nomi's right side.

Because of this, he was late to notice it. The fact that Nomi's right straight moved only slightly before stopping dead as Nomi launched a left hook in its place.

A feint?! He hurried to brace his right leg and tried to shift to the left. But his center of gravity, already inclined to the right, would not return to center so easily as that.

Nomi's left fist approached his face with a low rumble. At the same time, he opened his body up, and the right side Haruyuki was targeting danced away.

His efforts to correct its trajectory in vain, Haruyuki's fist simply brushed past Nomi's blazer. And then he felt Nomi's fist touch down on the right side of his jaw.

What? This punch doesn't hurt at all. The thought flitted through his mind right before the force of the blow pierced the several layers of fat accumulated around Haruyuki's neck and penetrated to his lower jawbone. There, it communicated its true mass and mercilessness to his nerves. Haruyuki felt soft structure being destroyed and capillaries breaking at one-tenth regular speed. Heat and pressure slammed against him, a slow exploding, and he started to fall to the left.

At the edge of his angled vision, he watched as Nomi followed through on his punch, spun his body around, and brought his right leg up, all with the same taut power. At wits' end, Haruyuki stared as Nomi, in an incredible motion like a frame-by-frame playback of an action movie, unleashed a spinning back kick.

The heel of his extended right leg connected with Haruyuki's right side, dug in, and pierced deep, so deep it was scary.

For a few seconds, Haruyuki experienced pain beyond his wildest imaginings, as if an enormous pole were gradually being thrust into his stomach, as he rose lightly into the air. From the corner of his eye, he saw Chiyuri's painfully distorted face blurred by tears. They had sprung up without him realizing it.

It was another seven seconds or so before he landed on the ground on his back.

All Haruyuki could do for the remaining thirty seconds of the Physical Burst's command period was roll around pathetically and endure the agony.

Vvvvp. The pitch of the environmental noise returned to normal, and the glue of the air thinned back into a gas.

"*Nngaah!*" He gasped fiercely as his accelerated awareness dropped down to regular speed, and he found himself rolled into a ball, clutching his battered stomach. Dry heaving repeatedly, Haruyuki saw Nomi's sneakers approach, parting the grass with a *crunch*.

"Aah, really now, Arita. If you had thought about it for a mere second, you would've realized that winning a fight in a state of physical acceleration depends entirely on reading your opponent and feinting, now wouldn't you? And that you had never actually fought anyone before? In which case, I suppose there was no need for me to use the command. Which means I just wasted five points." He stopped right in front of Haruyuki, placed his right foot on Haruyuki's shoulder, and then kicked him hard in the stomach. "Three minutes until next period? Well, I suppose we've got time. I will respond to your request and be your opponent, Arita."

"Oppo...nent...?" Haruyuki groaned, enduring the dull pain that was finally abating. *This is enough already. What now?*

The answer to his unspoken question came not in words, but in the glitter of an approaching XSB plug.

Nomi stooped, stepped on Haruyuki's back with his left foot, stabbed the plug into Haruyuki's Neurolinker, and yelled, "Burst Link!!"

8

HERE COMES A NEW CHALLENGER!!

Haruyuki stared dumbly at the text displayed before him, which followed the now familiar sound of acceleration.

A duel?! Why now?!

After all, Nomi had been keeping himself off the matching list through some unknown means and single-mindedly avoiding battle. So why now, and why would he be the instigator?

Thoroughly confused by the sequence of events, Haruyuki's brain couldn't readily fathom Nomi's intentions. He opened his eyes wide and simply stared as the world transformed with a dry vibration into a duel stage.

Every tree in the dense courtyard copse dropped its budding leaves at once, metamorphosing into jet-black deadwood. The sky instantly grew dark, dyed with the indigo of dusk. The school buildings, rising up on three sides around them, crumbled into ruins before his eyes, leaving nothing but the framework. Countless rods and planks popped up from the gray ground...Or rather, not rods—tombstones. Moss-covered crosses and stone monuments stretched out endlessly, as far as he could see.

When the stage generation was complete, two HP gauges materialized on either side of the top of his visual field. The name of

Haruyuki's duel avatar, Silver Crow, appeared below the bar on the left. And on the right—

Dusk Taker. Level five.

It was a name he had never seen, never heard before. And yet the avatar it belonged to was at a high level.

Most likely, Nomi had done this exact thing over and over again. Set a trap for another Burst Linker, grasped his weak spot, threatened him, forced him to "pay tribute" with his Burst points, and in so doing, leveled up without having to actually fight.

Haruyuki clenched his teeth, and the word Fight!! in large letters burned brightly in front of him before scattering into the ether.

Watching the last sparks disappearing, Haruyuki finally realized he was still lying facedown on the ground, just as he had been before acceleration. And that someone's foot was still resting on his back.

"......?!"

He quickly jumped to his feet, bounding back to create some distance. Readying both hands, he glared straight ahead, where the strange form of the avatar stood stock-still.

Its silhouette was a normal human shape. On the smaller side, it was not that different in size from Silver Crow. Its face also looked very similar: The entire surface was a featureless visor, beneath which the reddish-purple of the eyes hung sharply. The body and legs were also slim poles; the arms alone deviated sharply from this normalcy and appeared to be utterly bizarre.

The right was clearly of the mechanical variety. The inner side of the thick arm, made up of an assemblage of gears and shafts, was equipped with a brutal edged tool like bolt cutters.

But the left was, for all intents and purposes, organic. The arm was very much like that of some creature, with thin protruding segments and divided from the elbow down into three long tentacles.

The avatar's form had no real sense of unity, but the entire body was, as the "dusk" of its name indicated, a uniform dark purple. Its affiliation on the color circle was likely close-range and distant, but the saturation was fairly low.

Gleaning that much from his immediate observations, Haruyuki braced himself, guard up, and muttered the conclusion he had finally reached. "So you're going to try and suck my points away now. I don't fight back, you defeat me, and you get today's 'tribute;' that's what you meant?"

Nomi—Dusk Taker—remained silent a few seconds longer, and then turned his twilight-colored visor toward Haruyuki. "Once you get all dressed up in your duel avatar, you really take charge, hmm, Arita?" he said finally, sounding as though he was suppressing his laughter while the tentacles of his left arm writhed. "Even though you're still under my foot in the real world."

"And you! You so sure you should be leaving yourself open like this?" Haruyuki instantly fired back, ignoring Nomi's contemptuous snickering. "I know your face and name in the real world, and now I know your avatar name and appearance. You don't think my having all this information is just as lethal as you having that shower room video?"

"In other words, is this what you're trying to say? That if I release that video, you will counter by outing me 'in the real' and I'll be attacked by other acceleration users?"

"Is there any reason I shouldn't?"

"Ha-ha-ha! Tough talk! Well, I'll acknowledge that you have indeed managed to get ahold of one card. But to get your points, no matter which route we go, there is still the need for the duel. So I thought I'd hang onto one other thing for you."

"H-hang onto?" Haruyuki wasn't immediately able to grasp the meaning of Nomi's words, distorted by a metallic effect.

"Yes. Something very precious to you. Now then...we went to all the trouble of getting this stage, so perhaps we should fight? Although it is a little lonely without the Gallery. But this is a Direct Duel, after all." As he spoke, the blackish-purple avatar raised the cutters of his right hand and snapped the blades shut.

Haruyuki no longer had any idea what Nomi was planning. But if they were going to fight, Haruyuki had no intention of sitting quietly and getting beaten down. He definitely had Nomi's real identity in his hand; all he had to do was broadcast that information in the accelerated world, and Nomi would be hounded by point-hungry Burst Linkers until he couldn't move without getting challenged, something Nomi was likely interested in avoiding.

In which case, they just had to settle things now in a normal duel. He expected that Nomi's plan was to take this "something very precious"—i.e., his pride—with an overwhelming show of force, just as in the fight earlier, and make Haruyuki bend to his will.

But.

"If you think you can have an easy victory in this world, go ahead and try, Seiji Nomi!!" Haruyuki shouted, clenching his fist. With a single kick, he shot off the ground.

The battleground was a Cemetery stage, the main characteristics of which were that it was dark and the arms of the dead shot up from the ground occasionally to grab onto the legs of the duelers.

His opponent was a level higher than he was, but unlike online RPGs and other games, a difference in levels was not a determining factor in victory or defeat in the fighting game Brain Burst. Obviously, at the extremes of levels one and nine, overcoming the difference in fundamental abilities was difficult, but in a duel between four and five, the stage attributes and compatibility with them were much more important. And in this Cemetery stage, Haruyuki was confident he had a definite advantage.

"Aaaaah!" Sprinting in a straight line, he used his metallic fists and feet to smash the tombstones along his path as if they

were made of Styrofoam. The object destruction bonus he got from this went straight into charging his blue special-attack gauge.

Keeping the attacking Silver Crow in his sights, Nomi—Dusk Taker—barely moved at all. He shifted his feet unhurriedly and braced the bolt cutters of his right hand before him and the tentacles of his left behind.

"Chehhh!" By the time Dusk Taker waved his left arm with a high-pitched, assertive *kiai* shout just like in the kendo tournament, the distance separating them was still more than five meters.

The three tentacles bent, whiplike, and snaked out ahead.

But Haruyuki had been expecting this. In basically every game, tentacles always snaked out. The speed at which the glittering, pointed tips rushed forward was fairly decent, but even so, they were slower than a bullet. Haruyuki shook his head to dodge the one targeting his face, chopped at the remaining two with a sword hand, and closed in on Dusk Taker.

"Tchah!" With a short cry, he shrank into himself and slipped past the protruding bolt cutters.

"Haah!" He pushed off as hard as he could with his left leg, and the perpendicular elbow strike he unleashed, aim true, was a direct hit to his enemy's lower jaw. Haruyuki heard a crunch and a light effect exploded, illuminating the surface of the ground. A chunk disappeared from the HP gauge on the right. First strike.

Head hammered back, Nomi tried to stop himself from reeling backward, but Haruyuki gave chase, driving a right middle kick into Nomi's defenseless chest.

"Ngah!"

He pressed farther as Nomi groaned and staggered, left hook and right high-kick in quick succession. Silver Crow's body, more slender and lighter than his real world body could ever hope to be, flashed like a lightning strike, faithfully enacting the commands barked out one after another by Haruyuki's brain.

How do you like that? You see this?... You see this?! Haruyuki roared in his head, launching a kick from a showy three stories up in the air, looking for all the world like wire action in a kung fu movie.

You might not have realized this, since you're too busy running from duels, but when it comes to close-range, hand-to-hand fighting, there isn't anyone at my level who can beat me. Do you have any idea how hard I've worked to get this kind of speed? You don't know how many times I've taken a virtual bullet and thrown up in the toilet. A guy like you, obsessed with a dirty info war in the real, thinking you can reach the top of Brain Burst like that—

"You don't deserve to call yourself a Burst Linker!!" Slicing through the air laser-like, his right straight punch pierced the blackish-purple helmet, concentric cracks rippling out from the epicenter.

Dusk Taker flew backward and crashed violently into a tombstone, health gauge already down to nearly 30 percent.

"One more and you're done!" Haruyuki shouted, and at last focused his power in his shoulder blades. As he drew both arms to his sides, the sharp sound of metal *clanged* as he deployed his enormous wings.

After all this fighting, his special-attack gauge was completely full. If he got a dive kick in, dead-on, from way, way up, the last of Nomi's HP would be dust in the wind. There was nothing around them but the endless rows of tombstones, no cover of any kind for Nomi to hide behind.

In a single breath, he tucked his body in, and just as he readied himself to take off—

Dusk Taker's left arm twitched to life with no advance warning as its owner lay limp against a gravestone, the three tentacles flying at him like each was a separate life-form.

Haruyuki dodged two with some fancy footwork, but the third coiled itself around his right wrist. But he didn't panic, and instead grabbed onto the tentacle when it struck and yanked it up as he kicked off the ground.

He rose up about fifty centimeters, shifted the perpendicular thrust of his wings to the horizontal, and tried to drag Dusk Taker up with him. His opponent resisted, planting both feet firmly, but Haruyuki had enough momentum to make those feet scrape ruts in the ground.

He had come up against many enemies like this who tried to capture Silver Crow with whips and wires. But nearly all of them had either been pulled up high into the sky, still connected by those very whips and wires, or trapped awkwardly, scraping along the surface of the earth. The propulsive power generated by Silver Crow's wings was essentially inexhaustible so long as he had charge left in his special-attack gauge. He had even won a tug of war with Chrome Disaster, the evil Burst Linker with power greater than that of any king.

"Aaah!" At Haruyuki's battle cry, a silver aura surged from his wings. He would drag Nomi through the tombstones and whittle away both the avatar and his remaining health. Thinking these merciless thoughts—

Dusk Taker caught the elbow of his own left arm with the enormous cutters of his right hand. Without even the time to register his shock, Haruyuki heard an unpleasant *snip*, and his arm was severed as if it were made of butter.

Instantly, the tension of the tentacle clinging to him vanished, and without the extra load, Haruyuki cartwheeled backward through the air. He bounced twice, three times on the ground, destroying several tombstones before finally coming to a stop.

He stared up at the reddish-black twilight sky, temporarily stunned, before hurriedly springing to his feet. Suddenly, however, skeletal white arms erupted through the ground around him and grabbed his limbs: "Ensnare," a terrain effect of the Cemetery stage.

"Dammit!" Cursing, he tried to brush them off, but the arms kept popping up and persistently clutching his various parts. Forced to remain on his back, he spread his wings and tried to lift off straight up.

However.

Just as his body was about to break free of the earth, a shadow shot toward him, moving like some kind of insect, and came down on Haruyuki's shoulder with a kick. Haruyuki was nailed back down.

Above him, naturally, was Dusk Taker, whose HP gauge was now less than 20 percent thanks to the self-amputation of his left arm. In contrast, Haruyuki was still at 90 percent. A turnaround seemed impossible at this point, but the dusky avatar's entire body was strangely relaxed. He bent over languidly and drew near Haruyuki's featureless helmet.

As soon as the Ensnare wears off, I'll get up in the sky and finish this thing, Haruyuki thought as he said quietly, "Do you like stepping on people that much?"

"Ha-ha! Here you are saying that when it seems that you enjoy being stepped on," Nomi muttered with little inflection, and then lifted his left arm, half of it missing, to stare at the cross section.

Drawn by his gaze, Haruyuki looked in the same direction and observed with a faint physical revulsion three wriggling nubs— new tentacles poking out. "So they regenerate? Like a lizard's tail or something."

"If we're talking about it, it's more like octopi or sea anemones. Or wait, I think the *former owner* said starfish."

"Wh-what?" Haruyuki asked in response, unable to grasp the significance of this statement.

"I told you, didn't I?" Nomi turned toward him and began to murmur in an even colder voice, "That I would hang onto something very precious to you. And that—"

The blades of the bolt cutters clacked open around Haruyuki's left arm.

"—means—"

Light from the reddish-purple eyes swirled around in the center of Dusk Taker's helmet, which was so close now that it almost touched Haruyuki's.

"—this. 'Demonic Commandeer.'"

His special attack!

But the voice uttering the attack name contained neither fight nor exaltation; the words were simply spit out. Almost as if Nomi were distancing himself from the rule itself—that players must call out the name to activate their special attacks.

Dusk Taker's face emitted a pillar of black light that slammed into the mirrored surface of Haruyuki's helmet, and then bounced back in every direction.

"Ngh…!" Haruyuki gritted his teeth and readied to withstand the shock. Nomi could attempt to take him out at this extremely close range, but it just wasn't possible to bounce back from an HP gap like this in one blow. Haruyuki decided he would respond with a counterattack once Nomi's had finished doing whatever it was going to do, and he turned his attention to his timing.

But.

His gauge didn't decrease.

Silver Crow's health gauge continued to gleam a bright green, without moving in the slightest. There was no pain, either. Nor heat.

And yet Dusk Taker's special-attack gauge was plummeting from fully charged at an alarming rate. The blackish-purple vortex increased further in intensity, putting a cold pressure on Haruyuki's face, but otherwise, nothing changed.

No.

Haruyuki suddenly felt something being sucked from his body. He realized it the instant his enemy's special-attack gauge had dropped to half: The flow of the light reversed itself, erupting like a slithering liquid from Haruyuki's helmet. Spray scattered, swallowed up by Nomi's formless face.

Several seconds later, the phenomenon simply stopped.

His opponent's special-attack gauge was at zero, completely consumed. In contrast, Haruyuki's was once again full. His health gauge had taken absolutely no damage, and Nomi's was similarly unchanged, with 20 percent remaining.

"Whoa!" Haruyuki yelped, willing himself to fly in the same breath. This attack of Nomi's probably had a delayed effect, in which case, there was no point in waiting for it to be activated. If he got up to a very high altitude with Dusk Taker still on him like this, and then dropped his enemy to the ground from that height, he could settle this—

......

Silence.

A chilly atmosphere permeated the field.

The arms of the dead twisting in and around his body were gone. The only thing holding him down was the light touch of Dusk Taker's left foot and right hand, each claiming one of his shoulders. And yet.

He couldn't fly.

No matter how much power he concentrated in his back, no matter how he focused his awareness, the metallic wings that should have brought Silver Crow's body up and released it to the sky did not respond.

Dumbstruck, Haruyuki whirled his head around and peered over his shoulder.

They aren't there.

The silver fins, ten on each side, that should have been shining reliably and beautifully as always, had disappeared, without any trace whatsoever.

Completely bewildered, Haruyuki slowly turned to face forward again, and the blackish-purple avatar in front of him stood up soundlessly, casually releasing Haruyuki's restraints and taking several steps back.

"Heh-heh-heh." A thin laugh that was equal parts a young child's innocence and a veteran's tenacity slipped out from beneath the visor. "Ha-ha! Underneath that mask, you must be astonished, no doubt. Perhaps you're already thinking about the possibilities in that gaming head you're so proud of. 'What was that attack before; what's happening to me.' I'm not the sort to put on airs, so I'll just come right out and tell you. In short…"

Nomi crossed his arms in front of his chest as Haruyuki had a few minutes earlier, then thrust them out to the sides. "It's like this."

A hollow, wet sound filled the air, and, unable to speak, Haruyuki simply stared as two curving protuberances stretched out from Dusk Taker's back. They extended a meter or so before stopping, trembling, groaning, and then they deployed wide to both sides, scattering a dull, viscous black fluid.

Wings.

Composed of bones and membrane, like a bat or a demon, they formed a sinister black silhouette in the red of the evening sky.

The wings flapped loudly, and before the eyes of Haruyuki, within whom all thinking had ceased, the small avatar jumped up slightly, then quickly returned to the earth's surface. The avatar cocked its purple helmet.

"Goodness, this is fairly difficult, hmm? I suppose they're controlled not just by the physical order system, but also with input from other systems." Flap, flap. The wings beat fiercely over and over, and each time, the avatar's lift increased. "Oh! Like this? I guess I'll need to practice until I can control them without thinking."

Although it staggered and wobbled left and right, the avatar moved solidly away from the ground to float upward. It wasn't a jump. It wasn't hanging from a wire, either. This was…This was—

"No way." A cracked voice leaked from Haruyuki's mouth. "No way. No. Way."

There is and has ever been only one duel avatar with the ability of pure flight.

That's what she said, didn't she? Only me. The only one who can fly in this world is me. The one and only, my power. My hope. My…everything.

"Oh no, this is quite real." Hovering three meters above the ground, Dusk Taker spread both hands slowly. "My lone special attack, Demonic Commandeer, takes the Enhanced Armament, the special attack, or any one of the other abilities of the target avatar. Those tentacles, I got them from someone ages ago. Although I'm not really that good with them. Do you understand what I'm saying? Ultimately...there is no time limit. Although naturally, I can only keep so much in stock."

Stealing abilities. No time limit.

So that meant this midnight-purple avatar stole the silver wings that were the reason for Silver Crow's existence, never to return them...?

"N-no way! Give them back...Give them baaaaaaack!!" Haruyuki screamed, as if his voice could fight the bottomless sense of emptiness washing over him. He leapt to his feet, took several quick steps, and jumped with everything he had, stretching out his right hand to grab at Nomi's feet.

"Whoopsies!"

The feet were swiftly lifted higher and Haruyuki's hand cut through empty air. He fell to the ground with a metallic clatter and clumsily got to his hands and knees. His limbs grew cold, and his sensations grew distant. He tried to stand up again, but his avatar wasn't listening to him.

"Arita, Arita! Please don't be so dejected." The words rained down from high above, as if they were teasing—or, perhaps, as if they were consoling. "I told you, didn't I? That I'd hang onto something precious? Please don't worry. I'll give them back. The day you graduate from Umesato Junior High. Naturally, you'll deliver your quota of points to me every week. Two years' worth, paid in installments, as it were. And if you default even once... Well, you understand, don't you?"

As if to drive the point home, he flapped the strangely shaped wings loudly once and continued coaxingly, "It will be fine. You have that close-range fighting ability. You very nearly made me use my trump card, after all. You'll do quite fine without wings and such. I guarantee it! Heh-heh-heh...Ha-ha-ha-ha-ha!"

Haruyuki couldn't suppress the shaking that wracked his entire body.

This isn't real; there's no way this could happen. There's no way the system would allow such a ridiculous special attack as stealing abilities. This...This—

"Do you think I'm a coward, a cheater?" Snickering from his throat, Nomi continued mercilessly. "But, you see, isn't that how everyone who's faced you in a duel up to now has felt? 'Flying is too much; how is it even possible?'...Now then, I suppose I'll take this week's payment. Please stay still right there. Or I suppose you can no longer move?"

He heard the flapping of the sinister wings and felt Nomi landing very near him. But Haruyuki no longer had a shred left of the will to fight.

With the nonchalance of a bored factory worker, the large cutters grasped his left arm. The metallic snap, the sparks of amputation, the pain careering through his nervous system—Haruyuki felt it all from a distance, like the happenings of another world.

The duel ended, and as Haruyuki returned to the real world, Nomi's foot was removed from his back.

"Thank you for the duel, Arita," the small seventh grader said brightly, coiling the cable he had yanked free of the two Neurolinkers. "This concludes the clarification of our positions in both the real world and the accelerated world. It's inevitable, actually, that someone superior like me would use someone like you, at the very bottom of the ladder. I look forward to the next two years."

Glancing backward, he looked hard at Chiyuri, still on the ground after he'd sent her flying. "I'm tired after that serious duel, so I'll have to have you show me your avatar another time,

Kurashima. Please do remember your promise to be my pet. And…it goes without saying, but please keep this a secret from Mayuzumi and your boss—if you want your wings back. I have a few more preparations to make before I settle things with them. All right then, if you'll excuse me." After a neat bow, Seiji Nomi left the courtyard with the same composed air as when he'd appeared.

Haruyuki, on all fours, put some effort into it and raised himself up on shaking arms, only to collapse with a *thud* on the same spot. Although a minute hadn't yet passed in this world since he had been punched and kicked by Nomi, he was essentially oblivious to the lingering pain. His entire body was soaked in a greasy sweat, but he only felt an empty cold, as if he were hollow inside. Teeth chattering, he was unable to even take a deep breath.

Chiyuri's shoulders were similarly shaking, but she finally crouched down before him and forced out a hoarse voice. "Haru…Why…Why is this happening…Why would he…say such horrible things…"

It's supposed to be a game. It's supposed to be fun, her wide-open eyes said.

"Sorry, Chiyu." Haruyuki hung his head and pushed a voice that wasn't quite a voice from his throat. "I'm sorry I dragged you into this mess. I'm sorry for scaring you. But I…I can't do anything. He took my wings. I can't fight anymore. I don't have anything anymore, nothing." As he muttered, drops flashed to life in both eyes and poured down his cheeks.

I—Haruyuki Arita, Silver Crow, lost in every way to Seiji Nomi/Dusk Taker. In the information war in the real world, in the fistfight with real bodies, and even in a duel in the accelerated world, I lost utterly and completely. And—he took It from me. Everything.

He watched as two kneecaps, blurred by tears tumbling and falling one after another, sidled up to him. For a moment, he wondered if she was going to hit him. If she would jab him and yell at his cowardly, pathetic self like always.

But.

Chiyuri abruptly pulled Haruyuki's head toward her and buried her own forehead in his shoulder. "I hate this...I hate it, I hate it, this...It's all crumbling...We tried so hard, so, so hard...to go back to the way it was...So hard!"

The thin weeping in the pauses between her bitter words dug much, much deeper into his chest than the pain from Nomi's fists.

9

That day, Haruyuki had no idea how he got through his remaining classes, what he ate for lunch, or even which road he took to get home. When he came to his senses, he was flopped on his bed, still in uniform, and staring vacantly at the ceiling.

It was as if his memories of the day had all been placed in opaque wrapping and tumbled into soundless darkness. Almost as if the whole ordeal had been a dream.

Right, it was a dream. There's no way that could have been real, right? he murmured to himself.

Of course, if he accelerated right then and there, picked an appropriate opponent from the matching list, and went to duel, the truth of the matter would quickly be made clear. He would know without looking whether or not he had his wings on his back. But he wasn't the slightest bit interested in checking.

Rolling onto his side, he pulled up the blanket, from his feet to his shoulders, thinking he'd just skip his usual training and go straight to sleep. But that was when he heard the delicate chime of the doorbell in his auditory center.

He wanted to ignore it—probably some package for his mother—but whether he liked it or not, an image of the visitor popped up in a small window in his visual field. There stood his good friend Takumu, looking grim, and Haruyuki threw the blanket up over his head.

All day, Takumu had been asking Haruyuki what exactly had happened, including at lunch and after school. Given the bruise on Haruyuki's jaw and the state Chiyuri was in, it was plainer than day that something had happened.

Chiyuri had apparently only replied with, "Ask Haru," and Haruyuki could only respond with, "Nothing." He was likely betraying Takumu whether he told him the truth or not, so he excused it in his head, telling himself he needed time to think, and fled to his condo.

But Takumu was apparently not going anywhere. The chime ringing again had a resoluteness to it, as if saying, *I'll wait however long it takes for you to come out.*

Haruyuki sighed deeply and, half despairing, raised his hand to press the unlock button in the holo-dialog. When he got up and trudged out into the hall, Takumu had just opened the door and come into the entryway. With a look, Haruyuki urged him in.

They went into the living room, still not speaking, and sat down at the table across from each other. The silence continued for another three minutes or so.

"If there's literally no way you can tell me, I won't ask you about what happened anymore," Takumu said abruptly, looking at the faint remains of the bruise on Haruyuki's jaw. He took off his blue-framed glasses and met Haruyuki's eyes directly. "But just tell me this, Haru. What exactly is Chi to you? Why would you just leave her when she's looking so heartbroken—when she's crying? Whatever happened, she's my…friend, my best friend, you know, Haru?"

Unable to meet Takumu's eyes, Haruyuki turned his gaze down and to the left.

I would never just leave her! he shouted in his heart. But to settle this mess that he had gotten Chiyuri tangled up in, he would have to make this creature Seiji Nomi submit to him completely.

Unless he forced Nomi to delete the video of Haruyuki sneaking into the girls' shower room, defeated him in the accelerated world, and got his wings back, Haruyuki would have no choice but to follow Nomi's orders for all time. And Chiyuri would be stuck in the same position, with Haruyuki between them as a hostage.

If he considered things rationally, he should probably explain the whole situation to Takumu right now, regardless of what Nomi had said about keeping quiet. But Haruyuki wanted desperately to avoid telling Takumu about how he had been completely tripped up by Nomi's vision-masking program and had dragged Chiyuri into this as a result of charging into the girls' shower.

After all, that program was embedded in the photo you sent me. If you had just noticed the abnormal file size, this would never have happened, he murmured over and over in his head, conveniently ignoring the fact that he hadn't noticed, either.

This thinking, clearly nothing more than blame shifting, pushed words he didn't want to say from his mouth. "A-and you. How do you feel about Chiyu? If you're going to come here saying all this stuff, maybe you should do something about it yourself?"

"I want to. I want to, but... I—"

I already betrayed Chi once.

The instant he felt he heard these unsaid words, Haruyuki slammed both hands against the table. "T-Taku! I mean, you're just as bad as me!" he roared suddenly, letting the feelings overflow. "You always, always do this, keep your head down like this! You drag out all that old stuff forever and swallow all the things you want to say! I mean, you like Chiyu, don't you?! You want to go out with her again, don't you, Taku?!"

"Yeah, that's right! I do like her! I like her more than anyone!!" Takumu yelled back, making his chair clatter underneath him. "It's exactly because I like her that I want to do this her way! I'll wait as long as it takes for Chi to come up with her own answers!!"

"Wait?! And what are you going to do if the answer Chiyu comes up with is not you?! What are you planning to do if she decides to go out with some other guy?!"

"That's fine! I'm fine with that!!" Takumu gritted his teeth and the edge of the table creaked where he was clenching it in stiff hands. He choked out his next words from deep in his throat. "If that's what makes Chi happy. Even if that guy was, say...you, Haru. Even you. I'd be okay with that."

"...Are you seriously saying that, Taku?" Haruyuki asked, the voice that slipped out strangely monotone, even to himself. "So then...what? Are you saying you'll let me have Chiyu or something? Oh...or—"

No. No. I don't want to say it. Why on earth would I want to say something like this? I mean, I, I've always wanted you and Chiyu to go back to the way you were, that's it.

"Or do you like Kuroyukihime now? So then, if Chiyu and I got together, you could have her? Is that the plan?"

I just keep hoping and praying for you two.

Haruyuki accepted the heat and shock blooming in his right cheek half matter-of-factly. As well as Takumu's powerful fist thrust across the table, its connecting with his face, and how he and his chair flew back and fell to the floor.

Peering through a veil of tears for the second time that day, as he stood up, Haruyuki saw the thin, threadlike trail of teardrops on his friend's cheeks as well.

"Haru...Haru." Takumu's voice cracked and shook. "Haru, didn't we decide we wouldn't hide things anymore? Why...Why won't you tell me? Why won't you tell me the truth? I...Am I so untrustworthy a person?"

"Ta— Th—"

Taku, that's not it. But nothing more in the way of a voice would come from Haruyuki's throat. *I can't tell him.*

If he laid everything out, Takumu would probably immediately try and confront Nomi or something. And then he'd know.

That Haruyuki, that Silver Crow, had lost his wings. That he'd never fly again.

But he should actually confess that. If they were partners. If they were friends.

But Haruyuki couldn't tell Takumu. He just couldn't bring himself to spill the fact that he was so much weaker now than he had been at level one, that he was no longer qualified to be Cyan Pile's partner.

Takumu waited for another ten seconds for Haruyuki to answer him, but finally, the fight left his shoulders and he turned around, wiping his eyes on his sleeve.

"Sorry for hitting you."

Leaving the curt apology to linger, his tall, good friend walked heavily out of the living room. Haruyuki heard the front door latch, and then there was only silence.

How much time passed while he lay on the cold laminate floor?

Coming back to himself suddenly, he saw that the view outside the south-facing window had turned to night. He pulled himself slowly to his feet, brain still on pause, and changed into whatever clothes he could find before stepping out of the condo. He rode the elevator down to the first floor and crossed the lobby briskly.

The condo site was bustling with families visiting the adjacent shopping center. He saw a child clutching to her chest a bag from a video game shop, face shining, and was reminded that the latest in a popular RPG series came out that day.

...Maybe I'll pick it up, too.

Buy the game, go straight home, put it into his Neurolinker, and play intently. But the stuff they sold these days required a ton of capacity. He probably didn't have enough empty space in his local memory, but he could just erase some other game. That ridiculously large program...Brain Burst.

Right. I might as well stop playing that game. I mean, you do eventually get sick of any game. Now that I think about it, I can't believe I spent a whole six months obsessed with that one.

If he left the accelerated world and stopped being a Burst Linker, Nomi's stake in him disappeared. The video he had as evidence also lost its value, and he wouldn't be able to hold Haruyuki hostage to threaten Chiyuri.

Wasn't that the best choice right now? Of course, he wouldn't be able to help her in her quest for level ten anymore, but he also wouldn't drag her down and disappoint her with an avatar who couldn't fly anymore.

Everything'll just go back to normal. Something I had for a while will go away again, that's it. Is there any reason left why I shouldn't leave?

A little girl passing Haruyuki looked up at him with a strange expression. And that was when he realized he had tears streaming down his face as he walked along through the throng of people. Hurriedly, he wiped at his face roughly with both sleeves of his hoodie and started running for the gate to his condo.

Just duel with someone to earn the points to pay Nomi. Meet his quota like he was told and get his wings back someday.

If Haruyuki fought in Suginami, Takumu would be called to his duel's Gallery if he had "audience standby" switched on, so Haruyuki decided to change areas, and he walked up to Kannana Street.

After thinking a bit about whether to get on the inner- or outer-ring bus line at the Koenjirikkyo intersection bus loop, he waited for the bus to Shibuya. Nakano and Nerima to the north were the territories of the red legion Prominence, and he didn't feel like seeing its ruler Scarlet Rain.

When the rounded, electric-engine EV bus and its many wheels stopped, Haruyuki stepped onto the ramp. At the edges of his vision, the fare was subtracted with a *clink* from his e-money balance. He crammed himself into an empty seat in the corner and let his thoughts drift as he stared at the night scene flowing past.

There were about a thousand Burst Linkers in total, and Haruyuki had been taught that the majority lived in Tokyo. However, he didn't know the aggregate total—i.e., the total number of people who had obtained the power of acceleration, including the number of people who had lost it in the seven years since the Brain Burst program appeared on the network.

Just how did they, these former Burst Linkers, feel now? Were they biting their lips in regret? Did they simply remember it fondly? Or were they shaking with deep-seated resentment?

Haruyuki tried to imagine himself in their place. *If I lost all my points and ended up facing a forced uninstall, would I be able to walk away, to just think of it as "game over"? I mean, here I am clinging to the idea of being a Burst Linker, despite the fact that my wings, which are basically the reason for my existence, have been stolen.*

No, there's no way I'd be able to forget so easily. I'd probably scramble around trying to get Brain Burst back again.

And "beyond that"... there has to be some people at that stage. There's just no way there's no one out there, anger and despair only growing, brooding about trying to bring the accelerated world itself down with their expulsion. Kuroyukihime explained it before, how even if some kid did complain, without any physical evidence, no one would believe him or her, but is that really true? If the media or the police started getting anonymous tips one after another, wouldn't even the grown-ups start looking into it?

How exactly has Brain Burst been able to stay this completely hidden for more than seven years? And just what is the creator of the program trying to do by setting up this situation?

As he let his mind meander along this track half escapistly, the bus turned left at Koshu Kaido and entered Shibuya, Green Legion territory, where his privilege to go unchallenged in his own legion's territory would no longer be valid. Haruyuki—Silver Crow—would be registered on the matching list and could easily be trespassed upon at any moment.

...Anyone will do.

Haruyuki closed his eyes, leaned deep into the seat back, and waited for the moment. Silver Crow was now just a close-range type, weak to hits. Long-distance, close-range, mid-range—he had no advantage over any opponent.

Eight PM was the busiest time slot for duels, even on a weekday, and it was only thirty seconds later that the thunder of acceleration filled his ears.

Sucked into darkness, Haruyuki fell briefly as he transformed into his duel avatar and stepped onto the ground. Of course, the first thing he did was check his back; there was not a trace of the metal wings. He squeezed his eyes shut tightly once, and then looked around anew at his surroundings.

As before, it was Koshu Kaido at night, but the lines of vehicles that had been squeezed onto the road were gone, including the bus he had been riding. The road surface was cracked and caved in, the landscape dotted with mountains of rubble.

A Century End stage, huh? Haruyuki avoided the gazes of the Gallery members taking up positions on the roofs of the surrounding ruined buildings, and he cast his eyes at the ground. Without even checking the name of his duel opponent, he waited in the middle of the wide road. The guide cursor indicating the direction of his enemy twitched, and then pointed east.

Finally, from deep in the darkness, he heard the thick roar of an engine. For a mechanical type, it was approaching pretty quickly. So a locomotive type, then. In which case the sound he was hearing was coming from an old-school internal combustion engine, and the Burst Linker who owned such a device was—

Haruyuki finally raised his head.

The light of the round headlamp blinded him. Going for a ridiculously flashy spin turn, the American motorbike screeched to a halt, red sparks flying from both front and rear brake rotors, the surrounding bonfires reflected in its chrome parts.

"Hey hey heeeeeeeey!!" The skull-faced rider leaned back in the long seat and flipped the index fingers of both hands out at Haruyuki.

Haruyuki didn't have to look up at the name display; appearing before him was none other than his old friend, the motorcycle-using Ash Roller. Which meant both the stage and the opponent were exactly the same as the very first accelerated duel of his life, six months earlier.

"Mega crazy long time, man! What, you just so in love with me you came all the way to Pucker Valley??? Maaaaaan?!"

"...Huh?" Dumbfounded, Haruyuki forgot about saying hello or anything and countered with a question. "Wh-what is 'Pucker Valley'?"

"Whoa whoa whooooaa, come on, keep up! Yashibu, obvs! Yaaaashibu!"

"......" Giving it another second or so of thought, Haruyuki finally grasped that he meant Shibuya. "Um, hey, Ash. I don't think *shibui* means *puckery* in English; it's *bitter*, sure, but not in the way you're going for. Bitter-sour is *nigai*...So I think you should actually be saying *Nigaya*. So, um."

"...For serious?"

"...For serious," he retorted finally, caught up in the force of Ash's personality, despite the fact that he had never been more depressed, and the Gallery on the buildings alongside the road erupted in laughter. Ash Roller looked in their general direction and brandished the middle fingers of both hands.

"Nothing to LOL at, maaaaan! I'll kick all of your asses, just wait!!" He quickly turned his skull face back to Haruyuki and lowered his voice. "So then, what's *shibui* in English?"

"Uh, umm...*rough*, maybe?"

"Oh ho! So then it'd be 'Rough Valley,' huh?...But who cares about that!!"

"Y-you're the one who ask—"

"Keep it shaddap! Had a few wins and now you're all pumped full of yourself, aren't ya?! Watch and weep!!" he shouted, and pressed a button on the edge of his handlebars. *Clang!* Two bright red cones peeked out from mysterious pipes, one to either side of the handlebars' fork.

No way. But no matter which way he looked at it, they couldn't be anything else. "A-are those missiles?" Haruyuki murmured, stunned.

"One hundred percent! Missayles! Complete with homing, you flying monkey!"

"B-but missiles on an American motorbike, design-wise...I mean, how does that work aesthetically...?"

"Heeey! These things are totally Century's End, mega cooooool!! So go on, fly away! And then weep those tears!!" Ash Roller howled, and then craned his neck as though he had finally noticed what was different about Silver Crow. "So why you got your wings all shut up? The duel's started, y'know. Hurry up and spread 'em!"

Haruyuki shook his head slightly and said hurriedly, "I have my reasons. Today, I'll be fighting you on the ground."

"Huh? Well, you do what you want...But don't take me lightly or I'll seriously make those tears fall hard, got it?"

Haruyuki stared as clouds of white smoke flew up from the rear wheel, and the bike peeled out to the right. In his recent fights against Ash Roller, he had shifted to a game plan of slamming into the wall-climbing motorbike with hard drop attacks, but he couldn't use that strategy anymore, of course. All he could do was dodge the charge toward him and inflict incremental damage from behind.

The bike spun around some distance off and came barreling straight at him. Haruyuki lowered his stance and focused his mind on scrutinizing the incoming trajectory. The nature of a gamer meant that body and heart moved instinctively once the fight began, but obviously, Haruyuki hadn't gotten past Dusk Taker stealing his wings. That enormous hole still gaped in his heart, and he felt like he was now shoving his hand into that hole and poking around to see what, if anything, was in there.

"Hngah!" Baiting the hook until the last possible second, he dove to the right with a fierce battle cry, and the tread of the front wheel brushed his leg.

Now! He whirled around to slam his fist into the rider.

But.

"Hyaaaah!"

A boot launched abruptly from the side of the bike and connected with Haruyuki's helmet. As he soared through the air, he saw Ash Roller standing straight up in his seat, leg thrust out, following through on the kick.

The biker quickly dropped down with a *thud* and started accelerating again. Twenty meters out, he spun the machine around and stood in his seat again; apparently, he controlled the accelerator with his right foot.

"See this?! Maaaaan! That's my new jam! V-Twin punch, yo!!"

I don't know about the name, but the trick's amazing. Haruyuki admired it as he got to his feet.

Ash Roller maneuvered the enormous bike with just his legs, like a surfboard. Now it wasn't just the vehicle itself that attacked; the rider could strike, too, erasing the gap that used to open up when Haruyuki dodged the machine's assault.

. . . Maybe I'm screwed? Haruyuki murmured to himself.

In a simple contest of blows, Ash Roller, with his bike's charging ability, had the advantage. If they were both to strike simultaneously, for instance, Silver Crow would be the one taking serious damage. It was actually a waste of time to fight back now.

Haruyuki threw both arms down and stood stock-still as the bike's front wheel sprang up directly in front of him. He danced through the air like a broken stick, crashed into the road, and then tumbled two, three times before slamming into a mountain of debris and finally coming to a stop.

I guess the hole's empty after all, Haruyuki thought vacantly, head spinning as he lay there awkwardly. *Stripped of my wings, I have nothing. All I can do now is target low-level Burst Linkers, ones who are more compatible with me, and just keep fighting. Steadily earn points in fights and deliver what I've saved up to Nomi. For two whole years. Until the day he gives me my wings back.*

The engine was suddenly growling right next to his head.

Hurry up and finish the job, he thought and waited, but the hard, hot tread did not crush him even after several seconds. Instead, a voice came from high above him.

"Soooooooooo bad, yo. Hey, Crow. Why aren't you flying, man?"

Haruyuki lifted his head a little and caught the skull face in the corner of his eye. "...I can't fly," he replied thinly, at a volume inaudible to the Gallery. "My wings are gone. So I can't win at same-level duels anymore. I just wanted to test that today... Go ahead and end this already."

Once again, he heard nothing but the rumbling of the V-Twin engine.

"...Finish it?" The voice that finally reached his ears contained a stillness he had never heard before in Ash Roller. "What d'you mean?"

"There's nothing to mean. If you run that tire over me a few times, the duel will be over."

"Hmm. So this your deal, then? You can't fly no more. So you can't win. So you're throwing the duel and letting me have it."

Even in his current state, Haruyuki could tell he wasn't being complimented on his fighting attitude. However, even if he could use every bit of cunning he had to come up with some brilliant scheme to win this, there was no point. The only thing that mattered now was being able to hit his average in all the fights from now on, forever. And he knew that was already impossible. So—

"There's no point in standing up anymore," the still fallen Haruyuki muttered, and awaited Ash Roller's abuse.

But the reply he got was even quieter—so restrained it could even be said to be calm. "Hey, you remember, man? That second duel between you and me... That time you lifted up the ass of my bike."

"......" How could he forget? That was Haruyuki's first win, a fight to be memorialized. But saying nothing, not even nodding, he waited for Ash Roller to continue.

"You really had me. Ass up in the air, and my bike wouldn't move, like, even a millimeter, no matter how much I revved the engine. So then I was just stuck sitting there, and you went to town on me. It was like that checkmate thing. But, man…" Eyes glittered behind the skull of the helmet, and Ash Roller let out a low, strained voice, "That time, did I throw it? Did I give up like you are now and let you beat me?"

You didn't.

The Burst Linker before Haruyuki, who had sunk pretty much all his potential into the Enhanced Armament of the motorcycle, leaving the rider himself with essentially zero fighting ability at the time, had jumped down from his seat, swinging real punches at Silver Crow and his metal armor.

In the end, Haruyuki had unilaterally pounded on his opponent until he could no longer stand and won the duel. But Ash Roller had not capitulated, right up until the very last dot of his HP gauge was shaved away. Howling curses the whole time, he had been on his feet, swinging his fists, until the very moment Haruyuki knocked him unconscious.

"…No," Haruyuki answered in the negative, in a voice so thin even he could barely hear it. At the same time, below his own helmet, he felt tears welling up for the millionth time that day in his avatar's eyes.

"…But. But. I…My wings aren't coming back. You wouldn't get it. You get to keep fighting forever with that bike of yours."

Again, a long silence.

The Gallery on the surrounding buildings started to make impatient noises. However, Ash Roller appeared not to pay them any mind as he shook his head and spit out quietly, "Dick. You giga dick. No, tera. You fucking tera dick. You made it to level four and you still don't get it at all…When we dueled the third time and I watched you suddenly fly and all, do you have any idea how much I— No, not just me. Every single Burst Linker who learned there was some guy in this world who could fly. Do you have any idea how floored we were, how much we…"

The skull rider swallowed the rest and thrust his face forward abruptly. "Hey. Where are you now?" he asked in a near whisper.

"...Huh?" Haruyuki blinked eyes full of tears, not quite understanding the sudden question.

"I'm asking you where you dived from."

As a general rule, you should never be asked for the location of your real body during a duel. But for some reason, Haruyuki, thrown for a loop, answered without a single thought of the risk of being outed in the real. "K-Koshu Kaido...I'm on a bus."

Ash Roller clicked his tongue briefly and kept talking, his meaning becoming increasingly incomprehensible. "Okay, when we're done here, get back to your house ASAP. Go to the toilet, get in bed, and then dive up."

"U-up...?!"

"Keep your voice down, idiot. The Gallery's gonna hear! And what else does 'up' mean but the Unlimited Neutral Field? Once you dive, come to the lights at Kannana and Inogashira Street again. As for the dive time...right. Nine on the dot. You better not be even a minute late."

Having given the dumbfounded Haruyuki this order, Ash Roller yanked himself up and ran his finger through the air. A draw Offer opened up in front of Haruyuki.

"C'mon! Just say yes already!"

Pushed by Ash Roller, not understanding anything about anything, Haruyuki clicked the OK button.

The duel ended in an unexpected way, and once he had returned to the electric bus racing along a real world road, Haruyuki immediately cut his global connection. He almost tripped down the stairs in his urgency to get off the bus when it stopped at the next stop, looked both ways, ran to the nearest intersection, crossed to the opposite side of Koshu Kaido, and leapt onto a bus headed back the way he'd come.

As he tumbled into a seat, panting, he wondered what Ash Roller had in mind. Was he planning the coup de grâce? Did he invite Haruyuki to the Unlimited Neutral Field where there was no instant logout, to steal all his points and force the cowardly Silver Crow to leave the accelerated world forever?

No way, that couldn't be it. Ash was putting himself in the same level of danger, after all. He had no guarantee that Haruyuki wouldn't show up with a bunch of friends. But then, why—

"Well…whatever," Haruyuki muttered, and gave up on thinking altogether. Ash Roller might have been the foe he had most frequently come up against in the accelerated world, but Haruyuki definitely didn't hate him or anything. If an opponent like that was to be the one to deliver his final blow, then so be it.

When he returned to the Koenjirikkyo bus loop, the hands of the clock had swung around to half past eight. After running full speed all the way home, Haruyuki, as instructed, used the bathroom, drank some oolong tea, stuffed a slice of yesterday's leftover pizza in his mouth, and jumped into bed.

This might be my final acceleration.

In which case, I wish I could see the person who invited me into this world—Kuroyukihime. Even if I can't explain everything that's happening, I wish I could just say a few words to her.

Although this thought popped into his head, he was reluctant to call Kuroyukihime himself, when he knew she was in distant Okinawa, hands full, no doubt, with her responsibility to keep 120 students together. And yet, as the time display at the edge of his vision approached nine, he thought that, maybe, she might call him. He waited the whole time, but the receiving icon didn't flash even once.

When the digital readout reached 8:59:58 PM, Haruyuki closed his eyes tightly, took a deep breath, and murmured the command.

"Unlimited Burst."

10

It was the second time Haruyuki had visited the Unlimited Neutral Field, the infinite world built above the Normal Duel Field, and his first time diving there alone.

Under the faint yellow sky, the view of the reddish-brown megaliths lined up had a Wasteland vibe somehow. But this world employed a "Change" system, and so its characteristics switched periodically. Haruyuki ran intently along the dry earth to attempt to reach the rendezvous point while there were still good footholds.

Whatever the characteristics, the terrain of the accelerated world conformed to the real Tokyo. The ring road Kannana Street existed as a wide, dry valley, tucked in between the groups of megaliths.

As he raced forward, choosing the shadow of the rocks and avoiding the center of the road, Haruyuki watched both sides and kept his guard up. The Unlimited Neutral Field was inhabited by Enemies, monsters generated and moved by the system. He had only seen a large one once and hadn't yet fought any. Alone and unable to fly, if an Enemy with the strength of a high-level Burst Linker attacked him, the monster would easily beat him into next week.

Fortunately, however, all he saw were a few cow- and snakelike things moving sluggishly around a distant wilderness, and without getting in their sights, Haruyuki managed to reach the area of the nearby Daita Bridge, on the border between Suginami and Shibuya.

Just in case, he hid in the shadow of a stone a ways off and felt out the scene, but it didn't look like there was a large number of people lying in wait. That said, the instant he peered at the point where wide valley crossed regular valley, all the strength drained from his body. Leaping into his field of view was the rider in the flashy skull helmet, arms crossed, reclining on his American motorcycle, which was stopped right in the middle of everything.

"Laaaaaaaaaate! You're late, man!!" Ash Roller shouted, waving his right hand as he watched Haruyuki approach.

"I-I'm sorry. I had to run here, so—"

"And you prob'ly snuck over here, all spooked by the Enemies. Don't worry. The only ones who show up on a main road like this are the super big guys."

"Y-you should've told me that before! And what are we supposed to do if a super big one shows up?"

"Run away crying, obviously."

Haruyuki sighed beneath his silver mask, shook his head quickly, and changed the subject. "So why did you call me out here, then? Did you want to finish the duel or something?"

"You stupid? Even if I did beat you and get the ten points, diving here takes ten points. Never get nowhere like that."

Haruyuki stopped himself from pointing out that that was a double negative and contented himself with spreading his hands questioningly. "Then why?"

"Just get on," came the cool reply, and his jaw dropped to the ground.

"...Huh?"

"I said, get on, man. Grab a lid— Oh, guess you don't need one." Laughing, he put his thumb up behind his back, so Haruyuki, apparently an idiot for being on guard for a trap, straddled the seat in an unaccustomed motion.

"All right. Hold on tight. My pretty baby here accelerates like a monster!!"

Around the "like," he was already opening up the throttle, front wheel bouncing up high, and Haruyuki came very close to falling off the back. He hurriedly propped his body up with both hands, and the night-black bike tore out due east on Inogashira Street toward the city center, howling throatily.

"Unh...whoa!" he shouted, unable to stand the pressure of the wind hitting his face and the acceleration that made his whole body creak.

The roar of the engine grew louder, and every time he thought they were at top speed, a boot would kick hard at the pedal, and the higher gear would pull them ever faster. The reddish-brown road surface melted into countless flow lines, and the rocks approaching from the front screamed past, one after another.

"Isn't...this...too fast...!" He half yelped this complaint, but the answer that came back to him was laid-back to the extreme.

"What? Idiot. This isn't even half of what you do flying up there."

"B-but the bike is—"

Haruyuki had never even been on an electric scooter in the real world. Naturally, when it came to automobiles, he had ridden in the car his parents had before the divorce and in taxis, but electric cars didn't make any engine noise, and you obviously didn't feel the wind.

But this old-style motorbike was a polygon object in a virtual world, a totally different beast than modern machines prioritizing energy efficiency and safety. It was completely incredible that things like this had run wild on public roads in the real world until a mere twenty years ago. Except for a helmet, the rider's body was completely exposed, and the rider just sat there with no seat belt or air bags or anything.

"H-how fast can this thing go?!" Haruyuki shouted, since he was unable to see the gauge from his position, and once again, the response was unhurried.

"It's no racer, so it can only do like two hundred."

"T-two hund…"

If there was an accident, we'd be sooooooooo dead! Haruyuki freaked out in his head, before suddenly, sharply getting it.

That was the kind of vehicle it was. This machine wasn't for anything other than speed. The engine racing, unsparing in its explosive use of precious fossil fuels; the complex transmission; the desperately fat tires; all of it was designed and assembled for the sole purpose of going fast. The beast existed, as it were, as an unqualified manifestation of the desire for speed. A machine created by human beings without wings, creatures who sought only to go a little faster, faster, faster, as if fighting against their fate of living glued to the earth.

Haruyuki forgot his fear and tossed his head back to look up at the pale yellow sky with wide-open eyes. There, the silhouettes of pterosaur-like Enemies soared together in a small herd.

I—I didn't understand anything about the meaning of the power that was the wings I was given. A tool to fight, an advantage to win, that's how I always thought of them. But those silver wings aren't some special attack I got through leveling up, and they're not some Enhanced Armament I bought with my points. They're supposed to be the true nature of the avatar Silver Crow, an avatar my own heart created. They're supposed to be my salvation, my desire, my hope. It's because I forgot that… Because I only saw them as a tool… I know it's because of that, that he could take them from me so easily. And now… Right now I'd—

Realize how precious they are.

Haruyuki desperately swallowed the howl in his throat before Ash Roller noticed anything was up. He was no longer afraid of two hundred kilometers an hour. On the contrary, he even felt like the engine roaring diligently below him was a very industrious and reliable thing.

The bike went around to the south from Inogashira Street, avoiding the heart of the city, and then headed east once again.

Around the time they entered Minato Ward, Haruyuki finally asked the question he should have asked right at the start.

"Um…exactly where are we going?"

"Can see it now. That."

Letting his eyes follow the abrupt jerk of Ash's helmet, Haruyuki saw a stretch of huge, rough rocks and a hazy, long, and thin silhouette at their end. Probably a steep, rocky mountain—no: it was already a tower, drawing a perfectly perpendicular line up from the ground to reach into the distant sky.

Haruyuki took a few seconds to go over his mental map of southern Tokyo, wondering if there was a building like that in the place corresponding to that spot in the real world, and finally arrived at the answer.

"Huh? I-is that the old Tokyo Tower…?"

"Very yes!"

Ignoring the very dubiousness of the English that Ash Roller fired back, Haruyuki picked through his hazy knowledge of the landmark.

Tokyo Tower, in Minato Ward's Shiba Park, used to send out TV signals throughout the capital city area but had ceded that role to Tokyo Skytree in Oshiage, Sumida Ward, more than thirty years earlier. After that, it had continued operation for a long time as a viewing platform, but skyscrapers easily surpassing the tower's 333 meters were built in rapid succession all over Tokyo, so its role as a tourist spot also finally ended at the beginning of 2030. At present, the elevator no longer ran, and the building was preserved as a historical relic into which entry was prohibited.

The former Tokyo Tower—the spire he stared at as they drew nearer with every passing second—existed as bare rock in the Unlimited Neutral Field, seemingly with no internal structure. There was nothing other than the three-hundred-meter stone pillar soaring above the wasteland.

"Wh-what is there in a place like that?" he asked, stunned, and Ash Roller, uncharacteristically, started mumbling vaguely.

"Yeah, well, it's...Right. There's a person I want you to meet."

"A person...?"

Not a guy *or a* jerk *or an* SOB?

"Yeah. Uh, to be honest, it's my parent."

"P-pardon?!" Haruyuki shouted, shocked to his core. "Y-your parent...?! Then that means...He's even more incredible than you? Like beard, sunglasses, leather vest, tattooed, beer belly—"

"Just what do you think I am anyway?" he growled, sending a shiver up Haruyuki's back for some reason. "Just so you know, if you face 'er and run off at the mouth like that, you're gonna seriously regret it. Been a while since she stepped back from the duel frontline, so you prob'ly don't know, buuut...Way back in the day, she used to freak people out. People called her 'Iron Arms,' 'ICBM,' stuff like thaaat."

"Oh, ICBM...?" Haruyuki parroted back Ash Roller's words, the ends of which were getting weird, perhaps out of fear.

"Totallyyy. Oh, and one more...Had the nickname 'Icarus.'"

"Th-that doesn't sound so scary as all that."

"Well, you know. Started calling her that after she retired, I guess. She's, well...Until you showed up, she was the *Burst Linker who got closest to the sky in the accelerated world.*"

Haruyuki gasped sharply, and at basically the same time, the motorcycle stopped in a cloud of dust.

In front of them, the stone pillar rose up maybe twenty meters in diameter from the rufous, dried earth, so perpendicular it could have been used as a triangle ruler. Nearly a perfect circular cylinder, there was, as expected, nothing like stairs or an entrance anywhere. Maybe because the old Tokyo Tower was off limits in the real world, it was reproduced in a form like this.

Haruyuki looked at their surroundings and wondered just where this "ICBM," aka Icarus, was, but the only thing that stopped his eyes was a stone turtle-like silhouette, moving slowly in the distance.

It can't be, he thought, but he asked anyway. "Ummm...so is that her?"

"Idiot. That's an Enemy. I'm just waiting for the wind to stop."

"W-wind?" He hadn't noticed while the motorbike was racing along, but now that Ash mentioned it, there was indeed a strong wind gusting, a result of the Wasteland stage terrain. But it wasn't as though they were in the middle of a duel, so why would he—

The instant this thought entered his head, the howling of the ceaseless wind stopped abruptly.

"All right! Let's go! Hold me tight!"

Initially baffled by Ash Roller's sudden shouting, Haruyuki soon grasped the meaning of his instruction.

The front wheel of the bike, throttle wide open, jumped up, and Haruyuki reflexively wrapped his arms around the avatar's torso. While the engine emitted a high-pitched whine and the rear wheel kicked up gravel, the front wheel slammed up against the vertical stone wall, and Haruyuki barely had time to wonder at what was happening.

The massive American motorcycle, with pair onboard, started to climb straight up the towering precipice.

"Whoa...whooooaaaa?!" Screaming absurdly, endlessly in his heart, Haruyuki had a vivid premonition of the bike flipping over and falling back, upside down.

However, the bike rode up the vertical pillar without even wobbling, almost as if some mysterious gravity were at work to keep the tires glued to the wall. After five seconds or so, he finally understood and allowed himself to relax.

This was Ash Roller's wall-climbing ability. Now that he thought about it, he had seen this bike run freely along a building's walls more than a few times during duels. But he hadn't known it could climb for long periods like this, with no approach run. Put another way, Ash Roller was right now casually revealing the upper limits of his own abilities to Haruyuki, a member of an enemy Legion. But unable to ferret out Ash's true intentions, Haruyuki simply held his breath and stared at the peak of the spire.

Obviously, the bike couldn't manage the same speed as it had on the ground, but it still climbed forcefully in a low gear. Glancing down, Haruyuki saw that the earth was already so dim in the distance that it looked like it was a different color.

Flying with his wings, this height would have likely been no big deal, but now, his stomach tightened sharply and he hastily brought his eyes back to face forward. The top of the spire finally coming into view seemed to have been cut flat, and the edge traced a beautiful arc in the yellow sky.

When they were about ten seconds or so away from arriving at that arc, he felt a wall of air about to rush at them from the left.

"Shit! Wind! Shiiiiit!" Cursing, Ash Roller turned the handlebars and shifted the motorcycle's trajectory to the left. The squall that blew in seconds later sideswiped the bike mercilessly.

"Fly hiiiiigh!!"

"Aaaaaaaaaah!!"

On top of the bike shooting up vertically, riding the wind, Haruyuki and Ash Roller paddled the air, a crawl stroke in the sky. Perhaps because of their efforts, they made it to the peak in a parabola, steadily sliding to the side as they came down. Then, the rear tire of the falling bike landed solidly, about five centimeters from the edge of the top of the tower.

"I-I-I-I-I am never riding this thing again! I'm never getting on anything that doesn't have at least four tires again!!" Haruyuki moaned, tumbling from the seat and pressing hands and feet against hard stone.

Ash Roller, however, still straddled the motorcycle, waving the index finger of his right hand in annoyance. "You don't get it at all. It's fun because the bike could fall over, man."

"That back there wasn't about falling over!!" Haruyuki shouted, shoulders heaving, and shook his head before finally taking a look around.

The summit of the stone pillar/old Tokyo Tower in the real world was a circular space with the exact same twenty-meter diameter as the bottom. But it looked completely different from the world below.

The words *heavenly garden* popped up in the back of his mind. A soft lawn shone greenly over the entire area, a small spring in the center. The shimmering water there was clearer than anything he had ever seen.

In the center of the spring drifted a small floating island—and on top of this, Haruyuki saw something unexpected.

An elliptical blue light turning slowly, shimmering like a mirage. A portal. The sole means of returning to the real world of your own volition from this Unlimited Neutral Field.

He was surprised there would be one in a place like this; the majority of portals were located in landmark-type buildings like large train stations and tourist attractions. In which case, maybe it wasn't so strange for there to be one in the old Tokyo Tower. But it seemed like only people who could scale vertical walls like Ash Roller, or people who could fly like Silver Crow used to, could use one way up here.

He brought his gaze back, cocking his head to one side, and saw another unexpected something on the opposite side of the garden.

A house.

The adorable toy-size house was surrounded by countless flowering plants and stood quite quietly. The walls were painted pure white, and the pointed roof was a deep green. It matched the green of the ivy crawling up the walls, and the sight was so beautiful it could have been mistaken for a page from a picture book.

As he stared attentively, no words escaping him, the door of the house abruptly opened with a light creak. Next to him, Ash Roller leapt off his bike and stood at attention.

So then the person coming out was likely Ash Roller's "parent." Probably a macho Hells Angels type in leather pants. The house was a bit of a mismatch, but Haruyuki wouldn't be surprised if an enormous Harley came growling out that door. He braced himself for anything.

But, in the end, he couldn't begin to prepare himself for the situation he found himself in.

What came rolling out, creaking as it did, was indeed a two-wheeled vehicle. But rather than front to back, the wheels were side by side. The spokes were extremely thin silver lines, and the tires were also silver, perhaps a centimeter wide, rather than rubber. On this vehicle was a slender chair, also knitted from silver wire.

A wheelchair. The total opposite of an American bike, with no engine, no muffler. And the person sitting there was about ten thousand light years away from the image in Haruyuki's mind.

There was no doubt that it was a duel avatar. The arms resting in her lap were tinged with a smooth, hard blue brilliance, and the lower jaw of the downward-pointing face was in the shape of a sharp mask. He couldn't see any more of the face because of the wide-brimmed hat the avatar was wearing. Not the witch-like pointy hat of Chiyuri's avatar, Lime Bell, but a pure white bonnet. The body was also wrapped in a dress the same white.

... *Huh? So it* is *a girl?*

As if to give an affirmative answer to Haruyuki's surprise, the stirring wind caused the long hair beneath the hat to flap. The straight, waist-length hair was a sky blue so clear it could suck you in—the color of a clear fall sky.

The wheels creaked once again, and the wheelchair started to advance slowly. And yet both of the avatar's hands stayed as they were folded up on her lap. Apparently, the wheelchair was equipped with some kind of self-propelling mechanism.

The wheelchair rode smoothly forward, approaching them via the same brick path that circled the spring in the center of the lawn. The avatar stopped about two meters away from Haruyuki and Ash Roller and lifted her hat gently, revealing her face. Haruyuki stood stock-still and stared at the visage, unable to believe he was looking upon the parent to Century End rider Ash Roller.

Her face was the kind often seen on female-type duel avatars, a mask fitted with nothing more than lens-type eyes. But Haruyuki felt like this face, without nose or mouth, was more beautiful than similar avatars he had seen so far. The avatar looked straight at Haruyuki and then Ash Roller, date-shaped eyes glittering a pale red against glowing, pale blue skin.

"It's been a while, Ash. I'm happy to see you haven't forgotten me yet."

"I-it has been a while, Master. A-a-as if I could forget you."

Unfortunately, Haruyuki did not get the chance to retort, *Shouldn't that be "mega" ages,* to Ash Roller while he bowed respectfully. The sky-blue avatar turned her intense gaze back to Haruyuki.

"So you're Silver Crow."

The calm voice was like a gentle breeze, and Haruyuki also felt keenly compelled to lower his head deeply for some reason. "Y-yes. Nice to meet you. I'm Silver Crow."

"A pleasure. My name is Sky Raker. Glad to meet you, too, Corvus."

Feeling her gaze flicker up to his shoulders, Haruyuki shrank into himself abruptly. From the tone of her voice, she seemed to know about Silver Crow, but the silver wings—the ability to fly—that this name was so known for in the accelerated world were no longer upon his back.

Avoiding Sky Raker's gentle gaze that somehow seemed to penetrate into his mind, Haruyuki cast his eyes down to the ground. But after a short silence, he threw his head back up, forgetting his shyness, when he heard Ash Roller.

"Um…okay then, Master. I—I'll be on my way now."

"Wh-what?!" Haruyuki pressed the skull-helmeted rider turning to return to his bike. "Y-you're leaving?! Wh-wh-what am I supposed to do?!"

"How should I know?"

"How should you know? You're the one who brought me here!!"

"'Cause you were all wah wah, boohoo, whine whine. Total mess, I shouldn't have even bothered to get out my missiles. And after I worked so hard to get them…" Ash Roller grumbled, scuffing the bottoms of his boots against the stone paving as if he were trying to get off dirt that wasn't there, but then changed his tone abruptly and said, "Look, Crow. I don't know how you lost your wings, but right now, you're prob'ly thinking, 'Can't fly, can't win, no point in fighting.' But, man…you know how many Burst Linkers there are in the accelerated world who can't fly no matter how badly they want to? You ever thought about that?"

Taking a shallow breath, Haruyuki reflexively dropped his eyes to his feet. However, Ash Roller's cutting words continued. "I mean, you duel long enough and you see all kinds of shit, man. Including people losing their power. But, y'know, your wings aren't the sort of thing where you can just, like, give up on the sneak attacks or something for having lost 'um. You keep fighting half-assedly like this and just disappear, all those guys who looked up, all this time, to watch you flying up there…All of us…" Ash Roller kicked fiercely at the ground, almost as if he couldn't get the rest out.

Head still hanging, Haruyuki murmured quietly in his heart, *I don't want to give up, you know. But my wings…After my flight ability has been deleted from the system, what is there I can do?*

"It's true my attitude in that duel wasn't great," he somehow managed to choke out, slowly raising a leaden head. "But…what does that have to do with this?"

"Uh, oh…That's the thing…I mean—"

"Corvus." He heard the quiet voice of Sky Raker, Ash Roller's parent, silent up until that point. "Ash was merely thinking that perhaps I could assist you in getting your wings back."

"Huh?" Haruyuki's eyes opened wide, as did his mouth. "M-my wings…? Assist…But Ash, you're Green Legion—"

"Oh! Right! Sorry!!" Ash Roller cried, throwing himself into the motorcycle seat with a *thump*. "Listen! Don't get the wrong idea!! Now you owe me! This is serious strategy here! A secret operation to raise your popularity parameters and get you to betray the Black Legion, jerk! Yeah! I am mega cooooooooool!!"

"That's vulgar, Ash." Sky Raker's quiet voice snapped at the skull rider, who was waving the raised middle finger of his right hand.

"Yes! I'm sorry, Master! Th-th-then I'll just be getting on excusing myself, yes!" He revved the engine loudly, and the American motorcycle plunged toward the spring in the center of the lawn, jumped high at the water's edge, and leapt into the glittering blue portal—

And disappeared.

More stunned than he had ever been, Haruyuki stood stockstill and somehow managed to mutter, "A secret operation's... pointless..."

Sky Raker giggled. "Other than the way his brain works, the way he talks, and the way he looks, he's a pretty decent kid."

What is there other than that? Haruyuki reflexively wondered for a few seconds, and then pushed Ash Roller out of his mind and took a few steps toward the silver wheelchair stopped near the spring.

A veritable mountain of questions swirled around in his heart as he timidly opened his mouth, still stuck on which one to ask first. "Uh...um...Ash said this, but. He said you were the person in the accelerated world who'd come closest to the sky..."

At this, Sky Raker's smile became transparent somehow, and she nodded. "I suppose I would be the representative of those Burst Linkers who can never fly no matter how much they want to, who Ash was talking about. No, I guess I shouldn't say that I couldn't fly. It's just that, in the end, these hands didn't reach the sky."

Haruyuki unthinkingly winced at this response, which he had anticipated to a certain degree. *In that case, she actually should be telling me off instead of trying to help me*, he reflected, but he couldn't stop himself from jumping at the single thread of hope glimmering faintly before him.

Blinking, he raised his gaze and uttered his next question in a hoarse voice. "Then…is it true…? That you can get my wings back…?"

This time, the answer didn't come right away. The avatar gently brushed aside dazzlingly lustrous sky-blue hair and stared at Haruyuki for a while.

"That's impossible," she said crisply.

"What…"

"When you lose something from your duel avatar, there is a reason you had to lose it. Here in this place, I have no means of negating that reason."

"……"

His faint hope instantly cut down, Haruyuki started to hang his head, crestfallen. But just as he was about to tear his gaze away, Sky Raker casually lifted the hem of the white dress she wore, and his eyes popped open.

"Please take a look."

What he saw—or rather didn't see—was from the avatar's knees down. The round knee joints drew a supple line up to the thin thigh area, but the calves that should have stretched out below them were nonexistent on both legs.

Perhaps he should have considered the idea that there was something wrong with her legs when the avatar came out in a wheelchair. But what would cause the legs of a duel avatar to disappear?

It was true that during duels, you could take damage through the loss of limbs for whatever reason. Haruyuki himself had lost arms and legs in fierce battles a countless number of times. But once the duel was over, the loss was immediately canceled, and you were back to brand-new in the next battlefield.

Haruyuki held his breath and, unable to avert his eyes, was forced to wonder, *Maybe Sky Raker, too…?*

Maybe she had her legs taken from her forever by Nomi, aka Dusk Taker, or another Burst Linker with the same ability?

But the next words from her mouth refuted that idea.

"I chose to cut them off myself."

"What...?!"

"I decided that I no longer needed legs, and I had a certain person cut them off for me. Understanding the whole time that it was the height of arrogance, egotism—no, madness. Since then, no matter how many times I dive into the accelerated world, my legs have never returned. Which means...even now inside me, the embers of madness smolder. As long as they do, my legs will remain like this."

Sky Raker stared closely at Haruyuki, rooted to the spot, with eyes the color of dawn, and pronounced softly, "Your wings are the same. If you do not face the reason that led to their loss and overcome it, you will most certainly never get them back."

Reason.

In other words, Nomi/Dusk Taker's special attack, Demonic Commandeer.

No, that wasn't it. It was the defeat itself. Unless Haruyuki got past the pain of defeat etched so deeply into his heart at being forced to yield to Seiji Nomi in every way, he would never be able to get back his wings. That's what it was.

But overcoming that was absolutely impossible. Because Haruyuki had lost his lone ability, the power of flight, and Nomi, who had taken it, possessed at that very minute its capacity to fly freely. Haruyuki didn't have a hope of beating him.

He dropped to his knees on the lawn unconsciously, and Sky Raker threw him an unexpected line.

"No matter what we do in this garden, your wings won't come back. But I didn't say you wouldn't be able to fly, Corvus."

Let's sit down before we talk about the rest.

The self-driving wheelchair started to move with a squeal, so Haruyuki followed, seriously confused.

White benches were installed at the edges of the round garden in the sky, each at a cardinal direction. They were the type with no backrest, only a seat, so that you could sit facing either way. Sky Raker brought her wheelchair to a stop next to the northern bench, facing outward, and Haruyuki shyly sat next to her. When he lifted his face, he gasped at the spectacular sight before him: an unbroken view of the heart of Wasteland Tokyo, three hundred meters below.

The government district area in Nagata-cho had changed into immense ruins hewn from red sandstone. The Shuto Expressway curved across the chasm, supported by an arch of piled stones. Even farther off stood a vivid red castle, remarkably majestic in appearance: the Imperial Palace in the real world. No matter what the stage was, that always existed as an enormous castle, sometimes beautiful, sometimes brimming with an unearthly aura.

As Haruyuki idly wondered if anyone lived there, Sky Raker broke the silence.

"I had thought I might like to meet you, Silver Crow."

"Huh...oh, th-thanks," he stammered, pulling in his shoulders.

Watching him, the sky-blue avatar radiated a lingering, gentle smile before continuing softly. "Seven years have passed since the foundation of the accelerated world, and finally a flying ability appears. When Ash told me about you, I was deeply surprised and also greatly interested. I thought, what kind of spirit...what kind of wounded psyche's scars could realize a power so great as to cut free of the tremendous gravity of this world?"

"No, it's— I-I'm sorry. My scars are really nothing big at all." Making his body even smaller, Haruyuki shook his head in short bursts. "In the real, I'm just fat and bullied and wishy-washy... Lately, I've been thinking it's kind of presumptuous to call that kind of thing a mental scar."

Even bewildered as he was at himself for telling this to a Burst Linker he had just met—a Burst Linker who was closer to being an enemy than a friend—the words tumbled smoothly and mysteriously from his lips.

Sky Raker smiled again and shook her head gently.

"The mental scars that Brain Burst reads from the owner's unconsciousness and uses as a resource for the duel avatar do not necessarily indicate only the strength of anger or resentment."

"Huh…? B-but, I mean, scars, that's like feelings of failure, right?"

"True, but those are not everything. Duel avatars generated from an enormous loss—say, a seething anger—without exception, manifest this power as a simple destructive force. Like with that Chrome Disaster, which brought such monumental calamity to the accelerated world."

Hearing that name, Haruyuki took a sharp breath. It had only been a few months prior that he had been trembling right down to the marrow of his bones in the presence of the Armor of Catastrophe, Chrome Disaster, and its terrifying attack power. It was an Enhanced Armament, but it definitely seemed to be stained with thoughts of extreme anger.

"And avatars with malice as their source acquire midrange fighting abilities like a curse, while avatars created from despair often become self-destructive types, hurting themselves to defeat their enemies. But you do know that not all avatars house destructive powers like this?"

"…Yes." Now that she was saying it, that was exactly it. Haruyuki's wings were not a direct attack power, and Ash Roller's bike was the same. However, in that case, what exactly was this "wounded psyche—"

"The wound, in other words, is a lack," Sky Raker replied, almost as if reading Haruyuki's mind. "A hole in the heart where something important is missing. You have this futile hole, and you get angry, you resent it, you despair—or you reach out your hand for the heavens again. That choice determines the nature of your avatar."

"Reach…your hand?"

"Exactly. In other words, *hope*. A wounded psyche is also the flip side of hope," Sky Raker said crisply, and then raised her face to stare directly into Haruyuki's eyes from under her white hat. "Silver Crow. You must have had more hope for the sky in your heart than any other Burst Linker who came before you. The strength of your desire to aim for the sky gave birth to the flying ability, to wings. Do you see? It isn't that because you had wings, you could fly. Just the opposite. *Because you could fly, you gave concrete form to your wings.*"

"Because...I could fly..." Haruyuki murmured hoarsely, and after repeating this several times in his heart to try and understand what it meant, he twisted up his face under his silver mask and shook his head vehemently. "That's—that's ridiculous. If you could fly just through the force of your will...Are you saying that those wings were just for show?"

"Taking it to the extreme, that's exactly it. Due to some kind of phenomenon, your wings and your flying ability in the system have been taken from you in the form of a removed object. But that doesn't mean that the force of will that is the source of that ability has been. Because, no matter what the special ability or avatar, taking that is impossible."

"No way...What you're saying, it's not possible!" Haruyuki threw his head down and clutched both knees tightly. "Even if I did have this desire to fly in my heart, it would just be...a trigger. Brain Burst read it, and then made those wings and their flying ability for me. So in this world, the ability itself is reality! U-unless I get it back, I'll never..." Haruyuki nearly howled, tightening his grip on his knees so much that his fingers were almost creaking.

For a while, only the wind sounded, blowing past at three hundred meters above the ground. Stretching toward the sky from the edge of the garden, the flowers in front of him—the names of which he did not know—rippled and scattered petals soundlessly.

"In other words, what you're saying is this." Sky Raker's voice rode to him on the wind, unchanged. She was still quiet after Haruyuki's anguished outburst, but her voice was tinged with a faint echo of humor. "That in this accelerated world, the force of your will and such are meaningless. That the numerical data prescribed and calculated by the system alone determine any and all phenomena."

"...But I mean, it is. We're in the middle of a VR game. You're saying there's something other than digital data."

"This wheelchair."

Her sudden, seemingly unconnected statement made Haruyuki yank his face up.

"Look at it closely. This is not a separate Enhanced Armament. It's just an object, just as it looks, assembled from a chair and wheels. I'm sure, however, you saw earlier that it drives itself?"

"Y-yes," Haruyuki replied, bewildered all the while, not seeing the true meaning of the question. "It's equipped with some kind of propulsive device, isn't it? A motor or something somewhere."

There's obviously something. I mean, it drove all by itself. She probably has a small controller in her hand, he thought, craning his neck to run his eyes over the slender silver wheels. His eyes flew open as the enormous shock of realization hit him.

There was nothing. He couldn't see any motor-type parts at all, not on the thin axle, not on the hubs, not on the rims. So then maybe some kind of injection-type device? He peered around at the back, but there was no nozzle or anything similar anywhere.

"B-but, I mean. Before, it moved by itself," Haruyuki muttered in blank amazement, and Sky Raker gently spread her thin hands out to the sides. Neither contained a trace of anything controller-like.

The wheelchair on which she sat perfectly still slowly rolled backward, wheels creaking.

"...N-no way."

Creak, creak. The chair pulled even farther back and suddenly began twirling on the lawn, before gracefully sliding back and forth and side to side, almost like a figure skater on ice. Finishing its brief dance, the chair stopped neatly, in exactly the same position as before.

"How was that?"

"How was that...?" Haruyuki's shoulders shook and his eyes were as far open as they could get.

It shouldn't move. This world created by the Brain Burst program was so faithful to authenticity that it could even be said to be another reality. All machines required a motive device, and all motive devices required an energy source. For instance, Ash Roller's bike had gasoline in the tank, and the drive wheel spun because of a chain connected to the engine. Which was exactly why, when Haruyuki lifted the rear wheel during their duel, the bike had no longer been able to move. In some other game, the bike almost certainly would have dashed ahead with just the front wheel, with no regard for how drive systems work. So this wheelchair propelling itself without any driving noise or injection light whatsoever—

"It can't be...There's no way. What...Exactly what force is moving that chair?" Haruyuki asked, gasping.

A serene smile graced the small mask of the duel avatar whose hair was the color of the sky. *"My will,"* she replied.

"Huh...?!"

"I moved it with nothing more than the power of my will."

"B-but-but-but!" Haruyuki shouted, stammering like a corrupt sound file, so floored by this that his heart nearly leapt from his mouth. "Th-that's almost. Almost...like ESP, isn't it?! S-so then, that's the ability 'Psychokinesis'...or...?"

Here, the smile turned bitter, and Sky Raker shook her head loosely. "Ha-ha-ha, it isn't that. This world...whether it's the normal duel field or the Unlimited Neutral Field, every Burst Linker fighting in the accelerated world has this power."

"Wh-what?!"

"Please think about it. You were able to fly freely in the sky when you had wings. Isn't that so?"

"Y-yes..."

"But how exactly did you control those wings? After all, the real you does not have wings."

He blinked successively at the question, one he had never considered before. "Th-that was…" Haruyuki responded hesitantly, unconsciously moving his shoulders. "A movement in my shoulder blades…"

"If you were doing that, you wouldn't be able to fully swing your fist while flying. Please try to remember. Even if you weren't aware of it, you were controlling your flight with the power of your will. Am I wrong?"

"……"

Even at a total loss for words, he still was struck with a thought: *Now that you mention it…*It was true that as Silver Crow, he moved both hands like crazy and could just take off on the spot, without running into the takeoff. And now that someone was asking what kind of physical movements he made when he did, the answer was—none.

But he still had trouble swallowing Sky Raker's explanation. "The power…of my will," he began, shaking his head sharply. "But, I mean, that's, how would it read that? The Neurolinker doesn't have a function like that…It's not supposed to—"

And then Kuroyukihime's voice from long ago reverberated in his ears: *Neurolinkers also have the ability to access things other than the sensory or movement regions of our brains.*

But she had been talking about mental scars, like discussed earlier. In which case, he could wrap his brain around it—because scars equaled memories plus interpretation. But how could this vague "power of will" or whatever be digitized?

"Perhaps you'd understand if, instead of 'will,' I said 'image power'?"

At Sky Raker's voice, Haruyuki gasped and lifted his head. "Image…?"

"Exactly. You could also call it 'the power of imagination.' During flight, you create a strong image of how much you're going to accelerate, when you'll turn, when you'll decelerate.

Your Neurolinker reads that and moves your avatar. Do you see? *Image* power! It is precisely this that is the true power hidden within us Burst Linkers. I have total control over this wheelchair through a stable imagining of the two wheels rotating. Admittedly, it did take me quite a long time before I was able to do this, but it's not impossible. Absolutely not."

Once again, the right wheel turned with a slight creak, and Sky Raker and her wheelchair faced Haruyuki again. When she spoke, she sounded majestic and mysterious somehow—an oracular echo.

"Those Burst Linkers who manage to attain control via the Image Power System—which lies beneath the Movement Command System normally used to control the avatar—have a name for it. This desire straight from the heart—in other words, your will."

She paused for a beat.

"Incarnate System."

"In…carnate?" It wasn't a word he had heard in either the accelerated or real worlds. But Haruyuki could feel a kind of definite power in the sound of it, and he repeated it several times in his head.

He didn't immediately understand what Sky Raker was saying. The Neurolinker might differ in its very foundation from the old-generation VR machines, and Brain Burst might be a mysterious super-application, but how on earth could they digitize the imagination of the diver?

And yet the delicate silver wheelchair had, in fact, danced easily for him on the lawn, without any kind of propulsive device at all.

Accept it. Haruyuki squeezed his eyes shut and murmured to himself. It was circular, but if the will—if believing had real power in this world, he felt it would certainly become the truth for him if he just believed Sky Raker.

"So then...So then." Something large and hot choked his throat, and Haruyuki worked to put the rest of his thoughts into words. "If I learn to use this Incarnate System, I'll be able to fly again even without wings...I-is that what that means?"

Haruyuki stared at Sky Raker's face as if devouring it and waited for her reply with a longing that almost burned.

The words she uttered quietly a few seconds later, however, were neither an affirmation nor a denial. "I showed you before how I move the wheels with the power of my will. But I could easily do the same thing with my hands, instead of working so hard to focus the image. Do you see? Using the will as an agent for work is possible to do with the normal control system, but manifesting something with the will phenomena is normally impossible; there is a very wide, deep ditch—no, a vast canyon—between these two concepts. To speak figuratively, it's like hitting a bullet with a bullet in the real world. It's possible, in terms of physics, but the execution is difficult. Extremely."

Sky Raker took her eyes off the speechless Haruyuki and cast her gentle eyes up at the sky. Then she began to speak again, still tranquil but sounding like she was having a hard time suppressing the would-be tremor in her voice.

"I wasn't able to do it. I threw away my legs, my friends; I abandoned everything I could think of, and yet I wasn't able to detach myself from the virtual gravity of this world...I said so earlier, didn't I? That the Burst Linker who can't fly no matter how she might want to is me."

"Uh...uh-huh..."

When he agreed, spellbound, the sky-blue avatar waved her supple right hand up at the heavens and continued. "Drawing near but never quite there...Since the beginning, this avatar of mine has had a certain Enhanced Armament. The power to move away from the earth and approach the sky. However, you most certainly could not call it flying. I leapt to an altitude of a mere hundred meters or so through a momentary thrust force, before I simply fell back down."

"......" Unable to reply, Haruyuki merely held his breath.

Once, a long time ago, he had tested just how high he could go with Silver Crow's power of flight. The normal duel field was surrounded on all sides by semitransparent barriers marking the boundaries of the area, but he had wondered about the sky.

In the end, Haruyuki's fingers had not come into contact with any wall before his fully charged special-attack gauge was completely spent. He remembered his altitude at that time as being three times higher than the Shinjuku government building he could see off in the distance. The government building, which had been rebuilt in recent years, boasted an imposing five hundred meters. In short, Haruyuki had effortlessly risen to a height of fifteen hundred meters, and that had been purely to satisfy his curiosity.

I didn't even think about the meaning of the power I was given.

Carried away by the same regret he'd felt on Ash Roller's bike, Haruyuki pulled into himself as much as he could and turned his ears toward Sky Raker's voice.

"I ended up possessed by the desire to someday fly higher, go farther. I spent every level-up bonus on enhancing my jumping ability, and all my time fighting so that I could get even more points. The few friends I had, and even my parent, lost patience with what I became and left me. All alone, only the Master of the Legion I belonged to understood and helped me. And I tried to be useful to her as well; we spent many, many hours fighting side by side... But when I reached and turned that bonus again to my jumping, I had a flash of insight: It would never be enough to turn Jump into Fly... My desire had turned into a deep-rooted delusion—no, madness."

"Mad...ness."

Sky Raker glanced at Haruyuki as he muttered hoarsely, and the faintest of smiles rose up as she nodded sagely.

"I...I made my avatar itself more lightweight, and in order to enhance my ability to fly using my will, I decided to get rid of my legs, which held my greatest attack abilities. I asked the person who had been both my friend and Master to cut off my legs with her sword. She tried to stop me. But I no longer understood even her feelings... I said some terrible things to her, but she only looked sad until finally she granted my wish."

Sky Raker stroked her knees lightly with her right hand and brought her story to a calm end.

"I used all my bonuses, trained my will, and even abandoned my legs to make it impossible for me to walk. The maximum altitude I was able to reach as a result was three hundred and fifty meters. Three point five times my starting altitude. But I did not reach the sky. I just barely managed to reach the peak of old Tokyo Tower here, and then I finally understood. That the psychic wounds that were the source of my avatar and my hopes did not have that much power. 'Raker' means 'one who views.' Viewing the sky for a moment at the peak of a parabola... that is the absolute limit of the power given to me. But by the time I realized this, I had lost everything I cared about.

"So, Silver Crow?" Sky Raker asked, turning her shadow of a mouth up into a smile. "Even after hearing this fool's story, do you still want to train with the Incarnate System and learn to fly? Even knowing that it's most likely ninety-nine percent impossible?"

"......" Haruyuki hung his head and bit down on his lip.

I won't be able to do it. Why should a total gutless loser, crybaby wimp like me be able to do something even she couldn't do, when she's a powerful enough Burst Linker to get to level eight?

It's not like I'll be like this forever and never get my wings back. If I can just hold on for two years, he'll give them back to me. I can make something up about why I don't have my wings for Takumu and Kuroyukihime. I just have to lie and keep paying points in secret to Nomi for two years. I mean, back when Araya was bullying me, I did basically the same thing and I got through six months of that, didn't I? And Chiyuri, if I really beg her, she should be able to put up with being treated like a pet on the duel field. It'll be fine. If I just pull back into myself and keep my head down, it'll be fine.

"...I—"

I can't, Haruyuki tried to reply.

Answer, stand up, turn around, take the portal back to the real world.

"...I..."

But something in his chest resisted stubbornly, and he couldn't make himself say the rest. Almost as if the avatar Silver Crow itself were refusing to utter the words. Almost as if this avatar— which was now, having lost its wings, nothing more than a stick figure, a huge head sitting on wirelike limbs—were insisting to Haruyuki that it still had value.

He took a deep breath, filling his trembling chest with cold air, and held it.

"There's still something I have left to do..." Haruyuki said, bowing his head deeply. "Please. I want you to teach me...how to use the Incarnate System."

Sky Raker smiled again faintly and cocked her head slightly. "It will take a long—a very long time."

"I don't care."

"It will probably take much longer than you think. So long that, depending on how it goes, you might reach the Point of No Return as a Burst Linker."

Haruyuki immediately understood the meaning of those words.

He knew two kings—the Black King, Black Lotus; and the Red King, Scarlet Rain—and there was something quite remote from their real-world selves in both of them, in their words and actions. The reason was that they had spent a protracted amount of time in this Unlimited Neutral Field, so much so that a gap between their actual and mental ages had emerged.

So the time to make that choice had finally come for him as well. Even as he was terrified, Haruyuki took a deep breath and nodded. "I understand...Please, Sky Raker."

"All right, then." Turning the wheelchair with a creak, the accelerated world's hermit looked up at the sky. "Right now, in real time, it's after nine PM, isn't it? How much longer can you stay in the dive in the other side's time?"

"Um…I have school tomorrow, but I should be okay for another three or four hours. If you like, until morning."

Kuroyukihime had once warned him that if he spent too long in this world, his real-world memories from before the dive would grow weaker. But that didn't seem like much of a concern right now. No matter how much time passed, he would never be able to forget that Seiji Nomi had stolen his wings. That, at least, was guaranteed.

"Good." Sky Raker brought the fingertips of both hands together and turned to face Haruyuki. "Well then…we'll stop here for today."

"E-excuse me?!"

"Your heart is in turmoil with all the things that have happened today. You can't train your will like this. And in any case, it's night here. We'll sleep well tonight and then begin tomorrow morning. We have plenty of time."

"S-sleep well?" Haruyuki asked, baffled. "B-but if we sleep during a full dive, won't our Neurolinkers look at our brain waves and automatically link out?"

"You don't need to worry about that happening while accelerated. You know that popular manga artist who's actually a high school student? The one whose work was recently turned into an anime?"

Perplexed at this question out of the blue, he nodded slightly. "Y-yeah. I'm a big fan…"

"He's a high-level Burst Linker. He gets all his sleep on this side, so he can do something as absurd as have a weekly serialization while going to high school."

Whoa, that genius hit maker is actually a Burst Linker. So then this kind of thing's happened before. A faint sense of déjà vu making his head spin, Haruyuki trailed after the wheelchair's smooth advance.

The inside of the white-walled, green-roofed house he had been invited into was larger than he had expected. That said, it was still just one room, equipped with nothing more than a small kitchen, a table, and a bed.

Sky Raker brought her wheelchair over to the kitchen's stove, where she removed the lid off a pot, uncovering a burbling sound. Instantly, a delicious smell filled the room. Before the eyes of a stunned Haruyuki, she nimbly ladled something resembling stew into deep wooden plates, and then brought her wheelchair to the table, a plate in each hand. As she set them down together, complete with spoons made of the same wood, she said to Haruyuki, "No need to stand. Have a seat."

"Oh…S-sure." Staggering, he set himself down in a high-backed chair, looked at the steaming white stew before him, and murmured in his heart, *No, but, this is, here…*

"This *is* in the middle of a fighting game, right?" he blurted, and Sky Raker nodded with a composed expression on her face.

"Yes, it is. Is there a problem?"

"It's just, I mean, supper in a fighter…"

"My! In the background of a certain 2-D fighter game in the early years, the Gallery was eating ramen, you know."

"Th-that might be true, but!"

At the same time that he was struck by the urge to rip off his own head, Haruyuki realized that he was intensely hungry. He had just chomped down on that pizza in the real world not even minutes ago; where exactly was this hunger coming from?

The metaphysical question vanished like the mist when Sky Raker urged him, "Go ahead, please eat," and Haruyuki quickly grabbed the wooden spoon.

And then he was confounded once again.

"Oh, b-but my…mouth."

Silver Crow's face was covered by a mirrorlike silver helmet and had neither eyes nor nose nor mouth. However, since Sky Raker encouraged him with a gesture to eat, he timidly scooped up some stew and brought it to his mouth. When he did—

The lower side of his helmet slid up a small bit with a light humming noise. Taken aback, he touched it with his left hand and felt a definite mouth in there. No longer understanding anything, Haruyuki muttered his thanks for the food and stuck the spoon in there.

It was delicious.

More natural than any VR manufacturer's taste-reproduction engine, a nuanced flavor permeated his mouth, and Haruyuki spooned up potatoes and onions and chicken and more to stuff his cheeks.

"I'm glad you seem to like it, Corvus," Sky Raker said with a smile, elegantly moving her own wooden spoon across from him while he greedily devoured his stew. "Please take your time and savor it. So that you'll have this memory for the time being."

"...Sorry?"

After emptying his plate without taking time to breathe, Haruyuki finally considered the meaning of her words. But without giving him the chance to ask her anything, Sky Raker agilely dumped the plates together on a shelf, so he could only bow his head and thank her for the delicious meal.

At some point when he wasn't paying attention, it had gotten completely dark outside the south-facing window. In the distance, he could see a light that was probably in the Odaiba area, rocking back and forth, reflecting off the black surface of the ocean.

Sky Raker snapped her fingers sharply, and whether it was a function of the house or telekinesis through will power, all the curtains slid shut. The wheelchair creaked over to the side of the small bed, and the amputee avatar nimbly shifted her body on top of the sheet, using her right hand as a support point.

"I know it's a bit early, but perhaps we should be getting to sleep?"

Huh?

Sleep?

One bed. Two avatars. Which means— What does that mean?

The pillow barreling into him cut off the instant expressway of his thoughts. He clutched it and cursed himself—*Right, of course, what was I even thinking, you stupid dumbass*—as he fell to the floor in his silver avatar. His entire body was covered in clanking metal armor; there was no great difference as to whether it was a bed or floor underneath him.

Having hung her hat on a hook on the wall, yanked off her dress, and laid down on the bed, Sky Raker snapped her fingers once more. The light on the ceiling and the fire in the wood stove vanished, and the inside of the house was shrouded in a light blue darkness.

"Good night, Corvus."

Just what I'd expect from Ash Roller's parent; she's not just a regular someone, Haruyuki thought admiringly and replied, "G-good night..."

At the same time, he cried in his heart, *As if I could sleep in this situation!*

But surprisingly, the instant he laid down next to the table and closed his eyes, a white fog began to gently envelop the core of his head. It was just like Sky Raker said; he was seriously spent mentally because of all the things that had happened.

Of course, it wasn't as though he had forgotten the humiliation and despair Nomi had inflicted on him. But right now, in this house in this world at least, he felt he could leave the black things at a distance. Although this perhaps might also have been due to utilitarian and gluttonistic reasons, given that he was pleasantly stuffed with a stomach full of delicious stew.

Haruyuki fought for a while against the sleepiness trying to pull his eyes shut with an almost violent heaviness, and murmured very quietly, "Um, Sky Raker? Can I ask you something?"

"Go ahead," she replied right away, so he glanced over toward the bed and directed his question at the graceful curve of her silhouette.

"Um...has Ash Roller already learned the Incarnate System?"

"Not completely, not yet. But I've just given him hints. It seems he is trying a variety of things in his own way."

At this reply, something fell into place for him. Haruyuki had felt that Ash's new technique of standing on the bike while riding it was just too over the top, but it probably had some image control incorporated into it. After he nodded slightly, still on the floor, he gave voice to his next question. "If you're his parent, then are you also in the Green Legion...?"

The answer to this came after a slight pause. "No. I have only and will only ever belong to one Legion."

"Then...that's...?" Raising his head unconsciously, Haruyuki dared to utter the question he really wanted to ask. "That Legion... It wouldn't happen to be Nega Nebulous? And the person you asked to cut off your legs—"

"Black Lotus. Stronger, nobler, and kinder than anyone, my only friend."

Haruyuki dipped his head at her voice, so still and yet echoing beautifully like a song.

"That's exactly...what I thought. You're somehow like—"

"It was a long time ago." Curt words from the bed reached him in the dark, as if to cut him off. "A long, long time ago. Now go to sleep, Corvus. Tomorrow's going to be an early day." He heard the sound of her rolling over sharply, as if to refuse any further conversation.

I still have questions. About the past, about her.

But an incredible weight pressed down on his eyelids, and Haruyuki entrusted himself to the warm darkness that visited him, sinking endlessly into the deep abyss of sleep.

The next moment, his head slammed into the floor. He opened his eyes reluctantly.

What the hell? I just laid down; who yanked my pillow out from under me? he thought as he raised his upper body. But his eyes flew open in surprise at the sky on the other side of the curtains, now open wide: It was dyed a beautiful orange and purple.

"Huh?! It's already morning…?!"

"It is. Good morning, Silver Crow."

Turning his face toward her voice, Haruyuki saw Sky Raker return to her bed the pillow he was convinced had been yanked out from under his head. She had already put on her white hat and dress.

"G-good morning." He returned the greeting and asked, "Um, what time is it?"

The sky-blue avatar pointed silently toward the kitchen. A small brass clock sat in the display case on the wall, the hands of which were pointing at five in the morning. Considering the fact that they had laid down right after the sun set the previous night, he calculated that he had slept a full ten hours, but he felt as if he hadn't even been asleep long enough to dream.

However, the inside of his head did feel refreshed, like he had splashed himself with cold water. In fact, this was actually the most refreshed he could ever remember feeling upon waking. And in the real world, only thirty seconds or so had passed.

"I get it. Sleeping here, that's a pretty good way to use your points," he hummed without thinking, and Sky Raker grinned.

"Although you run the risk of someone killing you in your sleep."

"…Huh?"

"You're much too late to try and save that head now. I called you five times and you still didn't wake up."

So that's why you pulled that dirty pillow-snatching trick. Nodding his agreement, Haruyuki shrank into himself. "I-I'm sorry. I'll be sure to wake up next time!"

But Sky Raker returned only a mysterious smile and rolled her wheelchair toward the door.

The Unlimited Neutral Field in the early morning shone with a beauty different from that of dusk. Although the affiliation was still Wasteland, the reddish-brown, rocky mountains were lit up by the morning glow, turned into colossal chunks of raw ruby.

The wheelchair creaked along the lawn wet with morning dew, approached the same bench on the north side as where they had talked the day before, and stopped. Haruyuki moved forward to her side and waited for Sky Raker to speak standing up this time.

The level-eight Burst Linker, former Nega Nebulus member, and current hermit of the accelerated world took a deep breath before beginning, in a voice that was a fair bit sterner. "Silver Crow. We will now begin the Incarnate training."

"Y-yes. I await your instruction." Haruyuki dropped his head in a deep bow.

This training alone, learning to use the Incarnate System to control his avatar through nothing but images, was the sole hope left to him. It might take several days, several weeks, but he would master it.

Burning with resolve, a soundtrack like something out of a Hong Kong kung fu movie's training montage playing in his brain, Haruyuki awaited her first instruction.

However.

"That said, the essential point of the will can be expressed in a single word. Anyone can use the system once they understand this word."

"…O-okay?" His knees buckled at Sky Raker's smooth voice. "J-just one…? And then your initiation into the secret art is complete?"

"It is."

"Please tell me what it is," he said, naturally enough.

"Of course. The next time you are able to come see me," was the response he got, so he hurriedly took a step closer.

"N-no, I won't go back to the real world until you tell me!"

"I didn't say 'decided to come see,' I said 'able to,' didn't I? In other words—" She cut herself off and beckoned him closer, so Haruyuki took another step toward her. The sky-blue hair swung, and the elegant avatar gently touched her right hand to Haruyuki's back.

"This is what I'm talking about." She shoved him to the side.

"Huh? Oh! Oh oh!" Haruyuki tottered two steps along the lawn. The third step took him into thin air.

"...Huh?"

"I pray for your health, Corvus."

The figure of Sky Raker smiling sweetly above him quickly receded. More correctly, Haruyuki's body plummeted through the sky from the peak of the three-hundred-meter-tall tower.

"Huh? H-hey! Ah!"

He hurried to flap his arms like wings, but naturally, this had no effect. Dragged down by the virtual gravity, he plunged in free fall straight down.

"Ah! Aaaaa—"

Haruyuki died.

11

An hour later, he was resurrected.

Dying in the Unlimited Neutral Field was an entirely bizarre thing. The scene around you changed to a monotonic black and white; your body became see-through like smoke; and, although you could move, at least in a haphazard way, you couldn't get any farther than about ten meters from the spot where you died. Tiny digital numbers carved out a countdown in the center of your vision, and when they made it all the way to zero from 60:00:00, the field finally recovered its color and your avatar its substance.

Haruyuki looked down on the fairly decent-size crater he had made and noted out loud, "There is absolutely no doubt that she was Kuroyukihime's friend." Then he put both hands on his hips and looked up at the vertical stone wall soaring up before him—the old Tokyo Tower.

"So then by, 'if I am able see her again,' she meant…she meant…"

Climb to the top of the tower. That's what she meant, huh?

After giving his head a quick shake, he sighed heavily. There was that whole bit about pushing the baby birds out of the nest to teach them to fly, but that only ended up a success story if the babies managed to survive the fall.

But unlike birds, Haruyuki's avatar had two dexterous hands. And his body was as light as possible, and powerful enough to drill into rock.

"Guess I'll get climbing," he muttered, as if telling himself to get doing just that, and then clenched his fists.

Even if it were a stone wall that continued straight up for three hundred meters, it wasn't as though the surface were perfectly slippery-smooth like glass. There were countless gaps where it looked like he could stick his hands and feet, and he should be able to dig out small holes at least.

Steadying his resolve, he crouched slightly and readied his right fist at his hip.

"Hnyaaagh!" With a fierce cry, he shot a straight punch forward.

The blow dug deep into the reddish-brown rock, carving out an indentation about twenty centimeters in diameter. He stuck in his right foot and raised his body up, grabbing hold of a fissure just within the reach of his left hand.

He ran his eyes from side to side and mentally traced out his route. He yanked his avatar up with just his left hand, then set the tip of his left foot firmly on a slight ledge that he had his eye on.

If the truth be told, this wasn't exactly the first time he was rock climbing like this in a virtual space. In shooting games where you carried a rifle and ran around the jungle or some mountain region, crawling up the side of a cliff like this and catching the enemy team off guard was a great strategy. So to adopt this fighting technique, Haruyuki had even borrowed VR rock-climbing training software from the library.

The secret to free climbing was to first clearly visualize the optimal route. And then not to cling too much to the rock. Haruyuki peered as far ahead as he could see and continued scaling the tower at a steady pace, planning in detail where he would put each of his four limbs.

Almost as if it were competing with him, the red sun in the

eastern sky gradually rose above his position. The morning glow disappeared at some point, and the sky became a foreboding yellow.

He already no longer had any idea of how many holds he had grabbed onto. The peak melted into the sky, almost beyond the limits of his vision, and if he had looked down, the ground should have been disappearing from view below him. But he did not look down at his feet once; keeping his face turned to the sky, he simply, wholeheartedly attacked the cliff. He had almost no awareness of himself, and there was no doubt that this concentration when it came to any and all games was essentially the sole and greatest ability of the human being named Haruyuki Arita.

These honed nerves captured a faint, distant vibration transmitting through the air: an omen of the sudden gusts that were a feature of the Wasteland stage. Instantly, Haruyuki thrust both hands into fissures in the rock, pressed his body flat up against the wall surface, and held on tightly.

A few seconds later, the atmosphere roared and shook, and a strong wind, the breath of a giant, assaulted Haruyuki and threatened to shake him loose. But still not feeling much in the way of fear, he calmed himself and waited for the wind to stop. To start with, Silver Crow's slim, smooth body completely lacking of any protrusions didn't offer much in the way of air resistance. So he felt sure he wouldn't be blown away by this much wind, and, in fact, that turned out to be the case.

When the grumpy giant finally gave up, Haruyuki let out a tiny sigh and resumed his ascent.

It was around the time the sun had arrived directly above him and was starting to incline a little to the west. The tip of the rock wall, which had seemed to extend infinitely, finally cut a crisp arc in the sky: the tip of the cylinder, i.e., the peak where Sky Raker was waiting.

It was still more than a hundred meters away. But at this pace, he should be able to reach it before nightfall. And thinking about it now, Sky Raker telling him to make sure to remember the taste of the stew, and her smile when he said that he would definitely wake up the next morning, were probably because she had anticipated him not being able to finish climbing the old Tokyo Tower in a single day.

I'll reach the peak today and show her! Haruyuki decided to himself, and he tackled the rock face with sure movements, without letting his guard down. The squalls, which had changed direction in the afternoon, assaulted him with increasing frequency, but Haruyuki glued himself to the wall and weathered them all.

The color of the sky gradually deepened, and the ascent that had started with the dawn started to come round on nine hours. As he began to feel an equivalent exhaustion and gritted his teeth determinedly, Haruyuki's nose captured the faint scent of flowers. And then his ears caught the burbling of the spring, and his eyes made out even the faint blue light of the portal.

A little farther. Twenty—no, fifteen more meters.

If he could climb the whole way on his first try, even Sky Raker would probably be surprised. Haruyuki grew enthusiastic and picked up his pace.

And then.

A high-frequency buzz that he had never felt before shook the air like a howl. A sound, like an infinite number of individual bells rung all at once, came from off in the distance, and Haruyuki lifted his face with a gasp, shooting his gaze over to the horizon in the east. And then he wailed, "Ah! Crap!"

What he saw on that horizon was the shining of an aurora pouring from the sky to slowly caress the earth.

The Change. The super massive phenomenon that transformed the affiliation of the entire Unlimited Neutral Field.

Haruyuki yanked his face back and started scaling the wall at double the speed he had been doing to that point. He slipped sometimes, causing him to break out in a cold sweat, but each time, he narrowly managed to shove his fingers into a gap and grab hold. Without waiting for the pounding of his heart to subside, he leapt once again upward to the next hold.

As if to hurry him along even more, the aurora approached from the east at an incredible speed, the sound of bells growing steadily louder. The reddish-brown Wasteland color of the earth scattered under the embrace of the seven-colored curtain of light, and the land was reborn in a new form. The world was *refreshed*.

After the Change, any defeated Enemies would be replaced and any stage destruction would be repaired. There were no Enemies in the vicinity of the tower; his problem was the latter issue. If he was caught up in the aurora, the holes that Silver Crow's sharp hands had carved out of the rock wall would probably—

"Wh-whoa!" Haruyuki shouted, and he tried to climb up the final stretch essentially crawling on all fours. However, he didn't make the remaining five meters.

The sound of countless bells overwhelmed his ears; the shining of seven hues painted his vision; and in the next instant, Haruyuki's hands and feet were forcibly flicked off the wall by some repulsive force.

"Dammit! Nooooo!" Flapping in midair, he tried once more to grab hold of the wall, but his efforts were in vain.

"Aaaaaa—"

Haruyuki died again.

When he was resurrected an hour later, the world was blanketed by evening, and it was no longer the red Wasteland.

The surface of the ground was a tight, systematic pattern of paving stones. And the old Tokyo Tower before his eyes had transformed into a steel spire, covered with overlapping metal plates shining blue-black. A Demon City stage.

Haruyuki sighed heavily, clanking as he sat down on the hard stone paving. If this had been a regular game, he would be beating the hell out of his pillow in his own room to distract himself, but he couldn't log out now, and he didn't have the energy for that anyway.

But he had managed to make it almost all the way to the top on his first try. Sky Raker had been talking like this training would take several weeks or even longer than that, if it went badly. Taking that into consideration, he should chalk this one up as a job well done. He clenched both fists tightly. *Next time, I'll make it all the way for sure.*

He really wanted to set out again right away, but he thought a night climb was probably impossible. He decided to tackle it the second it started to get light in the morning, and after slipping into a suitable building in the area, Haruyuki laid down in one corner of a room that seemed safe.

Maybe it was a reaction to having concentrated so intently for nine hours straight, but he was suddenly overcome by a powerful drowsiness. Haruyuki dropped hard into sleep, without even a second to feel the emptiness of his stomach.

But the morning of the third day since he had dived into the Unlimited Neutral Field, Haruyuki peeled his eyelids all the way back at the sight before him.

The day before, he carelessly hadn't noticed that the old Tokyo Tower in the Demon City stage was made up of nothing but the same smooth, hard steel plates as Sunshine City when he had fought Chrome Disaster. It had no windows and no stairs. In fact, he couldn't even find a single indentation where he could hook a finger. Which was to say, there wasn't anything at all in the way of a handhold for him to climb.

"Then I'll just have to make some holes," he muttered, and rapped on the steel material with his fingertips. Just as he had the day before, Haruyuki hit the wall as hard as he could with his clenched fist.

And then jumped up with a cry of pain.

"Ow! Owwwww!"

He cradled his right hand, jumped up and down at the intense pain—amplified to twice that of the lower field—and stared at the place he had just punched, but there wasn't even a dent in the blue-black wall. An indestructible object— That might not have been the case, but unless you used a heat beam or a drill, you probably weren't going to have any luck digging a hole in it. And, naturally, Silver Crow was not equipped with such tools.

"So then that means I have to wait for the next Change...?" He gritted his teeth and cursed, but he had absolutely no idea if the next aurora would come several days later, nor if the next tower would be destructible. Haruyuki dropped to his knees in sudden frustration.

Out of the blue, something hit his head with a *thunk*.

"Wha?!"

He jumped backward, stunned, and saw that his assailant was wrapped in white fabric. He glanced up, but there was just the steel-colored spire stretching infinitely up toward the gray sky; he could see no one.

However, Haruyuki didn't doubt that this package had been dropped by Sky Raker's hand. Still dumbfounded, he picked it up and undid the knot to find a large, round bun inside, and a small piece of paper, too.

Instantly, a virtual sensation of hunger assaulted him, and Haruyuki, vexed by the slow pace of the lower half of his helmet sliding up with a whine, bit into the large pastry. It was just a regular bun with nothing inside, but even still, this faintly warm, fragrant thing was absurdly delicious to him, and he devoured it in a trance.

After polishing off half of the bun, he finally flipped the piece of paper over and read the words written there in elegant handwriting.

"The Incarnate training has begun. Think about why you were not sent flying by the wind yesterday."

"Huh?" He gleaned essentially nothing from this single reading. Haruyuki had understood the climbing of this wall to be a sort of basic training before the start of the actual Incarnate System training. In kung fu movies and things, you had to intently scrabble up the levels before the old master would teach you the way of the fist, after all.

And the question about why he hadn't been sent flying by the wind was also cryptic. Obviously, it was because he had held on tight. And Silver Crow's body had very low air resistance. So if he plastered himself against the wall, the wind just slid over his back—

"Oh!" Haruyuki cried softly, abruptly. He felt like he was getting close to something important. Chewing on the remainder of the bread unconsciously, he continued to ponder the matter further.

Incarnate was a means of manipulating your avatar or objects, using Image Power.

When he had pressed himself up against the rock wall yesterday and endured the wind, Haruyuki had, basically, not even thought about the possibility of being sent flying. With Silver Crow's slim, smooth body, he had believed he could get through any gust of wind, and that then became fact.

What if that—if the power of the Incarnate System was already at work, then? Had he decreased the pressure he actually received from the air by drawing out a solid image of himself getting through the wind? And if he had, could he do the same thing with this steel wall as his opponent?

Stuffing the last bit of bread into his mouth, he slid his helmet back down with a *whoosh* and stared intently at his right hand. The five fingers there could not be any slimmer or sharper. And the silver armor shone, quite hard-looking.

Not a punch—a spear hand strike.

The thought hit him spontaneously, and he lined his fingers up tightly against one another, stretched out straight. Fixing his wrist, his arm from the elbow down looked almost like a sword. He dropped his hips, extended one leg behind him, and this time glared at the wall in front of him.

The steel plates glittering blue-black did look formidable, but it was, after all, the stage background. It simply existed, without any meaning whatsoever. Put another way, the thing itself was nothing more than an enumeration of the code in the Brain Burst server somewhere.

If he couldn't dig a hole in a thing like that, how could he call himself a duelist? Without a doubt, if it were she, if it were the Black King, Black Lotus, without batting an eyelash, she would shred this wall like it was butter.

He positioned his arm, fingers aligned, at his hip. He took a deep breath and then another—

"Hah!!" He thrust straight ahead with a martial arts–style cry.

Pale sparks shot in all directions, accompanied by a sharp squeal. A pain so intense it made him dizzy ran up the joints of each finger, his wrist, and then his elbow. The HP gauge in the top left of his view was shaved down the tiniest bit.

Moaning involuntarily, Haruyuki dropped heavily to his knees, but when he looked up, it was definitely there. A sharp scar about a centimeter long and a millimeter deep, etched out of the smooth wall.

I can do it! he thought, immediately followed by him lamenting, *It's not enough!*

His image power wasn't strong enough yet. He got hurt because he was thinking of his fingers as fingers, his arm as an arm. Think sword. A sword that could pierce and mince anything, like hers.

He stood and snapped his fingers out again. After thinking for a minute, he bent his thumb toward the palm of his hand. Thus, his arm, from elbow to middle finger's tip, made a sharp line, almost as if it had been designed that way right from the start.

This time, rather than positioning it at his hip, he brought it a little higher, readying it near his shoulder, drawn back as far as he could. Then, he thrust his left hand far out in front, twisting it ninety degrees as he did so. He had seen Black Lotus move like that for her special attack, "Death by Piercing."

"Hiyaah!"

The crash of impact this time was a little higher and clearer than the last time. And although he was made to dance again with a pain like lightning and forced to grit his teeth, the scar gouged out of the wall was a tiny bit deeper.

That day eventually ended with him simply continuing to attack the wall.

He gradually stopped feeling the pain, and although he was able to dig his fingertips in about three millimeters when the sun was near setting, he was still nowhere near the level of being able to use that as a support to climb the wall. However, rather than trying to push himself, Haruyuki returned to the same roost as the day before, even feeling a kind of satisfaction in his profound exhaustion.

Was there a chance that his work was just ordinary escapism?

He couldn't avoid the thought as he laid down. Because it was a fact that by accelerating, he was stretching out time and putting off the problem of Chiyuri, Takumu, and Nomi. But right now, he was happy at being able to concentrate so intently and throw himself into something like this; the work was a blessing to him. Haruyuki closed his eyes and once again slept like the dead.

The morning of the fourth day.

He stood in the same place as the previous day and revised his thinking as he stared at the many scars cut into the wall of blue-lit steel.

The directionality of his Imaging thought process should be correct: imagine hardness and sharpness in his fingers and the power in his arms hammering out those holes. But he felt like one thing wasn't quite right somehow.

As he was hemming and hawing, a fabric package made a direct hit to his head once again. He quickly grabbed it from the ground and yelled thanks up at the sky before biting into the bread inside.

Again today, a single note was attached. Heart pounding, he opened it.

"Good luck, Corvus! ♥" was all it said, and Haruyuki snorted lightly, flustered by the symbol at the end of the sentence. He had been expecting a hint like yesterday, but nothing else was written there.

So then I guess this means I already know all the things I need to know, he thought, making short work of the bread before starting to desperately rack his brains once more.

Will. Desire straight from the heart. Image Power. Sky Raker's words came back to life in his ears. *Do you see? Image Power! It is precisely this that is the true power hidden within us Burst Linkers.*

Hold…on. Her speech sounded really familiar, something from a long time ago, way back, something *She* had said as well. As soon as the thought crossed his mind, Her voice played vividly from the depths of his memory.

Listen, Haruyuki. You're fast. You can become faster than anyone else. Faster even than me, faster than the other kings. And speed is a Burst Linker's greatest strength.

There was no way he could forget that. Those were the words she said to him right before she used the final command of Physical Full Burst to save him. Kuroyukihime had to have known about the Incarnate System hidden within Burst Linkers at that time. However, she had expressed the greatest power not as "image power" but as "speed." Which meant—

The two were the same thing.

The word *speed* that Kuroyukihime had used wasn't simply referring to the pace of a duel avatar's movement in the field. The signal speed output by the brain and the consciousness connected to the Neurolinker. The quickness of the response between this world and yourself. And that, namely, was *being closer to the true nature of the world.*

"Manipulation…through images…" Haruyuki murmured and readied his right hand.

It wasn't about power. It was about speed. What he should be imagining was that. Moving as fast as he possibly could. Getting as close to the world as he possibly could. Becoming one with it.

"...Foo!" With the faintest of cries, Haruyuki put the image of light on his right hand and sent it flying.

Although faint, a white light did trace out its trajectory through space. *Schwing*! The sound echoed beautifully, almost like something from a musical instrument.

Haruyuki looked at his own fingers, buried more than five millimeters in the steel wall, and clenched his left fist tightly.

For another three days, Haruyuki continued the same training in the same spot.

He rose with the sun and greedily devoured the bun tossed down from the peak. The heart symbol was sometimes there, sometimes not, on the accompanying note, but with the piece of paper's encouraging words as support, he turned to face the wall and focused on delivering spear-hand strikes over and over with both hands.

In the fourteen or so years of Haruyuki's life, he had never once concentrated on a single thing for so long a time. Or perhaps it would be better to say that this was a time that, right from the start, could not exist in the real world. A flesh-and-blood body frequently got hungry, quickly got tired, and he did have to go to school, after all. It was precisely because of the Unlimited Neutral Field, where the flow of time was accelerated a thousand times, and his duel avatar, which did not know exhaustion, that this intense focus was possible.

It didn't at all seem like the light emitted by his fingertips, the depth they dug into the wall, and all the things he could experience around him were increasing. But Haruyuki harbored no doubts about his straightforward training. And so, aware of nothing but the speed of the signal emitted by his brain and delivered to his avatar, he repeated the same action thousands of times, tens of thousands of times, hundreds of thousands of times.

He felt like this training might be something that would one day suddenly awaken his "true power." He understood he was setting his sights on something that could only be reached through the steady accumulation of something that was invisible to him. It was the same as with the virtual squash game where he had tried endlessly for the high score in the Umesato Junior High's local net. Concentration and accumulation. There was no short cut.

Sky Raker, waiting at the peak of this iron tower—along with the Red King Nico and the Black King Kuroyukihime, who stood at the peak of the accelerated world itself—also probably had gone down this road in the past. Although he was so far behind them on this long, long road, he couldn't even see their shadows.

Someday, I'll be there, too…I will definitely reach that place someday. Such did Haruyuki pray intently from his heart at sunset on the sixth day as he gazed at his right hand, which was finally able to dig into the thick steel up to the base of his fingers.

It took another half day until he was able to do the same thing while attached to the wall—near noon on the day that marked a week since he'd come to this world.

After staring attentively at the sun, which shone weakly on the other side of thick black clouds, and deliberating for a while, Haruyuki decided to at last start his second ascent. There were only another five or six hours until sunset, but he wouldn't need to look for rocks jutting out, pause in his route, or double back on himself like in the Wasteland stage. If he climbed straight up, he could make it to the top before nightfall.

"All right!" Haruyuki slammed his hands against the sides of his helmet, let out a battle cry, and inflicted the first strike on the wall.

With a clear ringing, the white light traced out its trajectory, and his swordlike hand pierced deep into the wall. Hand reliably jammed in as a support, he yanked his body up and then struck in a slightly higher place with his left hand.

Speed. The speed of light. That's all you think about.

At some point, Haruyuki even stopped repeating the word *speed* to himself. All that existed in his brain was the image of a sword tip, of a white light being thrust forward.

Pierce. Lift body. Concentrate. Pierce again.

Since he needed to plunge his fingers in as level as he possibly could, the distance he gained with one cycle was just barely thirty centimeters. When he thought about the fact that he was trying to climb 333 meters, a simple calculation told him he would have to pierce the wall 1,010 times.

But Haruyuki absorbedly, intently repeated the same action. Without looking at the peak or the ground, he forgot the past and the future; the wall in front of him and his own fingertips became his entire world.

Pierce. Pierce. Again. Again.

Already, his striking hand was emitting a dazzling, laser-like light. The depth to which his sword hand dug rapidly increased, to the point where it was work to pull it out again, but he was unaware of that as well and simply continued to pierce and climb.

Haruyuki sank into a deep, abnormal concentration, even greater than when he was tackling the bullet-evasion game he had created. The information from his sight and hearing lost its meaning, and the steel wall eventually disappeared as well. In the seemingly endless darkness, there were only the flashes emitted by his hands, alternating flickers—

No.

He could see something.

Far, far in the distance in the darkness was a blue rippling like the surface of water.

The portal? Someone was on the other side of it. Vision filled with a golden radiance, all he could see was the silhouette, but he was sure…someone was…

Haruyuki broke through the dense darkness with both hands and tried to go to the silhouette. He felt like it was calling him.

"Who…are you…?" His voice rang out in the gloom and echoed loudly, and to this, some kind of response, no, something like a signal—

Then a faint trembling raced along his body, and Haruyuki opened his eyes wide with a gasp.

Before his eyes was the blue-black steel wall, unchanged. The sky was already dyed a deep red. Sunset was near.

But a light that was not the sun reached him from the east, and Haruyuki stared at it. A seven-colored aurora surging from the sky. The sound of bells. It was the Change.

Except that this time, Haruyuki couldn't hurry.

He continued to move both hands at the same fixed pace as he had been. Even without looking up, he could feel the edge of the peak close above him. As if aiming to make Haruyuki fall, the aurora advanced aggressively. The snapping and roaring of the land being rebuilt filled the world.

Pierce. Lift body. Pierce. Lift body.

Simultaneous with his next strike, his vision was assaulted by the seven-colored beam, and Silver Crow's slender body was instantly sent flying into the sky, flicked by the finger of an unseen giant.

The summit of the tower, so tantalizingly within reach, grew distant as the virtual gravity reached out its hand for Haruyuki, practically salivating.

But.

"…Hng!" With a low cry from the sky, Haruyuki set his sights on the wall two meters above him and launched his final blow.

Schwaaan! The simple sound reverberated through the air, and a sword of pure white light reached out and pierced deep—deep into a wall it should not have been able to reach.

At the same time as he felt sure resistance, Haruyuki used his arm as a fulcrum to vault himself upward with all his might. Whirling around and around, he flew through the aurora, and where he landed with a *crunch* was—

The lawn of the garden in the sky, which he hadn't set foot on in a week.

"Welcome back, Corvus."

Still crouching on one knee, Haruyuki heard the gentle voice from above. An intense despair washed over him at that, but he fought back against it and earnestly raised his head.

The sky-blue avatar in the silver wheelchair was looking down on him with a smile. "You came back very quickly, just as I had expected. No wonder you are the 'child' she selected."

Haruyuki responded from a totally different place. "I shouldn't have made it." Because in his head, only the sensation of his final strike burned too brightly. "With my short arms, that was a distance that I completely could not reach...But I believed— No, I knew that I would. That...If that's the power of the will, then..."

Here, he finally focused both eyes on Sky Raker and continued. "That's not 'playing' in any sense of the word. It's something... deeper...connected to this world. It's a...It's..." Haruyuki fumbled fervently through the limited number of endings for that sentence and managed to somehow put into words what he wanted to say. "It's like a rewriting of the facts..."

"Yes. That's exactly it."

Sky Raker's smile disappeared as she clasped her hands together tightly. When she continued, her voice was weightier. "Overwrite. This one word is precisely the key to the Incarnate System. However, you can't comprehend if you simply hear the word. You have to experience it."

"Over...write," Haruyuki repeated hoarsely and Sky Raker assented softly.

"The Incarnate System—in other words, the control system

built into the Brain Burst program—is essentially assistive at best. It's nothing more than a system to support movement control and supplement the avatar's motion. But images released too quickly and too strongly by the consciousness can surpass even the constraints of the program and become manifest. Wheels that shouldn't turn turn, an arm that shouldn't reach reaches. A resolute intention, a *will* overwrites events."

Haruyuki had supposedly reached the first level in the Incarnate System, but these words invoked a sense of wonder in him.

It had already been six months since he started playing Brain Burst. It was supposed to be nothing more than a game. But of all the countless titles he had played up to that point, he wondered if there was even one that questioned the strength of image power—that is, of the will.

The wheelchair advanced with a creak and stopped directly in front of Haruyuki, who was still squatting there, struck by these feelings. He timidly accepted the proffered hand and was pulled up with an unexpected strength; somehow, he managed to stand, albeit with a wobble.

Sky Raker took her hand back and smiled once more before uttering even more unexpected words.

"And now I have nothing else to teach you."

"Huh?" Haruyuki gasped and shook his head side to side several times. "B-but I'm still…I mean, I just finally climbed the wall! That's a long way from flying. I still have so many things to learn—"

"I told you, Corvus," the sky-blue avatar said calmly, shaking her head slowly, "that I never reached the sky in the end. Perhaps you are the one who will be able to fly one day with Incarnate alone. But that will probably take a very long time. Even if you focus hard on forging yourself in this world…Yes, probably ten years."

"Te—" Haruyuki was at a loss for words and clenched his teeth together tightly before saying, "I-I don't care. If it means I'll be able to fly again, I'll—"

"You mustn't." Instantly, a severe voice cut him off. "Six months, a year, you can still go back. But those who spend ten years in this world can no longer return to reality."

"Huh?"

"They no longer care about anything happening in the real world. They quit school, forget their friends, and lock themselves up in their rooms, thinking that everything is fine as long as they have this world. More than a few such Burst Linkers roam the Unlimited Neutral Field. No longer dueling or training, they hide themselves here for the sole purpose of running away from the real world...Silver Crow. Why do you play this game Brain Burst?"

Although Haruyuki was slightly confused at the sudden question, he answered right away, absorbed. "T-to become stronger. To get stronger, reach level ten with her, and...beat this game. To know what lays ahead, I..."

"In that case, you mustn't stay here. If you don't go back, you will finally begin to fear the end of the world. You'll end up praying for nothing other than eternity for the accelerated world. If you don't want to lose this feeling now, go back to reality."

"B-but, I-I—" Shaking his head fiercely, Haruyuki shouted, "I want to fly! No! I...*have* to fly one more time."

Two arms reached out to support Haruyuki as he dropped to his knees on the lawn with a *thump*. Held tightly against Sky Raker's chest, his entire body frozen solid in surprise, he heard a still voice murmur very close to his right ear, "It's okay. I'll give you my wings."

"Huh?"

"My Enhanced Armament, Gale Thruster. You should be able to master it now. I know you'll be able to flap those wings up to the heights I couldn't reach."

Haruyuki, very close to fainting at the sensation of touching a certain un-avatar-like well-roundedness under the white dress, somehow pulled himself back together and asked in a trembling voice, "Wh-why? Why would you do all this for me? I-I know it's kind of late to be asking, but...you're Ash Roller's parent, and he and I are—"

"Friends. Aren't you?"

He held his breath again at her swift response.

"Every time he has a duel with you, he never fails to tell me quite excitedly all about how he won or lost. Having an opponent like that is a delightful thing. Even if, for instance, you serve different Masters. Which is why for his sake as well, I want you to fly again."

After a long, long silence, Haruyuki earnestly squeezed out, "Thank you. So much."

At the same time, albeit very belatedly, he thought about his attitude the last time he and Ash Roller dueled, and how it had made the man despair somehow—it had even hurt him. Very much unable to put into words the myriad emotions swirling around in his heart, Haruyuki simply repeated the same word over and over.

"Definitely...definitely, definitely."

"Yes. Definitely. You are one who will be able to make it over the wall. Now then. It is time for you to depart from this garden, Corvus. The next time we meet will be in the real world."

"Wh-what?!" When he lifted his face at the unexpected declaration, red eyes were smiling gently at him—from extremely close up.

"Naturally. For the transfer of Enhanced Armament, you must either go through the Shop or direct in the real. If I sold it, it would have quite the hefty price tag, one that you most certainly would not be able to pay with the Burst points you have."

"S-something that valuable—"

"It's fine. I know he wants you to fly again as well. Now, for the time and place, let's see...Seven in the morning real time, in front of the west exit of Shinjuku Station, there's a..."

Haruyuki knew the burger shop Sky Raker specified, so he bobbed his head up and down, stunned at the speed things were moving.

"Good. Well then— Hmm?" Releasing the arms embracing him and moving to pull herself away from Haruyuki, Sky Raker cocked her head slightly. Her fingertips repeatedly traced the center of the now wingless Silver Crow's back.

"Uh, um...is something...?" Enduring the ticklish feeling, Haruyuki craned his neck.

"No...it's nothing. Now, you should be on your way." Sky Raker made Haruyuki stand and then she nodded, grinning in her wheelchair.

Not knowing how to express his feelings of gratitude, Haruyuki bowed as deeply as he possibly could and said in a shaking voice, "Thank you so much, Sky Raker. Um...the stew and the buns were delicious."

Then he whirled around before she could notice the tears streaming down his face below his helmet. Etching the night scene of the newly transformed Unlimited Neutral Field deep into his memory, he leapt straight into the shimmering blue portal at its center.

Having awoken on his own bed in the real world, Haruyuki just lay on his sheets for a while.

When he finally glanced at the clock, it was only 9:10 PM. Yet he had the definite feeling of having been away from his house for a terrifyingly long time. The taste of the pizza he had supposedly eaten immediately prior to diving was completely erased from his memory.

Just ten minutes— Passing just a week on the other side, he felt a separation from his present. How would it be if it had been six months, a year? He pursed his lips firmly, and his right cheek suddenly ached.

The reason for this pain alone was something he wouldn't be able to forget: Takumu hitting him after he had said those terrible things.

"I have to apologize," he muttered, caressing his cheek with his fingertips. To get his incomparable partner back, he had to reclaim what had been stolen from him, no matter what. His pride—and his wings.

Taking off his Neurolinker, Haruyuki set the alarm clock on the shelf and closed his eyes. Instantly, he was overcome by the exhaustion of climbing a tower in another world, and he tumbled into the deep abyss of sleep.

12

Fortunately, Haruyuki's mother didn't seem to notice that he was leaving for school an hour earlier than usual. Six thirty AM on a bright Tuesday, April 16. He said good-bye to her in her room and, after she sent five hundred yen to his Neurolinker, Haruyuki left the house.

Under an intermittently rainy sky, offering proof for the saying that you won't see three straight days of sun in the spring, Haruyuki walked to the nearby JR Koenji Station and got on the Chuo line. Dizzied by the unfamiliar crowds, he got off at Shinjuku Station, and when he left the west exit, the time was 6:55.

He moved at a trot toward the fast-food place that was their designated meeting place before suddenly wondering, *How am I supposed to know who she is?*

If he connected his Neurolinker globally, he could make a tag saying he was "Corvus" or make something float above his head, but this was the middle of Shinjuku Ward, controlled by the Blue King. Once he was discovered on the matching list, the information would make the rounds and he would be challenged to duel after duel.

And Haruyuki's real-world appearance had exactly zero in common with his duel avatar. Or rather, it was the polar opposite.

The real question here was why on earth he had been so quick to trust a direct meeting in the real; i.e., have it known that inside Silver Crow was this pudgeball.

The sad memory of the one time he had previously had a game-related offline meeting came back to life, and Haruyuki thought, rapidly rounding his back, *Yeah, I should just go home before she finds me. And then we'll just do the transfer of the Enhanced Armament through the Shop somehow*—

"Morning, Corvus."

"Eaah!" Haruyuki leapt into the air at the sound of the gentle voice and the pat on his shoulder from behind. Fighting to tuck his head and limbs into his torso like a turtle, he seriously considered replying, *You've got the wrong person*, for about 0.3 seconds, and just on the verge of actually doing so, he abandoned the idea and gingerly turned around.

Standing on the crosswalk was a girl he had never met, wearing what appeared to be the uniform of some high school, but Haruyuki instinctively knew that this person was Sky Raker herself.

Her long hair resembled the other's, and there was also the fact that the upper front area of her torso was extremely voluminous—just like her avatar. Of course this was reasoning that touched on harassment, but mostly, there was just a similar aura shrouding her.

Calm with a gentle air, she definitely didn't seem like a regular person. It was an aura she shared somehow with both Kuroyuki-hime and the Red King Niko. She wasn't in a wheelchair on this side, but Haruyuki bowed his head with confidence.

"G-good morning," he mumbled, looking at the very Japanese eyes of his interlocutor with an upturned gaze. "Uh, um...how did you know it was me?"

"The power of your will."

"Wh-what?!"

"I'm kidding. There aren't too many junior high students standing in front of a fast-food place by themselves at this hour."

Giggling, Sky Raker touched Haruyuki's shoulder and turned toward the door of the restaurant. At her urging, he slipped through the automatic door.

"Corvus, how about breakfast?"

"Oh! I already ate."

"Well then, just drinks should be fine."

After this exchange, he was treated to a medium oolong tea, not given the chance to refuse politely, and they headed for a table in the corner, seating themselves across from each other.

Wondering what she thought at seeing him in the real, Haruyuki at any rate bowed his head again. "Um…y-you've really done so…so much for me. And then you came all the way out here. Thank you so much."

"My school's in Shibuya, so it's not that far out of my way." Smiling, Sky Raker pulled a bundled XSB cable from her bag on the chair next to her. She plugged one end into the silver-white Neurolinker peeking out over the collar of her blazer, deeply reminiscent of the wheelchair she used in the accelerated world, and gripped the other end tightly with both hands.

There was no hint of hesitation in her gesture, but a look invoking the grief of separation flashed across her cheeks. As Haruyuki felt a sharp pain in his chest, the silver plug was already being gently offered to him.

He was aware of the many stares of the students and office workers in the restaurant settling on the back of his neck. In the dead of night, it maybe wouldn't get so many stares, but directing first thing in the morning, and in school uniforms no less, was pretty crazy.

Normally, directing in a place like this and with a girl in high school would have caused inevitable heart palpitations, copious amounts of sweat, and a beet-red face, but now at least was not the time for feeling embarrassed.

Having lost his wings, he understood, so much so that it hurt, just how valuable and precious this Enhanced Armor was, especially given that it was initial equipment and not bought in the

Shop. To be then nurtured all this time, fighting with her up to level eight…He understood to the point of absurdity.

But Haruyuki intuitively knew that any show of polite refusal for the sake of form alone would only insult her. Because this act was most likely based on the convictions of the Burst Linker Sky Raker.

He bowed his head deeply once and, taking the plug with both hands, Haruyuki stabbed it into his own Neurolinker.

Sky Raker's plump lips moved slightly in the shape of "Burst Link."

The transfer of the Enhanced Armament through a Direct Duel and the lecture on its use were completed within the 1,800-second count.

After they returned to the real world, the time was just seven fifteen. Aware of a lingering vague heat and a sense of excitement even after the direct cable had been removed, Haruyuki chugged the rest of his oolong tea. When Sky Raker had also emptied her coffee cup, she smiled with her eyes at Haruyuki and stood from her seat.

Feeling equal parts exaltation at the new power he had acquired and peaky unease at the thought that he might not be able to master it, Haruyuki trailed behind and to the left of the older girl as he walked to the station.

He noticed the sound when they were about halfway across the long crosswalk.

Each time her feet, clad in gray tights and dark brown loafers, stretched out and hit the ground, there was the faint but definite whine of a servo. Yanked back from his meditations, Haruyuki knit his brow, and after listening for several seconds, he understood.

Prosthetics.

Sky Raker's legs were artificial and electronically controlled. They were connected to her Neurolinker and received the order to move from her brain, and then internal actuators and dampers moved her. She would be able to walk without any hindrance in normal life, and she should be able to run, but even still, there would definitely be a limit.

Once they had finished navigating the crosswalk, Haruyuki stopped, hung his head, and clenched both hands tightly.

The reason Sky Raker longed for the sky, the reason she wanted wings, was probably not unconnected with those prosthetic legs. If that was the case, then her motive was so deep and maddening that Haruyuki couldn't even begin to understand it.

And yet she...

Because of that, she helped me after I lost my wings, without even trying to find out why I was given them... She encouraged me, gave me her own wings. Even though my own motives are totally nothing. Just wanting just to escape from the earth, I mean, that's it.

The backs of his eyes grew hot, and the depths of his nose popped painfully, but scolding himself that he could not cry there, that that was the last thing he could do, Haruyuki pushed past the feeling. Sky Raker was absolutely no less proud than any other Burst Linker Haruyuki knew, even the Black King, Black Lotus. Crying easy tears just because his heart thought it understood what was going on with her would be absolutely unforgivable.

He let his head hang straight down as he pinched his right cheek as hard as he could, an attempt to pull back what was trying to flow out, and the tip of a loafer entered his field of vision with a *clack*.

"You're quite kind, aren't you?"

At the almost consoling words spoken from above his head, Haruyuki shook his head fiercely several times. "I-I'm not. Not at all." His voice shook, and the end of his sentence had a strange choked sound to it, so he pulled at his cheek with his hand even harder.

A white hand reached out to grab that hand and pull it back forcefully. Crouching down, Sky Raker clutched Haruyuki's hand to her chest and their eyes met.

"Listen, Corvus. I most certainly did not help you out of pity, and I know you don't pity me or anything. Those tears are proof that your truth exists in the accelerated world."

"Tr-truth?"

Nodding gently, Sky Raker brought her face so close that the tips of their noses were nearly touching. The curious stares of students heading for the station on their way to school pooled on them, but seemingly completely unbothered by this, she told him in a quiet but firm voice, "Those who think that Brain Burst is simply a tool to accelerate their thoughts and make the real world easier would absolutely never cry like this. For them, the duels are a means of earning points, and the accelerated world is nothing but a hunting ground where they can trick and trap others. But we know that that is not everything. We believe that there are encounters with the truth, there is friendship and love, and other bonds in that world as well. Isn't that right?"

"...Yes...Yes." Finally, unable to hold them back, Haruyuki felt the tears fall in large drops as he nodded deeply.

Sky Raker wiped away the water on his cheeks with the fingers of her right hand, and continued in a voice shaking slightly with emotion. "Because of my own foolishness, I once lost friendship, those bonds. I deeply regret that I was part of the reason she threw herself into battle with the other kings with such extreme recklessness. But I don't want you to make the same mistakes. I want you to fight to protect what you really should protect."

Haruyuki closed his eyelids tightly and prayed hard. *I must never forget how lucky I am, even now with my wings stolen from me. This time, for sure, I have to burn that deep into my heart. All the people who I've met and created a bond with... Ash Roller, Sky Raker, Scarlet Rain, and of course Takumu and Chiyuri, and... Kuroyukihime. That is what I really should protect.*

"...Okay!" Once again, his voice was nasal, but he replied firmly and raised his head, wiping his face roughly. "Thank you. I-I'm definitely going to fly again under my own power. When I do, I'll definitely come to return them... Your wings."

"All right. Good luck, Corvus." Standing and smiling, Sky Raker started to move away after bowing, but Haruyuki stopped her.

"Um...um. I don't think it's lost or anything. I'm sure she's waiting even now...for you to come back."

Hearing this, Sky Raker opened both eyes wide and blinked several times in succession.

Haruyuki finally saw a faint but definite smile rise up. He smiled awkwardly himself, before running through the thronging crowd toward the Chuo line platform.

13

He slipped through the Umesato Junior High school gates mere seconds before the merciless tardy bell began. Checking that his Neurolinker had indeed just barely connected to the in-school net without penalty, Haruyuki panted and wiped the sweat from his forehead.

There was already practically no one in the schoolyard. If he didn't reach his classroom within the next five minutes, he'd still be marked as late. Begrudging the time needed to stuff his feet into his indoor shoes, he raced up the stairs. As he flew in through the rear door, his two childhood friends seated ahead of him whirled around. Chiyuri's eyes were colored with hopelessness, while Takumu's were tinged with pain. Meeting each of their gazes in turn, he bit his lip hard and hurried to his own seat.

Chiyuri was probably worried about Haruyuki backed up against a wall like he was, and Takumu had probably lost hope in this Haruyuki who wouldn't talk to him. But the only way to tackle the root of this situation was for Haruyuki to somehow make Seiji Nomi/Dusk Taker yield in a duel.

Currently, Nomi was holding three cards: Haruyuki's real identity, the shower room video, and his flying ability. In contrast, Haruyuki only held a half card, knowing a little about Nomi's real identity.

But when he thought about it, a Burst Linker's real identity was too lethal; you couldn't cancel that out no matter how many other cards you got ahold of. Even in this era, it was the same as Russia or America sending an armed nuclear submarine, drifting ghostlike through the deep sea. One lone ship was a significant deterrence. If, hypothetically, Haruyuki made public a photo of Nomi's face, his real name and address, and the name of his duel avatar in the accelerated world, Nomi would be dead as a Burst Linker. He would be assaulted by the kind of extreme groups who didn't shy away from attacks in the real, and once they got him in their grip, they would suck him dry of every last point. Haruyuki had been told that actual cases of things like this happening, while rare, did exist.

So thanks to this hammer hanging over his head, the video that Nomi had set him up for was, in the final reckoning, a card that couldn't be played. If that video were submitted to the school authorities, it would be a disastrous development for Haruyuki's life at school, but Nomi had to know that if he did submit it, he risked having a desperate Haruyuki, with nothing left to lose, expose his own real identity.

Put simply, the only card Nomi could really play without any hesitation to make Haruyuki his "point-earning dog" was the flying ability. But since a duel was the exclusive method of point transfer, if he could just beat Dusk Taker, even having had his wings stolen, he could resist and maybe even turn the situation around.

Naturally, this course of action would mean saying good-bye to the silver wings that had shone so brilliantly on Silver Crow's back until just the day before.

But even that was okay, Haruyuki decided in his heart. It wasn't because Sky Raker had given him a new way to fly. It was because he finally realized that his attachment to and dependence on these wings, an external object, had pushed him into a small box.

I will defeat Dusk Taker, who now uses my own wings. And then one day, I will set aside my ability and any Enhanced Armament, and I will fly using the power of my will alone, Haruyuki declared to himself, clenching his fists tightly.

The front door clattered open and Sugeno, their homeroom teacher, came in. The air now tense, the chattering class fell silent.

As soon as they had finished the customary pre-lesson bow, Sugeno said loudly, "No one sit down!"

Students who had started to sit jumped to their feet again with confused faces, and the young Japanese history teacher issued a further order, a blood vessel on his forehead popping up beneath his short hair. "All of you! Faces down, eyes closed!"

The feel of the room grew even more questioning, but pressed by the menacing look on Sugeno's face, the students quietly obeyed. Haruyuki also did as he was told, lips twisting.

"Good. Stay like that and listen. I think you already all know this, but yesterday morning, it was discovered that a small camera had been set up in the girls' shower room off the heated swimming pool. Fortunately, a student noticed it right away, so there was no specific damage, but even so, this is something that absolutely will not be tolerated. I'm very disappointed. And I'm furious. That a student who could do such a despicable thing could be here at Umesato!"

Bang! The sound of the teacher's podium being hit.

"At the teachers' meeting this morning, we decided to handle this within the school, since there were no victims. So listen... if the perpetrator is here in class C, raise your head now and look at your teacher. If you come forward on your own, your punishment will be reduced. So... are you here?"

Is he serious?

Still facing down, Haruyuki was stunned. Even if they did have their heads down and their eyes closed, any of them could easily have the image from their Neurolinker cameras displayed on the backs of their eyelids with one flick on their virtual desktops.

He was sure some students were doing exactly that right now. You'd have to have nerves of steel to step forward after all his ranting about angry blah, despicable yada, punishment blah blah.

Naturally, Haruyuki kept his head down, and it seemed the other students did the same. Sugeno stubbornly made them all stand for more than a minute, but finally he said in a low voice, "You're sure? This is your last chance. I won't be this nice next time." He sounded almost convinced that the perpetrator was in this class.

Haruyuki feared that Takumu might actually challenge Sugeno on this—Kuroyukihime definitely would have—but fortunately, he heard, "Fine. Sit down and open your eyes." Forty chairs squealed, and once the noise had subsided, their teacher spoke again.

"If you're going to come forward, do it today. Before your punishment gets really serious."

Haruyuki felt like Sugeno was staring straight at him as he spoke, and he knitted his eyebrows. And then he got it. The fact that Haruyuki had come to school the day before yesterday on Sunday was in the local net logs. Sugeno was probably suspicious of his reasons for coming to school on a holiday, when he didn't belong to any clubs or teams. But he couldn't call him to the office with that level of proof.

Haruyuki shifted his gaze with a feigned ignorance, and his eyes met Chiyuri's sidelong. He could see a deep panic and fear there, and now he held his breath. It had still only been a short time since Chiyuri became a Burst Linker. She didn't know that with his real identity known, it was an enormous risk for Nomi to actually use that video.

He wanted to tell her in a mail not to worry, but Sugeno kept staring at him, so instead, he shot Chiyuri a short but firm look. Sensing something, apparently, his childhood friend moved her mouth slightly before turning around again, but the paleness of her cheeks persisted.

*   *   *

Haruyuki paid twice as much attention as usual in his morning classes and took lots of notes. If he relaxed his focus even a little, his thoughts were tottered in the direction of the revenge match with Nomi.

But he still had no way to challenge Nomi, blocked as he was from the matching list through some unknown means. His chance for a rematch would probably be when Nomi came for his "tribute" of next week's points. Somehow, he had to train with the extremely capricious Enhanced Armament he had gotten from Sky Raker. Taking that into consideration, one week was actually not enough time.

Classes were strangely short when you paid attention, and before he knew it, the bell for lunch was ringing. He checked on Chiyuri and Takumu, thinking he might talk a little with one of them, but Chiyuri appeared to be eating her boxed lunch with several girls, and Takumu left the classroom without looking at Haruyuki.

He sighed briefly and started to bring his butt out of his seat with the idea of chasing after Takumu when a small RECEIVED icon flashed in the center of his vision. It wasn't mail or a voice call, but rather a dive call requesting a conversation in full-sensory mode.

Who on earth— As soon as he saw the sender's name, Haruyuki fell back into his chair with a crash. He forgot everything in an instant and, closing his eyes, murmured the command.

"D-Di-Direct Link."

His Neurolinker received his hurried, slightly stammered order, and his senses were cut off from the real world. The classroom was painted with darkness, and a sensation of falling soon came over him. If he simply waited, he would land in the Umesato Junior High local net VR space, but before that could happen, Haruyuki stretched a hand out toward the access gate floating in front of him. His virtual body was sucked in, and he was spit out—

In the middle of a white beach, spreading out somewhere under a fierce sun and an impossibly blue sky.

He stood stock-still for a moment in his pink pig avatar, and then took a few staggering steps toward the water's edge off in the distance, before he realized that this virtual space was not made of polygons. He had no sensation of walking in sand. Which meant it was an optical image of the real world, taken with a video camera, and flatly projected into Haruyuki's vision. When he turned to both sides to confirm this, the scene did not follow but took on a strange, distorted perspective. It was completely dark behind him.

The information transmitted should have been just visual and aural, but strangely, he could even feel the hot, dry wind of a southern country and he took a deep breath. Then.

"Hey, it's been a long time...Or I suppose it hasn't. It's been three days, hmm, Haruyuki?" A familiar and yet endlessly fascinating voice sounded, and a human figure slipped out from the right side of his field of vision.

Large straw hat. Thin white hoodie. Sunlight shining over the jet-black hair that draped itself over those shoulders, casting it in sparkle.

Bringing both hands behind her with a slightly bashful expression, Kuroyukihime continued hastily, "There's no lag? I'm connecting to the local net there through the student council office server, so it might be a little slow."

"N-no, not at all, it's fine. There's no noise, either. Um...um, h-hi, Kuroyukihime." Haruyuki dipped his avatar's head and again drank in the person before his eyes.

Because it was an optical image, there was no sense of depth, but it wasn't a polygon recreation; this was the real Kuroyukihime. She had gone to the trouble of setting up a camera to show him the scene in Okinawa, just like she promised.

"I-it's beautiful, really beautiful. The sand and...a-and you." When he added the last part at an extremely low volume, Kuroyukihime broke into a smile, albeit half bitter, and turned toward the emerald green sea as well.

"Henoko Beach. Earlier, there were military planes flying around here. I think you might have liked them."

"O-oh really? I wish I had seen them." As he spoke, his eyes were glued to the bare white legs stretching out below the hem of her hoodie. Kuroyukihime turned around again, and he shot his eyes up at the sky and said stiffly, "I-I-I'm so glad the weather's good! The sky's so blue, huh? Almost like a desert stage!"

She was looking at a camera lens over there, and so shouldn't have even been able to begin to tell where Haruyuki's eyes were focused, but, even so, Kuroyukihime had apparently realized something with her characteristic intuition, and, pursing her lips slightly, she yanked down the hem of her hoodie.

At that instant.

"C'mon, Hime! How long you planning to keep that thing on?"

A new human shadow entered the frame from the left. The girl with fluffy hair was a student council member Haruyuki didn't know. She was in a pink one-piece swimsuit, and Haruyuki felt his throat close up suddenly, but as she came up from behind Kuroyukihime, she suddenly did something huge.

In some incredibly quick work, she tugged down the zipper on Kuroyukihime's hoodie and yanked off the thin covering.

"Ah! Hey! What are you doing!"

"I believe someone was supposed to do some serious hanging out with me on the beach in her swimsuit this morning?" Giggling, the female student turned toward the camera and waved. "Take your time, Arita."

And then she dashed out of the frame on the right. All that was left was Kuroyukihime, face red under her straw hat, hands clenched tightly together in front of her body.

The swimsuit that appeared from beneath the dismantled armor was, of course, black. And the fairly small two-piece revealed close to 90 percent of her snow-white skin. They were unassuming in size, but as soon as he saw the top of the two extremely lovely protrusions brilliantly reflecting the sunlight, Haruyuki felt his heart rate skyrocket. He forced himself to take several deep breaths, concerned that his Neurolinker might do an abnormal link out.

Finally, Kuroyukihime looked at Haruyuki with upturned eyes and said, "W-well, that's, what. I mean, it is Okinawa, after all."

"R-r-right! I-i-i-it is Okinawa after all."

He wanted so badly to hit the record button in the corner of his vision, but if he did that during a full dive, she would know. Left with no other choice, he focused every fiber of his being on carving the real-time image into his brain, and he worked hard to make his mouth move. "Umm, okay, huh, well... I-it! It l-looks really good on you."

"Th-thanks." With a faint smile, Kuroyukihime brought her hands behind her back again, and Haruyuki stared desperately at her body. Very close to passing out, Haruyuki was pulled back this time by an incredibly faint scar cutting across the smooth porcelain skin on the lower right of her abdomen.

"......!"

Eyes widening briefly, Haruyuki bit down hard on his lip and when the too-gentle virtual pain generated was not enough, he bit harder.

He was sure that scar was from six months earlier when she had been critically injured, on the verge of death, saving Haruyuki from a car running wild. In the present day, thanks to advances in regenerative medicine, the majority of the aftermath of medical treatment was erased, but this had its limits. Or perhaps her injuries had simply been that serious.

Kuroyukihime seemed, keenly, to intuit the reason for his silence, and, blinking slowly once, she brought a smile to her lips that was colored with a different kind of gentleness. The fingers on her raised left hand traced the scar gently.

"Normally, you can't really see it at all. But with the sun so strong here, I suppose you can a little, hmm?"

Haruyuki couldn't reply to her quiet voice. Lifting her head, Kuroyukihime stared directly into the lens—into Haruyuki's eyes—and said in a fairly strong tone, "You don't need to worry

about it. It's my lone medal, after all. The pain, this scar came from protecting someone, rather than fighting, for the first time in my life. And now, this scar is a support for me."

"...Kuroyukihime." Haruyuki somehow managed to murmur that one word and clenched his avatar's hands tightly.

I will never, ever hurt you again.

Once again, he made the same vow to himself that he had repeated countless times already, but at the same time, he couldn't help but be aware of the hint of guilt he felt. If at that moment, Haruyuki were to explain the crisis he currently faced, Kuroyukihime would get mad, ask why he hadn't told her sooner, and probably be hurt again. And then, most likely, she'd come up with some reason to come back from Okinawa right away, push herself to the limits of her abilities, and even maybe rescue Haruyuki.

But that was exactly why Haruyuki couldn't tell her. He felt like he had to fight with his own two fists now, so that he could someday be the knight to protect her from everything.

"...Kuroyukihime." Haruyuki said her name again, and then spoke as clearly as he possibly could. "I...I'll get strong, too. Right now, you're just protecting me all the time, but...one day, I'll definitely be strong enough to support you."

Her smile changed to something mischievous, and, taking a step forward, Kuroyukihime slid a gentle hand over the position of Haruyuki's avatar. "It's getting time for me to get back. I'll call you again. And I'll be back on Sunday, so you have to decide before then what you want as a souvenir."

As soon as she said this, "souvenir from the Okinawa trip" and "reward for the Territories" got mixed up in his head, and the words that came out of his mouth as a result—

"Oh! Then th-thirty centimeters, d-di..."

"Huh? What? Thirty centimeters in diameter...A *sata andagi* sweet bun? Now, now! I really don't think they sell them that big...Well, I'll keep an eye out."

At the tired look that said, *Honestly, such a glutton*, Haruyuki hurriedly shook his head. Sadly, however, she couldn't see this motion.

"No...um, uh...I mean, if they have one, sure. Please enjoy the rest of your trip."

"Mmm, thanks. Okay, see you," Kuroyukihime said, and about to reach a hand out to the camera, muttered, "Oh!" and stopped.

"Wh-what's wrong?" Haruyuki asked, working hard to keep his eyes from boring holes into the thin, snow-white legs that leapt into his field of vision the instant he hung his head in dejection.

"Now that I'm thinking about it, I got a strange mail from Takumu. About that seventh grader from the kendo team we suspected of being a Burst Linker..."

"Huh?!" Swallowing hard, Haruyuki continued, flustered, "Wh-what did it say?"

"Mmm. Let's see. He asked if I couldn't look into...Nomi, was it? This seventh grader's scores by subject on the entrance exam, so I sent him what I found in the student database. Has he said anything to you?"

When he heard this whispered report, Haruyuki's jaw dropped. "E-entrance exam? Why would he want that data now?...No, Takumu hasn't said anything about it to me."

"He hasn't?...Ah! I have to go. Okay, I'm hanging up now. 'Bye!"

The flash of her right hand waving was the end, and the connection to Okinawa was cut off, leaving Haruyuki alone in a dark plane. The super-detailed images of Kuroyukihime in her swimsuit flew from his mind, and he tried to guess what Takumu was thinking, but he didn't have the slightest idea.

Maybe he wants to fill in the data from the outside in, but the only thing left now is for Nomi and me to duel, Haruyuki muttered to himself before giving the link-out command.

When he returned to his real-world classroom, there were only ten minutes left in lunch. He stood, intent on hurrying over to the school store to get some bread, but glancing over at Takumu's seat, he found it empty. His eyes then roamed over to Chiyuri to see that she was in the middle of a rare full dive. After staring for a minute at the Neurolinker on the thin, hunched neck, Haruyuki left the classroom.

With the current state of things, nothing's going to change in a week.

That was what Haruyuki had anticipated. Given that Nomi had said he wouldn't lay a hand on Kuroyukihime or Takumu, he thought there would be no movement.

However, Haruyuki had underestimated the intelligence and ability to take action of his childhood friend, who had once stalked the Black King, Black Lotus. He was forced to this realization at the very end of gym class, right after he got the call from Kuroyukihime, fifth period on Tuesday.

While the girls practiced their original dance routine in the gym, the boys were told to do a three-hundred-meter run, a command that left the feel of a certain disparity at work. But Haruyuki did his rounds along the school track, panting heavily.

In the bottom center of his field of view, cruel digital numbers marked his time. Things he didn't want to know were displayed before him—the remaining distance, his expected completion time, everything from the average pitch value to his heart rate—and watching the pounding heart symbol, he worried that if he kept this up, his heart might explode.

The majority of the students had already finished, and the only ones remaining were Haruyuki and a few extremely bookish types. Maybe because the jerks on the sports teams had more energy than they knew what to do with, there was even a joker trotting along the inside of the track, imitating Haruyuki's plodding form, and, *Goddammit! I'll remember your little joke when I get to level nine someday. I'll use Physical Full Burst in the hundred meter and get the world record, then when some track-and-field team scout comes along I'll be all, "I'd rather watch this anime," and they'll turn you down cold and then you'll see, you stupid idiots.*

He left himself to these ridiculous thoughts while he tried to throw his everything into a final burst on the last straightaway. When he was nearly at the finish line, Takumu sitting quietly caught his eye.

His old friend was not even looking at Haruyuki's sad sprint. Haruyuki thought it might have been a kind of warrior's sympathy, but apparently not; he was staring at a fixed point in space—in other words, some AR information—as if he were going to devour it.

What is he even doing? Haruyuki wondered, wiping away the sweat that poured endlessly over his forehead. In the distance of his blurred vision, he felt like he saw Takumu's lips part slightly and mutter an order.

Naturally, he wasn't close enough to hear what it was. But the words formed a command that Haruyuki could lip-read by now: Burst Link.

Taku, why the hell are you accelerating now... With this thought, Haruyuki thrust his right foot out for a final push on the remaining several meters.

Instantly, a familiar, cold lightning exploded, and after passing through a semitransparent blue, the color of the ground changed to a sharp silver, tinged faintly with green. The backs of the students running ahead of him froze, the sports team guy teasing him disappeared, and the gym teacher waiting at the finish line vanished.

"Ah! Wh—! Whoa!"

A light enveloped Haruyuki's body, transforming him into his silver duel avatar. After falling forward a few steps, he put the brakes on with a suddenly nimble movement unlike anything his real body could manage. Standing up and stepping on the hard ground, Haruyuki let an astonished voice slip out from beneath his helmet.

"Ta-Taku?! Why are you dueling me—" Naturally, that's what he thought. That Takumu had accelerated, and his own acceleration that immediately followed was because Takumu had requested a duel via the local net.

But this was not the case.

Words roared and burst into flames in the center of his vision: A REGISTERED DUEL IS BEGINNING!!

In other words, a duel he was registered to watch was starting. Haruyuki wasn't one of the duelists—he was the Gallery. Takumu was starting a duel with someone, so Haruyuki, who was registered to watch Takumu, had been automatically accelerated and invited to the stage.

In the top left of his field of view, the name and HP bar of the duel instigator appeared: Cyan Pile. Then at top right, the Burst Linker who had been challenged—

The name *Dusk Taker* appeared.

"Wha…"

Haruyuki gasped. Dusk Taker—Seiji Nomi—always kept himself blocked from the matching list through some unknown means. The only way to challenge him to a duel within the school should have been to restrain his physical body and forcibly direct with him, like Nomi had done to Haruyuki himself the other day.

About three hundred meters ahead of him stood an imposing navy and light blue avatar. Here, Takumu finally shifted his gaze to Haruyuki, but, without uttering a word, he gestured with his right hand for him to get back. At any rate, members of the Gallery—other than parent/child or members of the same Legion—could not get closer than within ten meters of the duelists.

Quickly turning to face forward again, Cyan Pile took in the view of the upper side of the school, eyes shining blue in his mask and its rows of slim slits.

The General Classroom wing had already been transformed into something organic, shining with a slimy metallic luster. The countless windows had all been replaced with convex, glass-like black eyes, and innumerable protrusions resembling fins or gill-like pleats lined the walls. The sky was colored an abnormal green, and the large schoolyard was covered in pipes like blood vessels or wriggling metallic tentacles. No doubt about it, this was a Hell stage.

Haruyuki took a step back from the metal insects skittering around at his feet and tried again to ask Takumu what was going on. But before he could, a repulsive rupturing sound echoed loudly through the field.

Turning his eyes to the source of the sound with a gasp, he saw that one of the eyeball windows—around the center of the third floor, in the vicinity of seventh grade class B—had been pulverized from the inside. Buckets of viscous fluid oozed out of the new hole in the wall, fluid scattered by the feet of the small human figure exuded from the gloom.

"Oh dear. I had thought you to be more of the cautious type, Mayuzumi," the blackish-purple duel avatar, Dusk Taker, remarked in his clear boy's voice as he revealed himself, looking down on Takumu from on high, shaking his rounded, expressionless visor slowly from side to side. "I was expecting, or rather, I was hoping to give you the gift of the scenario where you gather up every little scrap of information on me, rack your brains for trends and countermeasures, and then when you actually act, it's too late."

"I've already collected plenty of info," Cyan Pile returned curtly, and waved his left hand lightly. "Which is why I was able to pull you into a duel stage like this, isn't it, Nomi?"

"......"

Turning toward Nomi, who let slip a sigh of displeasure, albeit a faint one, Takumu raised the metal stake of his right hand and continued. "Seiji Nomi. Unfortunately, I still don't know what trick you're using to keep yourself off the matching list itself. But I can guess almost to the second when that wall will be released."

"R-released?!" It was Haruyuki who cried out.

"Yes." Takumu glanced over at Silver Crow, finally speaking to him. "Nomi uses the power of acceleration in the real world to give himself an advantage. Even in kendo team practice matches. So naturally, he must be using it in other places. To beat people up, to take care of his homework...and, of course, during tests."

"Tests..." Instantly, Haruyuki felt like he finally understood why Takumu had made that strange request of Kuroyukihime.

As if reading his mind, Cyan Pile nodded lightly and shifted his gaze back to Nomi, above him. "Right now, at this very moment, the seventh graders are taking their first practical aptitude test. The subject of your fifth period class is, Nomi, the history you got full marks on in the entrance exam. Using the power of acceleration, obviously. But unlike a kendo match, where all you need to do is sign in, during a test, you need to be constantly exchanging information with the in-school local net. You can't shut it off. I figured you'd have to be connected to the local net and Brain Burst at least momentarily during fifth period, so I just sat and waited for you. And if you were going to use acceleration during a test, it would undoubtedly be when you were on the verge of running out of time. Because it's more efficient to do all the questions you need to look up with an external app all at once. As a result..."

Takumu gestured grandly with his left hand, as if to say, *Here we are.*

Listening so hard he forgot to nod along, Haruyuki unconsciously let out a deep sigh of admiration. Having reached the conclusion that Nomi would appear on the matching list for a mere instant—just as time was running out during the test for the subject in which he got full marks on the entrance exam—Takumu sat in the schoolyard and accelerated repeatedly to keep checking the list.

Nomi, seen through with such perfect clarity, stayed silent for a few more seconds before suddenly shouting brightly, "And why on earth do we have history tests and the like! It's the height of pointlessness, to be forced to answer through rote memorization tidbits you could look up in an instant, don't you agree? And although you're connected to the local net during tests, you're blocked from viewing the database! I do think it's some kind of a joke!"

Shoulders shaking as he laughed, Nomi continued, sounding increasingly self-controlled. "Mayuzumi. You said so now, didn't you? That I am using the 'power of acceleration in the real world to give myself an advantage.' Almost as if this were the most evil act imaginable. But if you ask me, what's incredible is that some people actually only use their Burst points for duels. If that's all you're going to do, why do you even need Brain Burst? There's a veritable mountain of other more brutal, violent, and—this is key—pain-free games out there. At the end of the day, in the bottom of your hearts, you both also believe you're part of a privileged class. That you're one of a mere thousand Burst Linkers in the world, that you're different from the other *normal* kids. You yourself are steeped in this sense of elite-ness, and yet you don't take advantage of your abilities? If that isn't hypocrisy, deceit, then what is it?"

"I don't actually blame you in the least, you know," Takumu returned, shrugging. "Until a little while ago, I used the power of acceleration to sneak around, too. How you want to use your points is up to you; you can do what you want. But if you'll let me give you one piece of advice as someone who's been there, a perfect score's too much, Nomi. You'll only attract unnecessary attention; there's no gain in it."

"That, I suppose, is a difference of opinion. For me, you see, my philosophy is to obtain the very best in all arenas. Whether it's a single point on a test or a single strike in a practice match. Or rather…perhaps it's more correct to say 'take,' hmm? Ha-ha!"

The avatar popped his upper body out through the hole in the wall and stuck his bolt-cuttered right hand straight out, palm up.

"There are a finite number of things in the world. Which means when someone gets something, someone else loses precisely that same thing at the same time. Such as with the law of conservation of energy, as it were. The fundamental principle of this world is 'struggle.' And I, well… I like taking, but more that that, I cannot stand losing things or having things taken from me. Right now, you're trying to take a maximum of one point eight seconds of my time. Precious time, at that, during a test. It's absolutely unforgivable. Naturally, you'll compensate me for it. With your Burst points."

"Nah. You'll actually be giving something to me. Something you got unfairly, Seiji Nomi. Something precious you took from my good friend."

The moment he heard those quiet words, Haruyuki felt his entire body stiffen with a gasp. Takumu already knew. That Dusk Taker had stolen Silver Crow's silver wings.

Cyan Pile's hard face took on a somehow mournful quality, and Takumu looked at Haruyuki briefly. "I heard rumors about your duel in Shibuya last night. Sorry, Haru, for not realizing. This time, it's my turn to fight."

"T-Taku!"

At Haruyuki's short cry, Takumu flicked the index finger of his left hand up, as if to say, *Leave it to me.*

Instantly, Haruyuki was overcome by a powerful sense of his own smallness. He had been thinking of nothing but how he didn't want anyone to know he had lost his wings, his power, and he had said terrible things to his best friend; he had hurt him. And yet here Takumu was trying to help him. For this purpose alone, his partner had planned and schemed, used his points, and made this duel happen.

"Taku…" Clenching both hands into tight fists, Haruyuki was ashamed of himself for trying to resolve the situation by himself and keeping everything hidden. He instantly forgot the long training he had undertaken to that end in the Unlimited Neutral Field and shouted out with his whole heart, "Taku, win this one! Not for me—win it to show him how strong you really are!!"

"I'll win. To get your wings back, Haru." Nodding firmly, Cyan Pile took a heavy step, and pale blue flames licked up around his foot, making the air shimmer.

Confronted with this zeal, Dusk Taker turned his face away, seemingly disgusted, and spat out in a low voice, "Oh, don't put on this unpleasant show, please. Things like this make my skin crawl. Seeing such naifs saying such things with straight faces, as if they actually believed in fairy tales like 'selfless friendship.'"

Here, the blackish-purple avatar finally emerged fully from the dark hole. He wrapped a tentacle from his left hand around the opening's edge and used it to make his slithering descent. After kicking aside the metal insects squirming along the ground to make his landing, Dusk Taker glared with upward-turned eyes at the much taller Cyan Pile, from a distance of about twenty meters. The tentacle disentangled itself from the school wall and snapped back, coming to lightly stroke two curved angles—the folded-up flight membranes—protruding from the avatar's back.

"Return them because I obtained them unfairly? You can't be serious. Once I steal something, it's mine forever. As long as I don't get bored of it and no longer need it, that is. I like these wings. Until Arita finishes paying back his two-year loan, I plan to enjoy them to the fullest."

Haruyuki clenched his teeth tightly, aware of an enormous fury and hatred in the pit of his stomach.

But before he could shout out in reply, Takumu whispered in the same quiet, and yet white-hot, voice, "Nah, you're wrong. No matter what it is, power you steal can never become your own. The thing about power is, the only way you can get it is to create it, refine it, train it yourself."

"Hrrk! Again with that." Nomi sneered, pressing his right hand up against his mouth. "I'm likely to vomit if you say another word, so I'll just be taking your points and sending you on your

way. I still have another five questions left on my test and all."
Then the small avatar dropped into a crouch and readied both
hands in front of his faceless mask.

In contrast, Cyan Pile simply thrust out his left hand: the
imposing ready position he used in kendo matches.

"T-Taku!" Haruyuki shouted quickly, while taking a step
back in the charged battlefield. "You can cut those tentacles off
but they grow back! The cutter on his right hand is super sharp!
And if he pins you down and gets you with a black beam from
his mask, he can take abilities and Enhanced Armament, so be
careful!!"

A member of the Gallery giving advice to one of the duelists
was seriously bad manners, but naturally, in this situation, he
had no reason to hold back. Nomi looked fleetingly annoyed at
Haruyuki's shouting.

Immediately, Takumu moved.

With a thunderous roar, the blue giant leapt forward in a blur—
an incredible forward dash that should have been impossible for
the heavyweight body. It carried a punch that was impossible to
read, to boot. The propulsive force sending him rocketing forward was the pile driver of his right hand, the tip of which he
had, at some point, thrust into the ground. He was taking advantage of one feature of the Hell stage—the fact that the surface of
the earth was hard metal—and transforming the launch power
of his metal spike into forward momentum.

Perhaps momentarily caught off guard by the attack, his enemy's reaction was delayed, and Cyan Pile's massive fist was up
and headed straight for the face.

Dusk Taker abandoned the idea of trying to dodge the blow
and crossed both arms to take a guard stance. The punches that
rained down regardless sent pale beams of light shooting in all
directions: the first attack of the battle. A sound like a hammer
beating a steel plate rang out, and the smaller avatar flew, spinning, through the air. Haruyuki thought he might keep going
and slam into the school building behind him, but the tentacles

of his left hand wrapped around some protrusion on the ground and yanked him to a halt, like a giant rubber band.

As Dusk Taker landed on one knee, his HP bar was down more than 5 percent despite the fact that he had guarded, offering a glimpse of the enormity of Cyan Pile's power.

"Ooh! That's quite a change from when we're in kendo, isn't it? So then that meat sack expresses your 'lack,' does it, Mayuzumi? You're so smart and clever, and yet what you truly long for is a rough machismo?"

Takumu had nothing left to say to the laughing Nomi. Almost before the stake in his right hand was reloaded, he hurtled across the distance between them, all the while keeping his guard up.

"And judging by your avatar's name," Nomi spat even more sneeringly, staggering backward as if overwhelmed, "I'd say the real essence of your mental scars is that metal skewer in your right hand. Hmm, I wonder what that could symbolize? Piercing…Perforation…Goodness, what's wrong? Your eyes got a little scary there…?"

"Stop it! Stop it, you coward!" It was Haruyuki who shouted. If his position hadn't been one of observer, he would have started pounding on Nomi himself.

A duel avatar is born from the mental scars of the person who lives inside of it. Every Burst Linker knew that. Which was exactly why Haruyuki had deliberately avoided bringing that topic up with any opponent he had faced. And when it came to Takumu and Kuroyukihime, he warned himself not to even guess at it in his heart.

Cyan Pile's spike probably *was* an expression of some scar Takumu was carrying around. But he had taken ownership of it and mastered it as a weapon. Which meant, in other words, that he continued to fight his own scars on a daily basis.

"I mean, Nomi! You—Your avatar, too! It's the manifestation of some pain you don't want to look at, you know!!"

Dusk Taker chuckled at Haruyuki's sharp words, his eyes still fixed in front. "Oh, ouch, Arita. I already said this, didn't I? My pain is having anything taken from me. Thus, my Dusk Taker has the power to take. It's actually quite obvious. About as obvious as your Silver Crow there!"

His last word was overlaid with a whipping sound as the three tentacles, previously lolling on the ground, undulated like snakes to fling their cargo straight at Takumu. Metal insects, one of the Hell stage's many terrain effects, shot through the air, thin legs kicking frantically. In general, they were harmless, albeit creepy, but the ones in the flashy shells released different kinds of poison when crushed.

The three that Nomi had thrown were all vivid red or green. He had to have fairly good eyes to be able to grab hold of only the poisonous bugs, especially considering he wasn't shifting his gaze away from Cyan Pile closing in on him for even an instant. It was no mean feat to pull that off *and* have a conversation with Haruyuki at the same time.

He's surprisingly used to fighting.

Haruyuki opened his eyes wide at this thought, as Cyan Pile's left arm knocked the metal insects out of the air in a reflexive motion. Together with a squelching crack, like an egg being broken, insect carapaces shattered and an even more loathsome-looking sludge flew out. The blue body was showered in the splatter, and white plumes of smoke rose up from all over it.

"Ngh!" His HP bar dropped only a little, but Takumu reeled at the unanticipated attack.

Not letting the moment slip away, Dusk Taker plunged forward like a bolt of black lightning, howling, and in the blink of an eye, his extended tentacles had seized Cyan Pile's pile driver. And then, Nomi thrust his bolt cutters toward Takumu's throat.

Milliseconds away from having his head cut off, Takumu just barely managed to grab one of the cutter blades with his left hand. Forced into this awkward position, his thumb was caught on the inside of the blade, something Nomi could hardly miss.

Immediately, the blades clanked shut around the digit, and Nomi gradually applied pressure, as if to drag out the pain.

"Unh...Ngh!" Takumu groaned softly.

"Didn't your mother ever teach you not to grab the blade of an open pair of scissors?" Nomi hissed from below. "See now, this is what happens."

Clang! At the dreadful sound, the thumb of Cyan Pile's left hand danced through the air. A chunk disappeared from his HP gauge while at the same time, his special-attack gauge shot up.

"And you. Didn't anyone tell you my attack power's not just in my right hand?" Takumu said in a strangled voice before quickly thrusting his chest out and crying, "Splash Stinger!!"

Shunk! From the alternating rows of small holes on Cyan Pile's chest, slim missiles popped their sleek faces out and shot forward en masse.

Dusk Taker looked appropriately shocked and dropped into a defensive posture, crossing both arms, but even still, the needle missiles hit their mark one after another at extremely close range, blossoming into exploding flowers. Huge hunks disappearing from his gauge as he was thrown backward, the blackish-purple avatar did smash into the school building this time, ending up half buried in the metal wall.

"Aaaah!"

Not letting this advantage get away, Takumu plunged ahead decisively. The earth shook as he barreled along to build momentum and crash into Dusk Taker with his left shoulder. The building wall crumpled inward, and the two avatars hurtled into the school. Haruyuki hurriedly ran after them, entering the school through a hatch a fair distance off, since he couldn't damage the stage himself.

The long first-floor hallway had been transformed into something even stranger than the schoolyard. Slits gouged in the wall undulated peristaltically, occasionally vomiting up steam. A viscous liquid drooled from what looked like bundles of protruding pipes, and the hallway trickled and dribbled.

On the other side of this repulsive scene, the two combatants were already standing up and away from each other. Cyan Pile's remaining gauge was just over 80 percent, while Dusk Taker's was down to 60 percent.

"Nomi, you've already lost," Takumu announced gravely.

"What? Have I?"

"You have. You can't destroy the walls of a Hell stage with your power. The exit is behind me. And in this small space, a speed type like you doesn't have a hope."

It did seem to be exactly as Takumu said. Haruyuki himself had also battled Cyan Pile once in the hallway of a building like this. That time, by focusing on getting past the pile attacks and escaping to the roof, he had managed to tease out a hope of winning. Right now, however, there was nothing but a dead end behind Dusk Taker.

His narrowed reddish-purple eyes glittered, and the slim avatar lunged forward with no warning. Perhaps in revenge for Takumu's initial dash, he had at some point grabbed onto a wall pillar with the tentacles of his left hand, and, contracting them now, he flung his body forward. Unwilling to admit defeat, he was trying to get as low as possible so he could slip out between Cyan Pile's feet and escape the dead end.

But Takumu was calm. Slamming his right foot into the floor, he generated the shock wave that was the particular domain of the heavyweight avatar and knocked Dusk Taker off his feet before jamming a left front kick into his staggering opponent. Nomi guarded but was still knocked back into the hall.

"It's hopeless." Takumu spread his arms, as if to block the path behind him, and advanced. "I'm not letting you have the rear. If we had been fighting in the school building from the start, this whole thing would've been finished a lot sooner. So if you don't want me barging in every time you take a test, give those wings back to Silver Crow. And then, at the very least, I'll stay out of your way. So...what's it going to be?"

Faced with this condition, the injured Nomi propped himself up with his right hand and remained silent for a while.

Finally, he let out a long sigh. "Mayuzumi," he said, shaking his head from side to side. "You would faithfully keep such a ridiculous verbal promise, too, wouldn't you? Honestly, that there could be people with such totally different values in this world—and in the same school no less..."

Nomi spread his hands almost exasperatedly and murmured a short, unfamiliar command: "Total Disarmament."

Instantly, the tentacles of his left hand and the bolt cutters of his right disappeared, as if melting into thin air. The arming and disarming of Enhanced Armament could be done through a voice command the player registered in advance on the Install menu. Those two simple words were the command Nomi had selected.

Does this mean he's accepting defeat and is ready to give my wings back? Seiji Nomi? Really?

Speechless, Haruyuki was once again filled with a sense of admiring wonder for Takumu, who had so perfectly maneuvered his opponent to this place, the consummate chess player.

"Taku—" Just as he was about to shout, *You did it!*, Nomi dropped his small, empty-handed, injured avatar into a very low stance.

"This doesn't mean I'm surrendering," he whispered at the same time. "Just that if both of my hands are full, I won't be able to play my trump card."

"Trump...card?"

Haruyuki was sure that Nomi had said something like this to him, too, right as their first duel was ending. At the time, he had thought it was just some contemptuous remark, but— It couldn't be, he still had something...

As Haruyuki sucked his breath in sharply, Takumu got his enemy in his sights with his right hand. "If you're planning to keep going, then I won't show you any mercy, Nomi! I'll take every single chance I get to fight you. And I'll beat you down. You sure you want that?!"

"Goodness me." The response was even quieter, completely devoid of emotion. "I don't like this at all. You looking so serious and everything. And I mean, it's not like I want to say the name of my special attack...But, well, given the situation, I suppose I have no choice."

Dusk Taker used both hands to make a small triangle in front of his body. He then began muttering under his breath words that sounded like a spell—or a curse.

"Steal. Get. Grab. Remove. Take. Take. Take. Ta. Ke."

Haruyuki heard the low whir of vibration, which soon turned into a metallic, high-pitched hum. And then he saw it: Nomi's hands enveloped in a dull, midnight-purple pulse of energy.

The air in the hallway shuddered, and sparks snapped and raced everywhere. *Special attack?!* he thought immediately, but quickly brushed that idea aside. If it was generating these kinds of effects, his special-attack gauge should start to drop before the attack itself even began. But Nomi's didn't even twitch; it stayed just over half charged.

Haruyuki had only very recently learned about a logic other than a special attack that could generate this kind of phenomenon. The Image control system. Overwriting phenomena with the imagination.

Or by another name—

"T-Taku! Forget about the wings! Kill him right now!!" Haruyuki shrieked.

After a moment's hesitation, Takumu cried sharply, "Lightning Cyan Spike!!"

Cyan Pile's special-attack gauge, also half full, plummeted, and backfire like an aurora surged from the end of the pile driver.

Fwoosh! The air sizzled and the iron stake, a beam of pure light, shot out straight at Dusk Taker. From that distance, it would be impossible to avoid Takumu's level-four special attack—or it should have been. However.

Vmmp!

With a sound like dense gas popping, the gleaming steel spike stopped dead without piercing anything. Held by a mere two fingers.

The index and middle fingers of Dusk Taker's left hand, enveloped in the purple energy, lightly pinched between them Cyan Pile's most powerful special attack, as if it were nothing more than a rolled-up tube of paper.

"Wha…" Haruyuki's hoarse voice slipped out, and then the gleaming lance itself was sucked into the pulsing energy field with a sound like scorched metal being plunged into water. It vanished without a trace.

Languidly lowering his hand, Nomi lifted his face slightly and looked up at the stunned Cyan Pile, who stood rooted to the ground. Judging from how things had played out thus far, this would be the moment when he sneered something contemptuous with a disparaging laugh.

But Dusk Taker remained silent as he bent the fingers of both hands into claws and kicked at the ground. He generated an even stronger purple aura, this time of ripples, before launching himself into an incredible dash so fast, both legs were nothing but blurs. Twice as fast as the tentacles he had been using earlier. He ate up the ten meters separating him from Takumu in less than the time it took to blink, and as he closed in, Dusk Taker drew his left hand through the air in a large arc, from bottom to top.

The purple crescent moon cut into the air sliced across Cyan Pile's thick chest armor diagonally. Then Haruyuki saw the impossible: Deep, cavernous valleys were carved out of the blue chest plate as if it were made of clay—no, pudding.

A moment passed, and then bundles of pale sparks jetted up, spurting like blood from the gouges left behind by the five claws.

"Ngh!" Groaning and reeling, Takumu immediately countered, even though he was likely more shocked at this attack than Haruyuki was.

He rammed the tip of his pile driver into Nomi's left flank, which had been left unguarded. At the same time, he brought his free hand across, up to the launching mechanism at his right shoulder.

Thuk!

By the time the shot rang out, Nomi was already gone. It was so quick, it had to have been a short teleportation. He slid to the right and nimbly dodged the pile driver attack, before this time grabbing the base of the steel spike, which extended to its maximum immediately after being launched.

Once again, the eerie *fwoosh* filled the air, and the spike was crushed.

Or more correctly, the part in Dusk Taker's purple shining hand disappeared instantly. With a sudden, mirror-smooth cross section as its end, the steel stake clattered heavily to the floor.

He was absolutely sure of it now: This was an Incarnate attack. The images produced by Seiji Nomi were negotiating with the system and making any object he grabbed with both hands disappear. Denial of existence. Overwriting the phenomena.

Most likely, Takumu still didn't know about the existence of the Incarnate System. Even as every fiber of his being radiated pure astonishment, he determinedly tried other counterattacks. Perhaps understanding that Nomi's hands deleted everything they touched, he jumped back and launched a kick attack from beyond Nomi's reach. It was a spectacular right-roundhouse kick, the kind that set the air on fire. If it hit its target, it would likely have sent even the heaviest avatar flying.

But the power of this kick was simply numerical data, the sum of avatar weight, armor strength, and muscle parameters. In contrast, Nomi was overwriting data through image control faster than Takumu's kicking power was being delivered to the system via movement control. As a result—

Thud.

The kick was cut short with a sickeningly wet sound and Nomi's left hand. The force of the blow was entirely swallowed up by the pulsating purple energy and canceled out. The wet sound was Takumu's right shin as Nomi's fingers dug into it, nearly to the knuckle.

"Aaah!" A strangled cry of pain made it out of Takumu's mouth.

Slowly wriggling the fingers buried in Takumu's leg, as if to torture him, Nomi finally murmured, "Mayuzumi. Before, you said I couldn't destroy the walls in this stage or something, didn't you?"

Then he dragged Takumu, right leg still imprisoned in Nomi's hand, left knee dragging, and walked toward the south wall. Dusk Taker carelessly thrust his free hand out and it was immediately, soundlessly buried up to the wrist in the sparkling metallic green wall of the Hell stage. As if pushing through jelly, he used the hand to dig a large circle in the wall.

"To be honest, I hadn't wanted to show you. Although I suppose even seeing it, you can't actually understand it. Because the only ones who know this logic are the six—no, seven kings and their close associates, and *us*. But you're a smart guy. Now that you've experienced the gap in our abilities, I'm sure you understand." As he talked, he drilled a gutter almost two meters in diameter into the wall. At a kick, the wall crashed to the inside and the outside light came streaming in. "That you all are out of options. That the moment I started at Umesato Junior High, your destiny to spend every one of the rest of your school days working as my dogs was already decided."

Nomi had barely finished speaking when he waved his left hand fiercely and tossed Cyan Pile's enormous bulk through the hole to the yard outside. Without so much as a glance at Haruyuki, he also exited the building.

A numbness spread up from the core of Haruyuki's brain. In the dim hallway, shoulders shaking fiercely, he stood rooted to the spot.

Why? Why would a guy like Nomi know the Incarnate System? You wouldn't even be able to see it exists without some outside help. You can't learn this skill unless someone is kind enough to guide you to it.

Pulling Haruyuki back from his own stupefaction was a low, distant moan from Takumu. He lifted his face with a gasp, dove through the hole Nomi had made, and leapt outside, shuddering at the smooth fingermarks in the thick, dug-out section of wall.

In roughly the center of the schoolyard, he saw the shadows of the two entangled avatars. They weren't fighting, however. It was more like a one-sided slaughter at this point.

Cyan Pile looked like he was just barely standing, oceans of sparks scattering from the wounds to his chest and leg. Even so, he launched attack after determined attack with both hands, but he didn't even scratch Dusk Taker. The twilight-colored avatar casually evaded the punches while superficially shaving away his opponent's armor with his fingertips.

Cyan Pile's HP gauge was already down to 20 percent. The destroyed pile driver unrepaired, his fully charged special-attack gauge glittered in vain.

"T-Taku…" Haruyuki squeezed out a crushed voice.

He wanted to say something to his best friend, who wouldn't give up despite being at an overwhelming disadvantage, but he couldn't find the right words. Up against Nomi's Incarnate attacks, likely the manifestation of the disappearance of objects including physical attacks, the simple, close-range blue Cyan Pile had no method of resistance.

The hundredth or millionth scar was etched into his mask, and Cyan Pile finally dropped heavily to his knees. In a normal duel field, the pain generated when an avatar took damage was about half that of the Unlimited Neutral Field, but even at half strength, the cumulative pain of many tiny injuries quickly became intolerable. This was no doubt Nomi's aim in deliberately attacking with multiple shallow cuts.

When Takumu fought back against the virtual pain torturing his nerves and tried to stand back up, Nomi kicked him down as hard as he could, and Dusk Taker set his slim foot down firmly on top of the fallen Cyan Pile's mask.

"Five hundred seconds left, hmm? Well, you fought a lot harder than I expected, Mayuzumi. You have more of a gift for this than you do for kendo." Nomi chuckled before holding aloft the claws of his right hand. The purple energy pulse generated regular concentric circles and had conspicuously increased in strength. "Now then, I'll have compensation for the one point three seconds of my real time that you took. Your Burst points and pain. And your humiliation."

He went to plunge his right hand into Takumu's throat.

"Wait, Nomi!!" Haruyuki shouted, at the very edge of the permitted spectator distance.

The hand pulled up short, and Dusk Taker's round visor glanced over.

"Just wait!" Haruyuki cried desperately. "If you want points, take mine! Takumu used a ton of points to fight you! But I still have plenty. If you're going to take some, take them from me!!"

He was half serious. But the other half was a plan, and the thin chance it was betting on.

He fell to his knees on the spot, pressed the forehead of his helmet to a ground crawling with insects, and shouted like a cry of pain, "It's just like this, I'm begging you, Nomi!!" Naturally, this was his first experience prostrating himself so clumsily in the accelerated world, but that wasn't the case in the real world.

Last year, before his fateful meeting with Brain Burst, Haruyuki had been the subject of harsh bullying by three boys in his class. They had extorted bread and juice from him at every opportunity, and when he didn't have any and couldn't buy any, he had been forced to apologize by prostrating himself like this. It was a memory stained with a shame he'd prefer not to remember, but right now, in this moment alone, he used that desperation in his voice and his bearing and scraped his head firmly along the ground.

"Ooh, this is the worst. In every sense of the word, this is the worst, Arita." Nomi sounded astonished. "Going this far in the name of friendship is clearly an illness. But you are, for now at least, the owner of Brain Burst, are you not? Even *I* think this sniveling of yours has no place on the duel field."

"Think whatever you want. I'll make sure to pay you next week's points, too, so please...I'm begging you!!"

"Yes, yes, I understand. Somehow this reminds me of torturing pill bugs in the garden when I was a child. But, well, I suppose it's because you're this kind of person that you obtained the flight ability." Despite the considerable loathing in Nomi's voice, Haruyuki heard the sound of Nomi's foot being removed from Takumu's face. Then he felt him open the Install menu from the HP bar.

Which was followed by a shrill warning noise accompanying a single window opening up in his field of view, a confirmation dialogue to change the field from a one-against-one normal duel mode to a Battle Royale mode that included the spectators.

Haruyuki momentarily lifted his face to look at Nomi, who was shaking his head in fake exasperation, and Takumu, who was still on the ground, before immediately pressing the YES button. Now, as long as Takumu accepted, the mode would switch, and Haruyuki would go from being a spectator to a duelist. He wouldn't have to wait for next week; he could fight Dusk Taker now.

However—and he had anticipated this—Takumu wasn't pressing the button. It was only natural. He was taking Haruyuki's words at face value, and his pride wouldn't allow him to let Haruyuki shoulder the burden of points that were rightfully hunted from him.

From a position almost touching the ground, which Nomi, standing, could not see, Haruyuki stared at Takumu, putting all his will into his eyes.

Press it. I'm not giving up. I want to fight him. I have to fight him. So please, push the button, Takumu!!

It might have been that the shout in Haruyuki's head actually made it to his friend. Takumu momentarily opened his eyes behind his scarred mask and finally raised a trembling arm to touch a point in space.

A few silence-filled seconds followed, and then suddenly, all the data displays disappeared from his field of view. Following a digital alarm, Silver Crow's HP gauge stretched out at top left. The previous gauge on the right side stayed gone, but small, completely replenished gauges popped up above the heads of Cyan Pile and Dusk Taker. Below the remaining time of four hundred seconds, the blazing text FIGHT!! appeared, and then scattered in flames.

Finally, Haruyuki murmured to himself, still prostrate. Finally, this moment had come. His rematch with Seiji Nomi/Dusk Taker. The battle to get back the many things taken from him, the battle he absolutely could not lose.

Klak, klak. The twilight avatar crunched across the metal yard and approached him. He glittered a strange color in the green light pouring down from the sky. Perhaps to maintain his connection to the Incarnate, both hands dripped with the empty pulsing.

Still cowering, Haruyuki carefully pulled his right hand to his chest, folded his thumb into his palm, and stuck the rest of his fingers straight out.

My arm is a sword. A sword of light, piercing any and all things, no matter how hard, even the dark of nothingness. As he stabilized the image in his mind, he felt an intense heat being generated in his fingertips.

The footfalls grew closer. A chill caressed the nape of his neck. The feet stopped directly in front of him. One foot was raised up and brought casually toward his head—

"Shah!!"

With a short battle cry, Haruyuki grabbed the foot about to step on him with his left hand, leveraged it to yank himself to his feet, and lunged straight out with his right arm at the same time.

"Ngh?!" Letting a short cry escape, Nomi reacted at a terrifying speed and tried to parry Haruyuki's thrust with his left hand.

An abnormal clanging crash sounded throughout the field. The claws of Nomi's left fingers slammed up against Haruyuki's fingertips, now transformed into a radiant sword of pure white light. However, neither side touched. White and purple, pure light and empty aura fought each other, emitting a high-pitched squeal.

"What!…This technique…?! You dog…When did you learn this trick!!" Nomi howled, and the power of the purple pulse increased. His dark imagination, to make anything and everything disappear, ate into the system and tried to scrape away Haruyuki's arm.

Haruyuki fought back with the image of a laser to pierce through everything in existence. Speed. The speed of light.

…*Right. You're faster than anyone.*

The instant he felt that faint voice's call, Haruyuki shouted, "Go…throooooooough!!"

A transient clarity filled the battlefield like a thousand icicles shattering and scattering.

Zzrk! The sword of Haruyuki's right hand extended more than a meter instantly, piercing the darkness created by Nomi's left hand. Soundlessly, it dispersed in all directions. Then.

Dusk Taker's left arm itself shattered from the inside, from palm to shoulder.

"Ngaaah!"

As Nomi staggered backward, rivers of reddish-purple sparks gushing out of him, Haruyuki released the avatar's leg and thrust out his own left hand.

"Aaaah!"

Regrettably, his enemy's right arm managed to deflect the attack targeting the center of his chest, and Haruyuki managed only to cut up the armor. Nomi dashed away in reverse at a serious speed, spread both legs out, and stopped.

This was his chance to go for the kill, but Haruyuki couldn't give chase. Maybe because he had managed to squeeze out such a strong image, white sparks crackled and dazzled his vision. He shook his head several times to shake them off, and when he opened his eyes again, Nomi was already back in a guarded posture.

"Oh, myyyy…" A bantering yet hoarse voice slipped out from under the rounded, expressionless visor. "How unexpected, an Incarnate attack…Which means that, the whole of last night, you were up on the mountain training, weren't you, Arita?"

"Didn't even take a whole night," Haruyuki answered in a deep voice, standing up. The fingertips of both hands were still perfectly aligned; the white light and the hum of vibration remained.

"Hmm? I had heard that you lost pathetically to a bit player in the Green Legion. I was worried you might not be able to earn your point quota, but on the contrary, I see that you still have enough energy to bite back. I underestimated you." Nomi followed this with a sneering laugh, waved his right hand, and blew away the purple pulsation.

"What, you already out of energy?"

"Ha-ha-ha! Impossible!!" Nomi cried brightly, and moved his right hand once more, raising it high up to the left, crossing the front of his body. "You see, I wasn't just sleeping myself!!"

As he cried out, he drew his arm back as far as it would go, like drawing a bow. In sync with this motion, the angles protruding from his back deployed with a dramatic flap to both sides.

Five axial bones on each side. A thin membrane connecting them. Demon wings—the flying ability he took from Silver Crow.

Gulping unconsciously, Haruyuki watched as the wings spread out in the sky and once again flapped fiercely.

Wham! The air shook, and Dusk Taker's body rose straight up.

There wasn't a trace of the awkwardness he had displayed after taking the wings the other day; this was a spectacular flight. After quickly shooting past the roof of the school building, he whirled his body around and hovered.

No, I can't be surprised at this, Haruyuki told himself, biting his lip. Nomi was a user of the Incarnate System. And control of the flying ability was also through image control. In which case, getting the hang of it would be no big deal for him.

A singsong voice came pouring down from the ominous silhouette carved out of the green sky.

"The truth is, they are actually quite impressive, these wings! You had such a unilateral advantage and yet still are at level four! But well, I suppose there's no helping it given that all you have for a weapon are those short little arms and legs of yours, Arita. Rest easy, I'm not like you! I'll be able to use and master this power to a much greater extent than you. Like this, for instance!"

Nomi had barely finished speaking before he stretched out his right hand and chanted quietly, "Equip Pyro Dealer."

Haruyuki stood stock-still and stared up as the system, receiving the voice command, manifested new Enhanced Armament on Dusk Taker's remaining arm.

An enormous piece of equipment now covered the entire appendage. From a large, tanklike object sitting on his shoulder, several pipes stretched to his elbow and then on down, to a firing device on the back of his hand.

Long-distance heat power! Haruyuki clenched his teeth tightly and strained every nerve in his body.

Point-five seconds later, with the artlessness of a child playing with fireworks, Nomi sent flames gushing from the short gun barrel.

These were the very definition of flames. Not a physical bullet, not a beam of light, but extremely dense, near-liquid fire. Like the blazing attack spewed forth by a dragon in some fantasy game, the attack raining down from high above his head, roaring as it did so.

He had no time to hesitate about how to respond. As soon as he dashed forward reflexively, a *fwoomp*ing howl was generated behind him, and a fierce heat beat down against his back.

"Hng!" Grunting from between gritted teeth, Haruyuki ran

for his life, zigzagging randomly, but the thunderous flames were always chasing right behind him. Fires flickered all around him, and his HP bar was shaved away a few dots at a time.

When he had run westward along the wall of the school building for nearly ten seconds, the roar was finally interrupted. Whirling around as the soles of his feet slid along the surface of the ground, Haruyuki gazed up in wonder.

Smack in the middle of the large schoolyard was a bright red pond, about five meters in diameter. A small river wound its way out from the pond, and burbling, melted metal flowed before Haruyuki's eyes.

The new Enhanced Armament Dusk Taker had called up was clearly a flamethrower. And one that produced a terrifyingly high temperature. If he took a direct hit from that thing even once, the ground below his feet would without a doubt melt, leaving him unable to move, and he would be burned to a crisp just like that.

Haruyuki ripped his gaze away from the gleaming red expanse and shifted it to Cyan Pile, still crouching near it. His HP gauge had been refilled and his visible injuries healed with the duel mode change, but it seemed the shock of the pain from his entire body being hollowed out still held him. He was going to need at minimum another minute before he could participate in the battle.

"Heh...heh-heh-heh!" Dozens of meters up in the sky above Haruyuki and his racing thoughts, Dusk Taker raised his voice in an innocent laugh. "Just as I expected, the combination of flight with long-distance fire power is incredible. I can recharge my special-attack gauge with field destruction bonuses as I hover up in the sky like this. A clear perpetual motion machine...To be perfectly frank, I'm invincible."

"I dunno about that," Haruyuki shouted at the avatar in a strangled voice, the flame demon changing the orientation of the flamethrower again. "There's still one condition you have to meet if you want to be truly invincible."

"Oh? What's that?"

"You'd have to be the only one...who can fly!!" The words had barely left his mouth when Haruyuki raised both hands up high and prayed briefly in his heart.

Sky Raker. My other teacher. Thank you for these... Your wings!!

"Equip!! Gale Thruster!!"

The voice command rang out, sonorous.

Dusk Taker halted abruptly.

Two streaks of sky-blue light streamed from the sky, hit Haruyuki's back, and coalesced—

Producing a big, strong, beautiful object: streamlined boosters about eighty centimeters long and ten centimeters wide. The pair settled in place on his back, side by side. The tips of the square thrust openings tapered slightly, and on the ends, there was a total of four small stabilizers around them, two horizontal and two vertical. Rather than boosters, these were the equivalent of having two small cruise missiles strapped to your back.

This was the Enhanced Armament that once earned Sky Raker the nicknames ICBM and Iron Arms.

Haruyuki stared at his opponent, who couldn't completely disguise his shock, and lowered his stance. The boosters whined. Pale reflected light shone on the ground at his feet.

A heart that wishes for the sky. That is precisely the source of Gale Thruster's power.

Once again, a distant voice echoed in his ears: *Now go. You of all people should be able to fly again, Corvus.*

"Aaaaah!!" Haruyuki howled and kicked off the ground with all his might.

An enormous crash shook the atmosphere, and a dazzling light filled the surroundings. And then Haruyuki was shooting up into the sky like a bullet, at a speed easily surpassing the vertical takeoff with his old silver wings.

Dusk Taker's black silhouette grew closer with each microsecond.

But at the same time, Haruyuki's perception also started to accelerate, and his relative approach speed seemed to decrease.

"Wha..." Letting slip this semi-cry of surprise, Dusk Taker tried to turn the flamethrower of his right hand on Haruyuki. As the muzzle was on the verge of generating a red light—

"Heeaaah!!" Battle cry sharp, Haruyuki thrust his left hand out in a strike.

His sharp fingertips, wrapped in a white radiance, touched the muzzle and split it top to bottom. Then kept on going, piercing all the way up to the fuel tank on Dusk Taker's shoulder.

With a thudding groan, the two avatars joined together and then separated. Haruyuki danced ever higher in the sky as scarlet flashes appeared below his feet, and he heard the rumbling of explosions chasing the flashes.

He opened his crossed arms and stopped his ascent. Looking down, he could see the familiar H-shaped school building and large grounds of Umesato, and the figure of Dusk Taker floating against them.

Having already lost his left arm, he now also suffered severe damage to his right. The flamethrower was completely blown away, and his arm from shoulder to elbow was cooked a burnt black. Fissures raced along armor shining like amethyst, and the dripping of dazzling sparks was constant. Nomi's HP gauge was cut down to half.

Adjusting his descent trajectory by spreading his arms, Haruyuki landed on a pole at the edge of the schoolyard. It was topped with rows of strange eyeballs, which had apparently been floodlights in the real world.

Unlike with his stolen wings, flying with Gale Thruster didn't consume his special-attack gauge. But just like Takumu's Pile Driver, once it used up its energy in a momentary thrust, it took a long time to recharge. Checking in the upper left of his field of vision that the third gauge newly displayed there was slowly increasing, Haruyuki readied his sword hands.

"I see, I see." Nomi also yanked up his injured right hand. The curved claws housed the purple pulsing energy once again. "So you were still hiding a card like that?" The voice was flat, as if squelching any hint of surprise or anger, but the echo of a sneer still coiled around it somehow.

"Say, please tell me, Arita. Where on earth did you find Enhanced Armament like that? You don't have enough points to buy it in the Shop, now do you?...Oh, is that it? You chased the avatar who owned it to a forced uninstall and then stole it. Is that the case? How awful. Even I wouldn't go that far."

Nomi chuckled from deep in his throat, and Haruyuki responded calmly, "You wouldn't understand, Nomi."

"...And what's that?"

"Even if I told you the wishes of the person who produced these sky-blue 'wings' and the hopes entrusted to me, you totally wouldn't understand at all. Not when you think that the accelerated world is nothing more than a means to an end. And... someone like that, like you, doesn't have the right to call himself a Burst Linker!!"

Haruyuki thrust his right fist, filled with white radiance, straight at Nomi.

The twilight-colored avatar remained silent for a while. Finally, he cocked his head abruptly and said, "You know, I've heard that line before. 'Burst Linker'?...When have I ever used those words?"

"...What?"

"Did you know? Burst Linker is what the initial owners of Brain Burst called themselves. You can look anywhere you want in the system, but you won't find that title anywhere. Which is why we would never use it."

"We...?"

Before he could think about what that meant, Nomi spat fiercely, "If you're going to refer to us correctly, it should be accelerated persons— No, accelerated users. We use the privilege we have been given to its fullest and obtain whatever we are able to obtain. That is how you and I should be. Well,...isn't it about time we settled this? Mine or yours, whose will—that is to say, whose 'desire' is stronger!!"

A whistling roar swelled, and the now familiar energy pulse radiated from Nomi's right hand.

"The will is not about desire. It's a wish!!" Haruyuki shouted, and swords of white light grew from both hands.

At the same time, he scraped together every bit of hope and desire for the sky in his entire body. A clear sky blue filled his chest and flowed into the boosters on his back.

This was the true purpose of Sky Raker training Haruyuki in the Incarnate System: so that he could use his will to recharge the Gale Thruster, which could normally only jump a short time on a single thrust. As long as he could do this, these boosters were no longer simply a jump-assist device; they could become real wings, allowing even continuous flight. The third gauge, on the verge of being empty, was at full change in the blink of an eye. Pale flames gushed from Haruyuki's back.

The two duelists burst forward at maximum speed, tracing silver and purple trajectories in the sky.

"Aaaaaah!" With a battle cry from the bottom of his stomach, Haruyuki sent out his left sword hand at the speed of light.

"Chaaaaa!!" Raising his hand like a sword, Nomi raked his claws downward.

The shriek of impact echoed and the sky shook. The different-colored beams of light swirled and tangled and burst.

Two arms were ripped off, both nearly in half, and blown away.

"Not…yeeeeeet!!" With a howl, Haruyuki thrust the sword of his right hand directly at the center of Nomi's chest.

His arm, now a dazzling beam of light, pierced the blackish-purple armor soundlessly and became buried up to the shoulder. But at the same time, Nomi's right foot, enveloped by the illusory energy pulse, dug deep into Haruyuki's left flank. Both of their HP bars instantly dropped 30 percent.

Enduring a fierce pain that nearly burned away the core of his head, Haruyuki mustered all of his remaining will, set his sights

directly below him—the ground of Umesato Junior High—and opened his boosters all the way.

The entangled avatars plummeted, tracing out a tail of flames like a falling star. The hard ground raced toward them.

If they crashed like this, Silver Crow would no longer have the power left to fly, even if they ended up having the same amount remaining in their HP bars. As if sensing this, Dusk Taker tucked his body in, a defensive posture.

But Haruyuki lifted his face, and with his eyes wide open, added a slight, final adjustment to their descent trajectory.

"Taku! Now!!" he yelled.

"What?!" Nomi gasped, and in the center of the face he lifted—

Charging up from the ground, the bolt of lightning that was Takumu's special attack—Lightning Cyan Spike—pierced him.

This attack worked like a brake, and taking advantage of the deceleration, Haruyuki spun his body one hundred and eighty degrees, yanking his right arm out of Dusk Taker's chest as he did so. The rest was a matter of reverse thrust with the boosters, at the full force of their remaining energy.

Even still, the instant his legs touched the ground, cracks raced up his silver armor and sparks flew. Fissures rippled out radially through the ground, and at their center, he dropped heavily to his knees.

A second later, tracing the trajectory of the remaining beam of light in the sky, Dusk Taker crashed a few meters away.

He was in such a state it was a wonder that he had anything left in his HP gauge at all. Both arms were missing, and there was an enormous hole in his chest armor. The rounded visor of his face was cracked like a spiderweb, and a blackened scar marred the center where Haruyuki had stabbed him, sparks spurting out with a dry crackle. The tips of the wings, glued to the surface of the ground, twitched, perhaps with the intention to move again, but they didn't manage anything close to an actual flap.

...*It's over*, Haruyuki murmured to himself. However they struck Dusk Taker now, at that point, their victory was assured.

But Haruyuki stayed crouched down and motionless, waiting for the footfalls approaching slowly behind him.

Finally standing beside him, Takumu—Cyan Pile—was in a terrible state. Very nearly his entire body was scorched black, smoke rising up from it. But this wasn't from being attacked; it was damage he had inflicted on himself. He had dragged his avatar, which was unable to move to his satisfaction because of the lingering pain, and sunk half his body in the magma pond created by Dusk Taker's flamethrower. To fill his gauge enough to at least be able to get one blow in with his special attack.

It wasn't like Haruyuki knew that by looking at him. If he had turned his eyes to Takumu even once during the battle, Nomi would have noticed the flow of his awareness and seen through to his friend's intentions. So Haruyuki made sure not to look down from the sky. He simply believed: that Takumu would come through.

"...Nomi." Haruyuki addressed the exhausted avatar who was the color of darkness. "The reason you lost wasn't my Incarnate attack or the Gale Thruster. It was because we weren't alone. And that's the reason you won't be able to beat us in the future, either."

He received no reply.

Looking up at his partner by his side, Haruyuki nodded slightly, strongly.

Takumu returned his nod and offered his burnt left hand. Haruyuki grabbed it with his right and pulled himself to his feet.

There were still two minutes left on the clock. Haruyuki advanced one, two steps to deliver the final blow to Dusk Taker.

...Ring.

It was at that instant he felt like he heard a faint ringing sound. Haruyuki stopped abruptly and quickly looked around.

There was no one. How could there be? This field wasn't created with the global net as intermediary but rather the Umesato local net. Which was why there was no way a new Burst Linker would appear—

Brrrring.

Again, he heard the crisp and yet somehow sad sound.

Haruyuki and Takumu both looked toward the source of the sound at the same time—the sky.

There was not the slightest shadow in the green sky of the Hell stage. But in the next instant, Haruyuki caught a small movement in the corner of his eye.

It wasn't the sky. The roof of the school building towered up in the south. On the other side of the pointed cast-iron fence encircling it like lances, shining a green much more vivid than that of the sky, almost like peridot, a small avatar—

"What…"

Haruyuki couldn't tell if he or Takumu spoke.

That, that avatar.

Lime Bell.

In other words, Chiyuri, Chiyuri Kurashima. But why? Chiyuri shouldn't have already been registered on the automatic spectator list for Silver Crow or Cyan Pile.

"Chi—" Haruyuki started to call out in a hoarse voice.

However, as if to interrupt him, Chiyuri lifted the large bell on her left hand up to the sky softly. He felt like he could hear her voice. Quietly, riding the faint wind of the stage, extremely thinly, as if it were more a response with the senses than a sound.

…Sorry, Taku…Sorry, Haru.

And then the yellow-green avatar waved the bell. At the same time, she uttered a special attack name.

"Citron Call."

The sound of the ringing bell was exceedingly beautiful, but perhaps because of the sound effects of the stage, it was distorted somehow. The emerald particles glittering and dancing down from the rooftop enveloped Dusk Taker, who was on the verge of death.

Haruyuki and Takumu could do nothing but stare as the deep wounds dug out of the blackish-purple armor began to heal at once from the ends.

"Why..." Haruyuki heard the cracked, broken voice coming from his own throat.

"Why on Earth...Chiyu."

To be continued.

AFTERWORD

It's been a while, or maybe this is your first time. Reki Kawahara here. Thank you for reading *Accel World 3: The Twilight Marauder*.

Accel World postures itself as a series of VR fighting game novels, but you can't say that these are game novels in the strictest sense of the term. I think there are likely a good number of people who felt this with the first volume, because ambiguous things like battle cries and miracles transcend the presented game system. These are the sorts of things you must not have in a game novel, and I wanted from the bottom of my heart to avoid this sort of development if at all possible, but (LOL) when I'm writing, it ends up being this way for some reason.

This is probably because the question of whether a win in conformance with the system is really a win at all took up residence within me quite some time ago. In rock-paper-scissors, one side offers scissors, the other side offers rock and wins. Is that okay? This is the kind of question I'm stuck with. Like if you're the hero (or if you're the rival), you should just win with paper already (LOL).

No, I'm aware that what I'm saying is absurd! A test incorporating such systemic indivisibility is the Incarnate System in this volume. This is an extremely ridiculous thing, made to cover up the ridiculousness of making the power of imagination or will an element of victory or defeat in a concrete game. But whether this story will be able to continue in the future as a game novel with this element, or if it will be thrown further into chaos...Either way, I hope you will continue to watch over it as long as you have the patience capacity for it! I would like that!

If you just think it over, the only energy source that seems like it could possibly surpass the various systems in the real world—that is, the framework of common sense—is simply the power of imagination, isn't it? This is a world where no matter which way you look, there's a wall and again a wall, and all you can do is let out a sigh, but at any time, it is possible to fly past these with imagination. So I write something good like this, throw up a smoke screen, and muddle along.

Once again, I have been greatly aided by the illustrator HIMA, whom I seriously intrude upon with design work for both the real-world and avatar versions every time a new character appears; and my editor Miki, who, as always, gives me her total focus to make the pinnacle of pessimism Haruyuki into something more like a hero.

And to you reading this far, you have as much gratitude as my will is able to manifest!

Reki Kawahara
July 23, 2009

ACCEL WORLD, Volume 3
REKI KAWAHARA

Translation: Jocelyne Allen

This book is a work of fiction. Names, characters, places, and incidents are the product of the author's imagination or are used fictitiously. Any resemblance to actual events, locales, or persons, living or dead, is coincidental.

ACCEL WORLD
© REKI KAWAHARA 2009
All rights reserved.
Edited by ASCII MEDIA WORKS
First published in Japan in 2009 by KADOKAWA
CORPORATION, Tokyo,
English translation rights arranged with KADOKAWA
CORPORATION, Tokyo,
through Tuttle-Mori Agency, Inc., Tokyo.

English translation © 2015 by Hachette Book Group, Inc.

Yen On
Hachette Book Group
1290 Avenue of the Americas, New York, NY 10104

www.HachetteBookGroup.com
www.YenPress.com

Yen On is an imprint of Hachette Book Group, Inc.
The Yen On name and logo are trademarks of Hachette Book Group, Inc.

First Yen On Edition: March 2015

ISBN: 978-0-316-29637-3

10 9 8 7 6 5 4 3 2 1

RRD-C

Printed in the United States of America